DEBUTANTES

Cora Harrison worked as a head teacher before writing her first novel. She has since published twenty-six historical novels for children and many books for adults. Cora lives on a farm near the Burren in the west of Ireland.

DEBUTANTES

CORA HARRISON

MACMILLAN

First published 2012 by Macmillan Children's Books
a division of Macmillan Publishers Limited
20 New Wharf Road, London N1 9RR
Basingstoke and Oxford
Associated companies throughout the world
www.panmacmillan.com

ISBN 978-1-4472-0594-4

135798642

A CIP catalogue record for this book is available from
the British Library.

Printed and bound by CPI Group (UK) Ltd, Croydon CR0 4YY

*For my friend Patricia Lyons of Tara Book
Club with thanks for all her help, advice and
encouragement throughout my years as a writer.*

Prologue

The girl's face was perfectly framed by the russet beech leaves. The early spring sunlight lit creamy-white skin, a Grecian nose, violet-blue eyes fringed with long black lashes, and a curtain of shimmering black hair.

The camera clicked and clicked again.

'Keep still!' said the director's voice. 'Good! Now breathe in and smile – no, not like that. Think of something. Think of a line of poetry.'

'Don't forget,' said the director as a look of boredom began to show in the lovely eyes, 'once this film gets shown in a cinema you will have offers from Hollywood. Think of the money! There will definitely be enough for you to have a London season, to be a debutante and be presented in court. Think of shopping in Harrods!'

An expression as of one who sees heavenly visions came across the girl's beautiful face. Suddenly it lit up, as she imagined the gorgeous ball gowns, magnificent jewels and well-cut riding clothes that could be bought with Hollywood money. The camera whirred as she moved her head, her eyes full of a burning ambition.

Chapter One

'You can come out now, Violet.' Sixteen-year-old Daisy Derrington lifted her head from the camera and looked across to the beech hedge which framed the face of her elder sister, Violet.

'I've got all sorts of creepy-crawlies in my hair,' complained Violet as she slid out from under the branches. Standing there, even in worn, darned riding breeches and an old short-sleeved shirt, she looked marvellous, thought Daisy. Violet had always been pretty, but now, at almost eighteen, she was annoyingly beautiful.

'Don't make a noise,' Daisy said. 'I want to film the horses while they're still grazing peacefully.' She picked up her small box-shaped camera and began to move towards the next field. 'That's what you are supposed to be looking at. I'm going to do that now until Poppy comes out with the horse food. When I finish filming the peaceful grazing scene, I want to film them galloping. Will you go and help Poppy, Vi?'

The Derrington family consisted of father, great-aunt and four girls. Violet was the eldest. One glance at those beautiful violet-blue eyes had been enough to give her the name of Violet. That had been understandable, thought Daisy. However, her mother (a woman of few ideas,

3

obviously) had then gone ahead to give flower names to the next three girls. Poppy – well, it was obvious from the start that she had inherited her mother's flame-coloured hair, so her name was appropriate too, and Rose, the youngest, had been a sweetly pretty baby with a wild-rose complexion, according to everyone.

But Daisy, Poppy's twin, disliked her name intensely. Coupled with her appearance – slightly chubby, with cornflower-blue eyes and pale blonde hair – there was something childish and stupid about the name 'Daisy', and as far as she was concerned, it was hardly an appropriate name for a famous film-maker, which was what she intended to be.

The Derringtons lived in Beech Grove Manor – a tall, three-storey house made from honey-coloured sandstone and set amid magnificent beech woods in west Kent. The house had been built almost two hundred years previously with a stately dining room, drawing room, library and study on the ground floor and a dozen bedrooms, a picture gallery and a ballroom on the two upper floors. It had been a wonderful place to live in when there had been money to pay enough servants to keep it warm, well-cleaned and comfortable, money to do the repairs and money to renew the furniture when necessary. Unfortunately, the family fortune had lessened over the years and the present earl had made some disastrous investments, including sinking a large part of his fortune in a hugely disappointing gold mine out in India. By the early 1920s there were only half the servants needed for comfort and the furniture, carpets and curtains all needed renewing and repairing. There was no money for anything. No money to send the girls to school or even to afford the cheapest governess for them, no money for new clothes, no money for enough coal to heat the huge house properly, and certainly not enough money for Violet to become a debutante and be presented at court to the King and Queen, in the same way as other girls from the families that they knew.

Daisy kicked a pile of leaves in exasperation. Everything was so frustrating, she thought. The Derrington family was so poor, the four girls were supposed to ask for nothing, demand nothing, achieve nothing, and eventually marry someone rich and most likely boring. But they all wanted more than that. Poppy wanted to be a professional jazz player and singer, she herself wanted to be a film director and Rose wanted to be an author. Violet, however, was determined to find a rich husband and believed that if she made a good match, married a man with money – well, perhaps that would be the way out for her younger sisters. But to make the match she had to meet the men, and virtually the only way to do that was to have a season. Daisy, however, believed that the key to the future for herself and her sisters lay in the small box camera, complete with an enlarger, a positive film printer, a copier and a projector, all of which had been presented to her by her godfather, Sir Guy Beresford, a wealthy businessman with interests in the film industry. The moment Daisy had seen what Violet looked like on camera she had suddenly become fiercely ambitious to direct and shoot a film which could be sold to earn them some money which would be spent on a season for Violet. Violet was (she had to admit) unusually good-looking in real life, but when shown on film, she became something else. A real film star!

We all have ambitions, thought Daisy, and our first ambition is to get out of Beech Grove Manor.

Chapter Two

❈

Daisy was busy with her film when the gong went for lunch. She pulled her head out of the dark cupboard in the dressing room off the bedroom she shared with her twin sister and clattered down the uncarpeted stairs, colliding with Poppy, who was running in through the back door, her long red hair, freed from its usual thick braid, tumbling around her shoulders.

'Great-Aunt Lizzie will have a fit if she sees your hair like that,' hissed Daisy.

'Oh, pish!' Poppy gave herself an indifferent glance in the hall looking glass.

'We must be the only girls in England who haven't cut our hair,' said Daisy discontentedly, conscious from the glass that her own hair was not too tidy either.

'You cut your hair,' pointed out Poppy.

'Only a quarter of an inch at a time,' said Daisy. 'First thing in the morning I just slice through a curl at the end of each strand. I think if I do that every day Father won't notice, and then after a year or so I'll have a fashionable bob.'

'He's just totally unreasonable,' said Poppy with a puzzled frown. 'I can't see what difference it makes to him.'

And she didn't, thought Daisy with amusement. That

was one of the things you had to accept about Poppy: she was totally incapable of looking at things from anyone else's point of view. She couldn't see that their father's strict Victorian upbringing made him shudder with horror at the antics of the girls in London, with their short hair and their short skirts. She couldn't see that it was better to coax him rather than to quarrel with him.

Of the four sisters, Daisy was by far the most accomplished at bringing their father round to her point of view. Michael Derrington was rather a difficult man. After his wife's death in 1916 he had gone to war to fight in the trenches at the Somme, leaving his four young daughters in the care of his wife's aunt. He had been severely shell-shocked during the war and returned to Beech Grove Manor physically well, but suffering from depression and severe headaches. You had to be gentle with him, thought Daisy.

'One of these days,' said Poppy darkly, 'I'll just take the scissors to my hair. Perhaps I should do it now – make lunch more interesting, wouldn't it? Just imagine Great-Aunt Lizzie's face if I arrived with a neat bob!'

'Except that it wouldn't be a neat bob.' Daisy thought she should put a stop to that idea. Once Poppy took up a notion she never thought of the consequences. 'Nothing looks worse than a bob that's not properly done. You'd have to go to a hairdresser and that costs money. Come on, Poppy,' she hissed, 'let's go in or we'll be late.'

Violet and Rose were already sitting at one side of the large table in the dining room and the twins slid into their places opposite. Their father sat at the head of the table, frowning heavily over a letter that the butler had just handed him – another one of those bills, thought Daisy – and Great-Aunt Lizzie, a trim, upright figure, sat at the bottom and looked with disfavour at Poppy's untidy hair and Daisy's chemical-stained hands.

The dining room at Beech Grove Manor was gloomy at this time of day. Four of its seven windows faced west and the other three faced north, and not even the looking glasses that were hung on the walls opposite the windows brightened it up much. The battered old furniture was dull from lack of polish, the silver on the sideboard was sparse and bore marks of heavy wear, and the original red velvet curtains had faded to a threadbare pink. The place depressed Michael Derrington and mealtimes were never cheerful. It might have been jollier, thought Daisy, if they all just served themselves, or even fetched the food from the kitchen, but Great-Aunt Lizzie would never permit what she called a lowering of standards. Following the tradition of the past thirty years, the elderly butler accepted the dishes from the hands of a young parlourmaid and shuffled around the table trying to give an air of formality to shepherd's pie, turnips and boiled potatoes.

'I've had a letter from Cousin Fanny,' announced Great-Aunt Lizzie once the meal had been served. Five pairs of uninterested eyes looked at her and four pairs then looked away again. Only their father continued to look at the elderly lady.

'Drink your milk, Rose. Yes, Aunt. You were saying?'

Rose made a face. The girls' mother had died of tuberculosis and because Rose was so skinny, her father continually forced pints of milk on her in the belief that it would strengthen her. *'Delicate Child Force-fed Milk by Brutal Relations. Earl's Mansion Hides Broken Heart,'* murmured Rose, who kept a scrapbook full of lurid headlines cut out from newspapers. She sipped a half-teaspoon of milk and curled her lip.

'I was saying, Michael,' Great-Aunt Lizzie's voice rose to its shrill, well-bred heights, 'that Cousin Fanny has written to me. She enquires whether Violet is to be presented at court this spring.' She waited until Rose had swallowed a gulp of her milk and then continued. 'She suggests that Violet's godmother the Duchess of Denton may consider presenting her – she was such a great friend of dear Mary's – and would perhaps allow her to share in her daughter Catherine's coming-out party. We would, of course, have to take a house in London – at least for a month or so – and get the girl some decent clothes.'

Violet jerked her head away from the window and looked at her great-aunt; her eyes were blazing with excitement. Daisy stretched out and linked her little finger with Poppy's under the table. They knew how much this meant to their sister – to be a deb one needed to be presented at court by someone who had been presented themselves, and their mother's death had meant they didn't have many options in that department. Great-Aunt Lizzie was too fragile and

Cousin Fanny had her own daughter to present.

'Impossible! You know that perfectly well. I can't afford anything of the sort.' The Earl avoided his daughter's eyes. 'Maybe next year, if times are better,' he added. Bateman the butler looked distressed and poured a little extra water into his master's glass, perhaps wishing that it was wine as in the affluent days. Michael Derrington swallowed it down and glared angrily around the table.

'Next year I will be too old, Father!' wailed Violet.

'Hollywood,' mimed Daisy, but it was no good. Violet got up from the table and went out, slamming the door behind her. Rose took advantage of the disturbance to tip the rest of her milk into a low bowl of spring flowers, but failed to avoid Great-Aunt Lizzie's eagle eye or a lecture about deceit and wastefulness, and Poppy absentmindedly tapped a rhythm on the table. Michael Derrington made the sound of a man who is driven to madness by his unreasonable family.

'Great-Aunt Lizzie is so stupid. Why talk to Father about hiring a house? She knows he won't do it,' remarked Poppy in an undertone as they left the dining room together after the disastrous lunch.

'Stupid is the last thing she is,' said Daisy with a chuckle. 'She never does things without thinking about them. I bet that business about Cousin Fanny was all carefully calculated. Now, if she manages to get the Duchess to offer to present Violet and to invite her to share the coming-out ball with her daughter, Father will be so relieved that he doesn't have to pay for it he will say yes straight away.'

'Gee, man, you sure do have some brains!' said Poppy appreciatively, trying to put an American twang into her voice.

'She's probably in the drawing room at this moment sitting in front of her desk and writing a letter to the Duchess,' said Daisy confidently. She thought for a moment and then added, 'I wonder if it would be better if Violet wrote – perhaps just to tell her that her eighteenth birthday is next week. What do you think, Poppy? Would it work?' Daisy wasn't sure. Could Violet write the sort of letter that asked for something without really spelling it out? Violet wrote a lot of poetry, but poetry was probably not the best way to get to the Duchess's heart. 'I suppose that it might sound like she wants a present,' she finished.

'I've got it,' she said suddenly. 'I'll take a photo of her and it can be a birthday portrait. She send it to the Duchess. Nothing wrong about that, is there? It's the other way round: Vi is sending the Duchess a present, not asking for one.'

'I suppose it's an idea,' said Poppy indifferently.

'It's brilliant!' Without another word to Poppy, Daisy turned and ran into the hall, opening the door to the drawing room quietly and closing it gently after her.

She had been almost right. Great-Aunt Lizzie was in the drawing room and she was sitting in front of her desk. The drawer filled with sheets of stiff white writing paper was open and the inkstand was pulled forward, but she wasn't writing. Her gaze was fixed on the magnificent portrait of the girls' mother which hung over one of the two fireplaces in the room.

Mary Derrington had been a beauty. Her colouring had been the same as Poppy's – red hair and amber eyes – yet her face and figure were more like Violet's, with perhaps a look of Rose about the slightly hooded eyes. This portrait had been painted when she was first married and she looked so young and so happy that Daisy could hardly bear to look at it.

'I was wondering, Great-Aunt Lizzie, whether if I took a photograph – a sort of portrait – of Violet to celebrate her eighteenth birthday,' began Daisy and then, as she saw a slightly impatient look come into the elderly woman's eyes, she rushed ahead. 'I thought it might make a nice gift for Violet to send to her godmother,' she ended demurely, trying to sound innocent of any scheme.

'What a good idea!' Great-Aunt Lizzie's troubled face cleared after a moment's thought. 'Yes, Daisy, I think that would be a very good idea. I don't think Her Grace has seen Violet since she was about twelve or thirteen years old.'

'I'll get Morgan to rub down a thin piece of wood and I'll stick the photograph to it and Violet can do some of her fancy lettering underneath . . .' It would be useless, she knew, to ask for the photograph to be properly framed.

'Lady Violet Derrington on Her Eighteenth Birthday.' Great-Aunt Lizzie was nodding energetically.

'I'll make it look really professional,' said Daisy earnestly. 'At least, I'll try.' Suddenly she knew this was the moment to ask for something that she had wanted for quite some time. 'The trouble is that I need plenty of space to develop and print a big picture like that. It's a bit difficult developing things in that cupboard in our dressing room,' she went on. 'Do you think that I could use the old dairy pantry?'

Her aunt opened her mouth as though to say no – her usual response to making any changes in the house – but then thought of the portrait and shut it again. 'I don't see why not, but have a word with Mrs Pearson,' she said after a moment.

'Yes, Great-Aunt,' said Daisy politely and edged her way out of the room before any more could be said. Mrs Pearson, the housekeeper, was an amiable woman, far too old to run the household with half the number of staff needed for a house of the size of Beech Grove Manor, but, like the elderly butler, still bravely struggling on in a poverty-stricken environment for which they were both quite untrained. She wouldn't care what Daisy did as long as it didn't make more work for her and the maids. In fact, she was snoring loudly as Daisy passed the house-keeper's room on the way down to the basement. Daisy decided to leave her in peace and get on with her plans.

There was a labyrinth of rooms in the basement of Beech Grove Manor House. There had been a time in the last century when all food eaten by the large household had been processed down there, but now many of the rooms had been shut up. The dairy pantry which Daisy had her eye on had not been used for years. It had originally been the place where surplus milk was turned into huge round cheeses and left to mature on the shelves for a few months. The large wooden casks and paddles for stirring the milk and the enormous sieves for separating the curds from the whey, the cheese moulds and the wire cheese cutters were still stored there, but nowadays there was not much surplus milk and what cheese was needed for household use was usually made in the back kitchen.

The room had a tiny window looking out on a small sunken area. The light that came through the window could be shut off with the wooden shutter to which Daisy reckoned she could nail a piece of black cloth to cover any cracks . It had a sink with running water which would be invaluable for rinsing the negatives. An ancient covered lantern with a shutter stood on top of the draining board – that might be useful if she just wanted a little light. There was a handy shelf for her chemicals and an array of old dishes and cheese moulds which would be good for developing the films, and there were hooks underneath the shelf which could be used to hold a small line with pegs for hanging up the film to dry. In the middle of the room was a rough pine table and a stool. The room was perfect except for one thing – all of its walls were whitewashed, the worst possible background for developing films.

Without wasting a moment, Daisy went out through the back door towards the stables. Whenever anything needed to be done there was one man everyone turned to and that was Morgan the chauffeur.

Morgan's actual job was to drive the ancient Humber car and to keep it in good running order. In return for that he got a very small salary and the free use of an ancient cottage in the woods. And that cottage was the reason why a talented man like Morgan stayed in a badly paid job where he had little to do. A jazz player with a set of drums would not be tolerated in most jobs, but in the depths of the beech woods he disturbed no one and made a headquarters for the jazz-mad local young people, including Poppy. While not playing jazz or attending to his duties as a chauffeur, Morgan did everything else that he could turn his hand to, from felling the odd tree for firewood to mending the roof or painting walls. Moreover, since he had been in the Corps of Royal Engineers during the last year of the war, the skills he had learned then were now employed in servicing the ancient generator in the woods and keeping in working order the pump that brought water from the lake to the house as well as overhauling the twenty-year-old Humber car.

When Daisy went in search of him Morgan was vigorously cleaning out a disused stable. There was now only one man employed at the stables and he, like most of the staff, was fairly elderly and his time was taken up with looking after the Earl's stallion and the girls' ponies. Without Morgan's work the stables would crumble away.

'You wouldn't do me a big favour, would you, Morgan?' Daisy knew that he would. He was very interested in her ambition to make a film. 'Might go off to Hollywood myself one day,' he often said. She explained about the dairy pantry, her need for a proper developing room and the snowy-white walls, and he nodded. 'Let me just finish off this job and then I think I know where there's an old pot of brown paint. That should do you.' While he was talking he was busy clearing out the feeding trough, handily set just inside the open window hatch so that the horse could feed from the outside as well as when it was indoors.

'This stable hasn't been used for about twenty years – apparently it was for guests' horses in your grandfather's day,' he said, pulling out handfuls of dried leaves and twigs and clumps of mud and stuffing them into a sack. 'Too good for a workshop, but at least I'll keep it clean and tidy. Hold that sack open for me, would you? There's just some solid stuff at the very bottom of the trough.'

'What's that?' asked Daisy curiously as she caught a glimpse of a wooden box amid the black compost.

'Dunno – some sort of cigar box, I'd say. Here you are – have a look.' The box had broken in his hand and he took out an old envelope and gave it to her. Daisy looked at the water-stained envelope carefully. There was a smear of ink as if once there had been something written on it – a person's name and address, no doubt – but now it was unreadable. She gave him the sack, pulled up the flap of the envelope and took out a sheet of paper.

Morgan had lost interest. 'I'll just burn this stuff and then I'll be with you in five minutes.'

'I'll wait in the dairy,' said Daisy, making an effort to

sound her usual self. She was glad that he hadn't wanted to see the letter. Somehow she would have been embarrassed to show it to him.

Poppy was coming down the back avenue when Daisy came out from the stables. She was running a race with her dog, an overgrown harrier puppy called Satchmo, and Daisy went across to her.

'Poppy,' she said, 'come into the dairy with me. I want to show you something.'

Chapter Three

The letter was written in faded ink, but the words were still quite legible. The paper was stiff and glossy as Daisy unfolded it and held it out towards Poppy. They both moved nearer to the window and Poppy peered at the faint handwriting.

'*My darling*,' she read, and then stopped.

'Hey, Daisy,' she said indignantly, 'that's someone's love letter. We can't read that.'

'Look at the date,' said Daisy. She knew what Poppy meant. She had felt quite embarrassed at first.

'What!' Poppy narrowed her eyes and peered at the faded numbers. 'Twentieth of March 1906! Before we were born!'

'Poor girl, whoever she was,' said Daisy. She read over the words again to herself. The message was short but its meaning unmistakable.

'*They'll have to allow us to get married,*' read Poppy aloud. 'And look – *They can't say that we're too young now*. She says that she's a month overdue so she must have been two months pregnant – that's right, isn't it? I wonder how old they were. Perhaps he was a stable boy and she was a housemaid.'

'Perhaps,' said Daisy. 'The paper seems good quality though. Look how it's lasted. And the handwriting . . .'

They stared at each other uncomfortably and were almost relieved when they heard a heavy step outside.

'Here I am,' said Morgan, pushing open the door. 'Yes, this would be very nice, my lady. You'd have plenty of room here to develop your films. You leave it to me – I'll have this done in half an hour. Give it a couple of hours to dry and then you're in business.'

'Thank you so much.' Daisy had wondered if she should offer to help, but she guessed that Morgan would probably be quicker on his own.

'You're the bee's knees, Morgan,' said Poppy affectionately. She and her friends in the jazz band were full of expressions like that. 'Come on, Daisy – let's go and find Violet and tell her about our brilliant idea.'

She opened the swing door leading to the hall, almost bumping into Rose.

'What are you doing down here?' she asked. 'You know Great-Aunt Lizzie said it's too cold and damp down in the basement for you,' she added in a lower tone as Rose put her finger to her lips.

'Looking for Maud to help me with my sums,' she said. Rose was a gifted child so far as English literature and writing stories were concerned, but she hated maths and was in despair until she found that Maud, the scullery maid, was a genius with numbers and was of far more help to her than any of her older sisters.

'Well, she's cleaning out the fireplace in the library while Father is having his after-lunch walk,' said Poppy.

'What's that?' Rose had spotted the envelope.

'None of your business,' said Poppy.

'Oh, let her look,' said Daisy. She hadn't a great imagination herself, and neither had Poppy. Rose would be the one who might reconstruct the story that lay behind the letter. With a cautious glance at the closed drawing-room door, she moved across to the window beside the hall door.

'That looks like Great-Aunt Lizzie's handwriting,' said Rose as she unfolded the sheet of paper, 'and it looks like her writing paper too.' Her eyes widened as she read the letter.

'I say!' she exclaimed. *'Romantic Past of Earl's Aunt Uncovered. Shocked Nieces Hang their Heads in Shame.'*

'It's a good job you have Maud to do your sums,' said Poppy with a giggle. 'Look at the date! Great-Aunt Lizzie would have been at least sixty back then.'

'Makes it even more shocking,' said Rose primly. 'She was old enough to know better. Anyway, I'd better find Maud and tell her that the fireplace in the schoolroom needs cleaning. If she doesn't come to my aid soon, I shall be found to have expired from brain fever.'

'Give me back the letter.' Daisy followed her sister into the sunny library. The windows there faced south and gave a view of the front lawn and the main avenue. There was a young man riding down it.

'Baz!' exclaimed Poppy and ran out to greet him. This was Basil Pattenden, son of a local landowner and Poppy's best friend. Soon Edwin and George would arrive with their instruments and then there would be a full-scale jazz session in Morgan's cottage in the midst of the beech woods.

Rose gave the letter back reluctantly, but her mind was on her sums so she did not make too much of a fuss. Already she was holding out a mass of figures to Maud, the scullery maid, who was on her knees before the fire, carefully removing the hot ash into a metal bucket.

Maud had been working for the Derrington family for over two years and as scullery maid all the hard, unpleasant jobs fell to her. She was an orphan and had been brought up in the village workhouse, attended the village school until she was fourteen years old and was then sent off to work as a scullery maid in the big house. The village schoolmistress had hoped that the clever girl might become a monitor, helping with the younger ones in the school, and perhaps eventually a teacher. However, the Orphanage Board were not prepared to house Maud for any longer and so she had gone into service. Daisy had listened to her explaining maths to Rose and thought what a good teacher she would have made if things had been different for her. Certainly her knowledge of maths was far beyond that of any of the Earl's daughters.

Some day, Daisy told herself, I must do a film about her. She has the most unusual face. She comes out really well on film.

'Why don't you stay here, Rosie?' she said. Maud would light the fire in a minute and would have an excuse to linger until it was burning well. Rose would be nice and warm there and her father had gone for a ride so they would be undisturbed for the next half an hour.

Violet was sitting on the window seat of the blue bed-room with a book of Tennyson's poetry on her lap when Daisy went in, camera in hand. Her face was tragic as she turned to her younger sister.

'I don't suppose it will ever happen,' she said sadly. 'I don't suppose I will be invited to London by my god-mother. I was just reading "The Lady of Shalott" and about how she floated down the river to Camelot. I'm like her – I'm sick of shadows, sick of reading about love and never finding it. If only I could be part of the real world.'

Daisy nodded sympathetically. She pushed away the thought that there was plenty of real life to experience in Beech Grove Manor. There were eggs to collect from the numerous hens that strutted around the woodland and late apples, stored in the attics, to be sorted; there were horses to be groomed and dogs to be brushed; there was stable manure to be shovelled . . .

'I've got an idea,' she said cautiously, watching her sister's face for a reaction. 'I thought it might be good to send your godmother an eighteenth-birthday portrait of you – it would be a subtle way of reminding her of you without making it too obvious. She'd think, "Eighteen! She should be one of this year's debutantes!" What do you think? Would it work?'

'Perhaps,' sighed Violet. She turned back to the book on her lap.

'And moving thro' a mirror clear
That hangs before her all the year,

Shadows of the world appear,' she murmured.

'Bring the book with you.' Daisy had suddenly got an idea. 'Come on,' she said. She seized the camera and ushered Violet out through the door, leading the way down the broad steps of the main staircase.

'We'll go out by the lake,' she said over her shoulder. The background would be perfect for Violet's starry beauty and the south-westerly sun would be in a perfect position.

The lake at Beech Grove Manor was a large one stretching over some twelve acres and reputed to be bottomless. A pier jutted out into it for about a hundred yards. Built by their father about twenty years previously, soon after he had inherited the estate, it was a good place to fish from on summer evenings if one did not want to disturb the fish by taking out a boat. There had been plenty of money to spend on the estate in those days, thought Daisy, as she positioned Violet on the pier railing, and their father had probably been extremely happy then, improving the estate's facilities, mending roads, rebuilding the stables, caring for the woods and the lake. These days he seemed to be sunk in almost permanent gloom, unless entertaining one of his old friends.

'Just read aloud to me, Violet,' she said as she retreated a few feet. 'Be quite natural about it. Read a little, then look at the lake, then read again.'

This was going to be a wonderful photograph. It was a beautiful poem and, although the Lady of Shalott was not her kind of girl, she liked the descriptions of the river and she liked even more the expression that it evoked on her sister's face.

Violet read in a voice filled with emotion:

> *'His broad clear brow in sunlight glow'd;*
> *On burnish'd hooves his war-horse trode;*
> *From underneath his helmet flow'd*
> *His coal-black curls as on he rode,*
> > *As he rode down to Camelot.'*

And there it was. The perfect look! Violet lifted her head from the book and stared straight at the camera.

Daisy snapped, and snapped again, and then for the third time, though she felt in her bones that she had already taken a superb photograph.

Suddenly Violet's whole face blazed with eager excitement. She looked like someone who had seen a vision come true.

Daisy snapped again and again and then turned.

There, behind her, was an unknown young man.

He was standing at the end of the pier, one broad hand resting on the rail, and looking at them both. He had a square, determined chin with a scar running through the centre of it, cleaving it in half and forming a dimple. He had dark hazel eyes, crisply curling black hair and a well-shaped, curved mouth. He was dressed in riding breeches and coat and the outfit suited his muscular form. He has an interesting face, thought Daisy. Instinctively she lifted the camera and clicked.

He blinked and looked taken aback.

'I'm Justin Pennington,' he said rather stiffly, looking crossly at Daisy's camera. 'Are you Violet?'

'I'm Violet.' Her sister sounded rather breathless, and she smiled beguilingly at the young man.

'Goodness!' He looked intently at her and then began to laugh in an easy and rather familiar way. 'I haven't seen you for about six or seven years, I suppose. I didn't expect you to look so old. I used to pull your pigtails. Do you remember me? I used to stay with my uncle over at Staplecourt.' He spoke with the easy assurance of a young man about town.

A look of recognition and then disappointment crossed Violet's face, and her smile faded. 'Did you have lots of spots, then?' she enquired sweetly.

'I really can't recollect,' he said haughtily. 'I came over to see your father. Apparently he's out riding. Your great-aunt sent me out here after you. I'm staying with my uncle for a week.'

'On holidays from school, I suppose,' said Violet, her voice a good imitation of the way that Great-Aunt Lizzie spoke to the village children.

'Just finished at Gray's Inn in London,' he said, his eyes roaming over the lake. 'Get any good fishing here at this time of the year?' he asked.

'I have no idea,' said Violet frostily. 'It's not a subject I am interested in.'

He must not be an elder son, thought Daisy. He wouldn't have been studying to be a lawyer if he were. Of course! She remembered now. He was the youngest son of the Earl of Pennington. Violet had a good memory for that sort of thing – that was probably why she was being so unfriendly.

'I recollect you now,' he said, turning his attention to Daisy. 'You're one half of the terrible twins. The blonde and the redhead! I remember you and your sister were up a tree one day and you dropped handfuls of wet mud down on my head.' His smile was friendly, but Daisy did not dare photograph him again. There was something rather commanding and forcible about him – an air of someone who was used to getting his own way.

'I'm awfully sorry about that!' she responded. 'Now, I must go back and develop those pictures. Vi, you show Justin the lake and then bring him back for tea. Father should have returned by then.'

Let Violet entertain him, thought Daisy. It was the least she could do. Meanwhile, Daisy would be working hard on her sister's behalf, to give Violet her heart's desire of going to London as a debutante, having a season and being presented to the King.

Morgan had finished painting the walls of the tiny room when Daisy got back. He had even nailed some black tar paper over the cracks in the wooden shutters and door.

'Looks good, doesn't it?' He glanced around proudly. 'Look, I've whitewashed a piece of board on one side and covered it with brown paint on the other. I've hung it on this nail behind the door. You can turn it to the white side when you want to project the film – so now you have a perfect studio. You can start using it tomorrow morning. Look, it's almost dry already.'

'Hollywood, here I come,' said Daisy, with a grin that stretched from ear to ear. 'You're wonderful. This place is perfect.'

'You'll be a bit cold, I'm afraid,' he said, 'but you couldn't have a fire even if there was a chimney. Those rolls of film burst into flame very easily. I have an idea though. There are shelves of those stoneware hot water bottles in the back pantry over there. Before you start work you could fill four or five of them with hot water from the kitchen and you could put your feet on one and warm your hands on another. The place is so tiny they will even warm the air a bit. Now I'd better be off. Your father will be back soon, and who knows, he may have something he wants me to do in the village.'

Daisy managed to thank him properly before he disappeared. She was amused at his concern for her. She and her sisters were used to the cold in this freezing big house. Morgan's cottage was definitely a much cosier affair, she thought.

She had just finished arranging things to her satisfaction when Rose came in.

'Oh, I say,' was her comment as she looked around, but a second later she blurted out what was on her mind.

'Daisy! That letter! Let me see it!'

Daisy took it from her pocket and handed it to her younger sister. She had suspected that Rose's busy imagination might be at work on the mysterious letter. Rose was now counting laboriously on her fingers. It took her two attempts, but then her face shone with enthusiasm.

'Do you know who wrote this?' she demanded, holding up the letter.

'No,' said Daisy, and could not help adding, 'but definitely not Great-Aunt Lizzie, so put that out of your head.'

Rose ignored her. 'I can guess,' she said triumphantly. She waited for a second and then hissed dramatically, 'It was Maud's mother.'

'What!' exclaimed Daisy. 'But who was Maud's mother?'

'I don't know,' returned Rose. 'And she doesn't know either. She told me that. She's an orphan. She was left outside the door of the workhouse when she was a tiny baby. Nobody knows who put her there – that's what she told me.'

'Yes, but—' began Daisy.

'But . . . don't keep saying "but",' interrupted Rose. 'Do you know how old Maud is?' She didn't wait for an answer but rushed on. 'She is sixteen – that's all she knows.' She held up the letter triumphantly. 'Look,' she said. 'Look at the date on that – 1906. This letter was written seventeen years ago.'

Chapter Four

'I've got an idea,' said a voice in Daisy's ear.

Daisy was glad to wake up. She had been having a strange, confused dream where Maud the scullery maid had taken over the house at Beech Grove Manor and had set all four girls to work in the kitchen. She sat up in bed sleepily and pushed back her curly hair.

Poppy was sitting bolt upright on her bed, an old rug round her shoulders and her breath forming steam in the cold air. Daisy pulled in her hand that had been outside the blankets and eiderdown and lay on it to thaw out her frozen fingers. There were frost patterns on the windows but the sun was beginning to melt their intricate designs. It was going to be another fine day – but getting out of bed and washing in cold water was always a bit difficult in the winter.

'Wake up,' said Poppy impatiently.

'I am awake,' said Daisy. 'I heard you. You have an idea.' She was going to say something sarcastic about Poppy and her ideas, but was still too sleepy to bother.

'It's about Violet – I was thinking that we should have a party for her eighteenth birthday.'

'Great-Aunt Lizzie will say that we can't afford it,' said Daisy automatically. That was her response to most of the girls' suggestions.

'Needn't cost much,' said Poppy laconically. 'The jazz band will provide the music. Free! In fact,' she went on, 'Morgan was saying that we should try to have some practice in playing at real live venues, not just amusing ourselves at the cottage.'

Daisy smiled into her pillow. She should have guessed that it would be about music. Ninety per cent of Poppy's thoughts were connected with jazz and her clarinet. Still, it was not a bad idea. If there was no response from the Duchess to the gift of the photograph, then Violet would badly need cheering up.

'Nothing to wear,' she said sleepily.

'Well, there are lots of mother's old frocks up in that trunk in the attic. Do you remember? We used to dress up in them. Violet could probably make something for herself – and for us – out of them. She's good at that sort of thing. And she spends all her pocket money on fashion magazines so she must know what to do.'

'A party . . .' Daisy was beginning to wake up. She half sat up and then lay down again. The room was very cold. Then she thought of an objection.

'Who's going to be dancing?' she asked.

'Violet, you, me, Edwin, Simon – all the gang. And what about that fellow who turned up yesterday? What was his name? Justin. He could dance with Violet. Then there's Baz for me and George for you – he likes you – and Simon's mad about Violet.' She giggled. The jazz band were forever teasing Simon about Violet – he always turned bright red when she appeared. 'And Edwin could dance with Rose – the jazz band would have to take turns, of course ...'

Daisy thought about it for a moment and looked at it from Violet's point of view. She hadn't seemed to like Justin much, but she would certainly consider the members of the jazz band too young for her – and she wasn't too keen on Simon, calling him 'wet behind the ears'. Yes, it would be a good idea to ask Justin. And it would be jolly to dress up and dance. Daisy forgot about being cold and sat up in bed.

'It would be fun!' she said. 'We'll do it properly – send out invitations and all that. Great-Aunt Lizzie has probably got plenty of invitation cards. I saw the label on her desk drawer and if it's anything like her drawer of writing paper, it's absolutely full up. They probably date from the good old days when money was plentiful. Let's get up.'

Before her courage could fail her at the thought of the icy cold water in the jug on the washstand in their dressing room, Daisy jumped out of bed, got washed and dressed herself in her riding breeches and her two warmest jumpers, pulling a pair of fingerless mittens over her cold hands. It was only then that she noticed the hands on their alarm clock.

'You've woken me up at seven in the morning, Poppy, you idiot,' she shouted through the door, where splashes were punctuated by small shrieks.

Still, now that she was up, she was glad to be early. Her mind was full of the photographs that she had taken yesterday. This portrait had to be something special. She grabbed the alarm clock – all those chemicals needed to be so carefully timed – and went down the back stairs, softly in order not to wake Great-Aunt Lizzie.

The dairy pantry was startlingly cold, but it had one addition since the previous night. A heavy black curtain had been nailed to the outside frame of the door and now not a single chink of light would come in to spoil her film. She picked up two of the stoneware heaters and carried them into the kitchen. For the film's sake as well as her own, that dairy needed to be heated up a little.

Maud was there, piling coal into the enormous black range that did all of their cooking and made the kitchen the warmest room in the house. Thinking about what Rose had said the evening before, Daisy examined the scullery maid carefully as she explained about filling the bottles with boiling water. Was it possible that the girl was anything to do with the Derrington family? Her mother could have been a maid in the house, but who was her father? Not my own father, thought Daisy; that was certain. Michael Derrington had been very much in love with his own wife – he could still hardly speak of her without a break in his voice and sometimes Daisy would come into his library to find him with a small photograph of Mary Derrington in his hands and tears in his eyes. In any case he would probably have been out in India when Maud was conceived.

But what about his younger brother? Robert Derrington was another subject that it was not safe to mention to their father. Robert had been the heir to the earldom as, after nine years of marriage, Mary had shown no signs of having a son. He had been killed in the Boer War in 1899, and that was when Denis – Dastardly Denis as Rose called him, a distant cousin of her father's – had become heir. Any mention of Robert's name threw the Earl into a state of depression as he brooded on how well he and his younger brother would have managed the estate.

It did seem odd for a scullery maid with so little education to be as clever as Maud was. I wonder whether Robert was good at mathematics? Daisy thought.

'I can fill some more bottles for you, my lady,' Maud was saying. 'It'll be perishing cold in that pantry. Lucky it's so small.' She didn't wait for an answer from Daisy, but took down some more of the stoneware bottles from the shelf above the range and poured boiling water into them, fitting the stoppers quickly and efficiently.

'Oh, my lady,' she called when Daisy was carrying the last two bottles out to place under the workbench, 'Morgan left this for you last night.' She held up a discoloured and water-stained print of a mouldering cottage with a hay wagon in front of it. The print had two large safety pins in its top corners. 'Look,' she said, turning it over. 'He's lettered that on the back. You see, my lady, it says No Admittance. Morgan thought you should pin this on to the curtain when you're working – so that no one opens the door accidental-like. He told me to make sure that you got it and to give you these frames too – you can choose which one you like the best when you have the photograph developed. I've washed the glass and polished the wood a bit. Morgan thought they looked like new.' The girl's voice was enthusiastic and her pale cheeks blushed at the memory of the chauffeur's praise.

'That's lovely' said Daisy admiringly. She smiled at the girl. 'You and Morgan are friends, then,' she said teasingly. Great-Aunt Lizzie would have a fit if she over-heard her. She and Mrs Pearson, the housekeeper, had gone to great lengths in the past to keep male and female staff apart. Nowadays the only men apart from Morgan were the elderly stableman and, of course, the butler, but he was seventy if he was a day.

'It's just that we're both orphans, my lady,' said Maud demurely. 'That makes a bond between us. Now, I'd better be getting on with cleaning the grates, if you'll excuse me.'

Daisy forgot about Maud as soon as she seated herself at her workbench, as she had named the old rough pine table. She put her camera in front of her and started to get ready for the work that had to be done in total darkness. Her godfather, Sir Guy Beresford, had trained her to do this, giving her some useless films so that she could prac-tise again and again until she almost felt that she could do it in her sleep. She laid out everything that she would need: the can opener, the metal film reel, the film tank.

Then she put the materials needed at the second stage on one of the shelves: a film developer, the dish for the stop bath, the fixer with hardener, and another dish for a hypo eliminator bath.

By this stage there were footsteps outside on the

kitchen corridor. Nora, one of the housemaids, was chatting to Mrs Pearson and the voice of Mrs Beaton, the cook, could be heard scolding Maud for not having enough hot water on the stove. Daisy felt a little guilty as she moved her feet on the warmers under the bench, but Maud did not reply. She was probably used to it.

Then Daisy forgot about everything. Now was the tricky moment. She lit the covered lantern, went across the room and turned out the light, came back and blew out the lantern. It was essential that there was not one chink of light while she took the film from the camera and fed it on to the metal spool. She had done this so often with her head stuck in the cupboard in the dressing room that she was able to do it quickly and neatly, especially now she had so much extra room for her elbows. Then she picked up the spool and carefully inserted it into the film tank, covering it over with an airproof lid.

When that was done she switched on the light again and breathed a deep sigh of relief. From now on things were easier.

Daisy carried on working quickly and methodically, adding chemicals, shaking the bath until the gong sounded for breakfast.

'Just right,' she thought.

'How's it going?' Morgan was coming out of the kitchen, wiping the back of his mouth with his hand.

Daisy showed him crossed fingers and he nodded understandingly.

*

'Shall we tell them about my idea?' Poppy was waiting outside the dining-room door for her twin.

'Let's get the photograph done first,' said Daisy. 'Come and help me choose the three best prints after breakfast, then we'll show them to the others.'

It was a good job Great-Aunt Lizzie had decided that the three older girls were now too old for formal lessons. As far as Daisy was concerned there did not seem to be enough hours in the day for all the things that she wanted to do and she knew that Poppy felt the same.

But what about Violet? Something had to be done about her! She seemed to spend the days reading or playing endless games of Patience with a pack of cards. Daisy decided that Poppy's idea was good. At least Violet would be occupied in making party dresses for them all. She remembered when they were young she and Poppy used to take elaborate dresses from the trunk labelled 'Lady Derrington' in the attic and trail around pretending to be at a ball for grand young ladies. Surely some of them would do for outfits for Violet's birthday dance.

'This one, definitely, this one and . . . and that one.' Poppy held the negatives to the light and, as usual, was decisive.

'I thought these three were the best as well.' Daisy carefully cut them from the spool of film and poured a chemical into the bath to remove all traces of the fixer. 'I just want to avoid white stains on the negatives,' she muttered, praying that all would go well.

'Have you talked to Morgan about the dance idea yet?'

she asked as she held the negatives under the running water for a final wash.

'Haven't seen him,' replied Poppy.

'Well, you might as well find him now and see what he thinks. This will take a good five minutes and then I'll have to put them in the enlarger and print them.'

It was mid-morning before the three photographs were ready. Michael Derrington was still out on his morning ride around the farms of the estate, Violet was crouched over the wood-burning stove in the hall, reading poetry, and Rose and Great-Aunt Lizzie were struggling with fractions in the schoolroom on the top floor – though why the unfortunate Maud had to toil three storeys up with her bucket of coal when the house was full of unused rooms Daisy never could understand. However, her mother's aunt had a great sense of what was fitting and fractions belonged to the schoolroom.

Daisy borrowed an old dark blue rug from the linen cupboard and went into the library. Maud was sitting on the floor beside the light from the crackling logs in the fireplace. She was chuckling to herself over some hand-written pages torn from an exercise book, but jumped to her feet when Daisy came in and hastily crammed the pages into her apron pocket. Daisy recognized Rose's large scrawl.

'I beg your pardon, my lady; just finishing, my lady.' Hastily she picked up a small log and put it on top of the others.

'It's nice of you to help Rose with her mathematics,

Maud,' said Daisy, 'and encourage her with the stories she writes.' Her eye was on Maud's apron pocket as she spoke, but Maud just muttered something and was out of the room before Daisy could say any more. Rose was clattering down the stairs now, jumping the odd one – no doubt Great-Aunt Lizzie was still on one of the upper floors.

'Have you read it?' Daisy could hear Rose's eager voice, but she couldn't make out Maud's reply. She hurried over to the door.

'Could I read it, too, Rosie?' she asked cheerfully, holding out her hand to Maud. If the story was what she guessed, the sooner it was burned or at least securely hidden from either the housekeeper or Great-Aunt Lizzie herself, the better. Both would be shocked to the core and Rose would be in deep trouble.

'*Juvenilia by Child Genius Collected by Elder Sister. Has Another Jane Austen Been Uncovered?*' said Rose happily as Maud handed the sheets of paper to Daisy.

'Come and help me,' said Daisy, smiling reassuringly at Maud, but the scullery maid just scuttled away through the door that led to the basement.

'You're embarrassing that poor girl,' said Daisy reprovingly, suppressing the thought that she sounded like Great-Aunt Lizzie.

'You're the one who is embarrassing her,' pointed out Rose, and Daisy laughed. 'I suppose you're right,' she said. 'Now spread that rug over the table for me.'

The dark blue background was just right, she thought,

but she did not arrange the photographs on it until after she had sent Rose out to summon the rest of the family.

And then she stood back and waited for their reactions.

The photographs were nearly all the same, but nevertheless one stood out from the rest, and that was the one that Daisy had taken after Justin arrived. Violet had been reading the lines of poetry about Sir Lancelot and his 'coal-black' curls, had looked over Daisy's shoulder, and had seen the dark-haired young man as if he were a figure from the poem.

One by one her father, Poppy, Rose and Violet picked out this photograph and then everyone looked at Great-Aunt Lizzie.

'Not that one,' she said slowly. Elderly though she was her voice, as always, was clipped and assured. 'Not that one,' she repeated. 'We must remember that the Duchess of Denton has her own daughter to bring out.' She paused for a moment, visibly weighing up whether more need be said or not and then coming to a decision.

'This one, dear,' she said firmly and picked up the first photograph. 'The other one, that you all like, should be hung in the gallery.'

'That's not the best one – you're right about that,' said Poppy as a disappointed Daisy wrapped Great-Aunt Lizzie's choice in tissue paper and placed it in a cardboard box and Violet penned a little note to her godmother.

'I don't care as long as she invites me to London,' said

Violet. She folded the piece of stiff, embossed writing paper and placed it on top of the portrait. 'I just want to be presented and have some fun like other girls. And marry someone rich,' she added. 'I don't think that I could bear to be poor again. I'm just so sick of it. And if you and Daisy help me, then I'll find husbands for the two of you when you come out in 1925. I promise,' she added.

'And me?' asked Rose.

'And you,' Violet assured her. 'But I have to get away from this place or I'll go mad. I just can't stand it – nothing new, everyone talking about being poor, and it's so cold and damp.'

'That's because you weren't born to it,' said Daisy wisely. 'You can remember times when Father and Mother were rich and there were fires in every room. Poppy and I can't really remember those times – neither can Rose.'

'Ah, but I have an imagination,' said Rose. 'I can feel in my bones what it must have been like. I think that Violet should make the ultimate sacrifice for her sisters. She must marry money. Otherwise I may fall into a decline and fade away.'

'I would, like a shot,' said Violet broodingly. 'The only trouble is that so far I don't think I've met anyone with money. When I asked Great-Aunt Lizzie for money to post this parcel, she went to her desk and handed out stamps one by one. Look at them – rows and rows of penny stamps from the time of Queen Victoria. I'd be embarrassed to take this to the post office. I'll ask Morgan to take it for me.'

'Tell him not to pay any extra for it himself though, if that's not enough,' said Daisy.

'Let's choose you a rich husband,' said Rose. 'It's a shame that Great-Aunt Lizzie has given up having magazines delivered. Still I've cut lots of society pictures out from *The Lady*. Wait! I'll get my scrapbook.'

By the time the penny stamps were all glued on to the parcel, Rose was back with her cuttings scrapbook.

'What about the Earl of Charleforth?' she asked.

'He's bald,' said Violet, glaring at the picture in Rose's scrapbook.

'He's probably even balder now,' said Rose cheerfully. 'That picture must have been taken about five years ago. He's still in uniform. He's rich though. It talks about him going back to care for his extensive estates. I found that newspaper on a shelf in the linen cupboard.'

'Father's got extensive estates, but he's poor,' pointed out Daisy.

'That's because of dastardly Denis; the 'orrible heir,' said Poppy knowledgeably. The shortcomings of the unpleasant heir to the Derrington estate were a popular topic during their father's more garrulous moods. 'He won't allow Father to sell the woodland and so all of the trees are falling down in storms and we're as poor as church mice. The Penningtons have sold another farm – Morgan told me that.'

'If only you were a boy,' said Violet irritably to Rose.

'Then you would be the heir. Everybody was sure you were going to be a boy before you were born. I remember Nanny talking to us about a 'little brother'. If you were the heir you could agree to Father selling the trees and a couple of farms and then I could have a season in London like all the other girls.'

'Look, here's the man for you,' said Rose, ignoring Violet's constantly repeated lament about the family estate going to a distant cousin who was an unpleasant individual, determined not to help their father in his money troubles. 'Go on, look! You can't say *he's* bald.'

Violet surveyed the picture framed by Rose's cupped hand. A slight smile tugged at the petulant corners of her lovely mouth. 'I must say that he is rather good-looking. Looks a bit like that Rudolph Valentino in *The Four Horsemen of the Apocalypse*. Who is he? I'm sure I've seen him before.'

'Prince George,' said Rose, removing her hand. 'Just the perfect age for you – three years older. He was born on the twentieth of December, 1902.' Rose was a great authority on the royal family and knew all their birthdays, the cars they drove, the house parties they attended, the sports that they were good at and even their second, third, fourth and fifth names.

'I'm sure that King George would love me to marry his son,' said Violet glumly. 'He would regard it as a very good match – especially if I turned up in darned breeches and a jumper that has been washed ten times too often.'

'Well, Prince George is his fourth son so he's probably

not too fussy,' said Rose wisely. 'After all, he has only managed to get one of them engaged so far. And they go to every party in London. There are pages and pages of the royal princes in all the copies of *The London Illustrated News*.'

Violet stared moodily at the parcel with its rows of penny stamps. Suddenly she picked it up and kissed it. 'If only the Duchess will invite me to one of those parties,' she said. 'I promise you that I will do my best. I'll marry someone rich and then I'll present you all in court and you'll make splendid marriages too. I swear I'll do that!'

And then she put it down and burst into tears. 'It's all so silly,' she said tragically. 'It's like Cinderella. I'm too old for fairy stories. Nothing is going to happen. We're going to go on living in this dreary place year after year, having no fun, being poor, poor, poor.'

Daisy looked at Poppy and found her twin's amber eyes fixed on hers. One eyebrow was raised. As usual the same thought had come to both at the same moment.

'Go on, you tell her,' said Daisy. 'It was your idea.'

'Well, we were thinking of having a surprise birthday party for you next week,' said Poppy.

'They're just telling you a week early so that you'll forget and then it really will be a surprise,' explained Rose. 'Poor things! Don't laugh at them – they haven't got their younger sister's brains,' she added in loftily condescending tones.

'We're telling her a week early, Miss Clever,' snapped Poppy, 'because she's the only one of us good at sewing and she'll have to make the dresses.'

'Weave them from spiders' webs.' Violet made an effort to stop crying. She brushed the tears from her eyes and managed a faint smile.

'We were thinking about Mother's old dresses. Up in the trunk in the attic,' explained Daisy. 'We could just chop them a bit so that they're nice and short and fashionable.'

'And the jazz band would provide the music and the boys could be dancing partners too.' This was the most important part for Poppy.

'But we thought we would ask Justin for you,' put in Daisy hurriedly. Violet was not interested in the jazz club boys, who were all Poppy's age.

'Justin!' Now a speculative look had come into Violet's eyes. Daisy and Poppy exchanged glances. Violet was obviously thinking hard.

'We'll have to have some decent dresses, but we can do it in a week,' she said in a determined fashion. 'Rose, you give that parcel to Morgan. I'm going to see Great-Aunt Lizzie about those old dresses of Mother's up in the attic. With a bit of work we might be able to do something with them.'

Chapter Five

'Well?' The twins were waiting in the hall when Violet came out of the drawing room, gently closing the door after her. She was flushed and smiling.

'She says yes – but we must talk to Mrs Pearson first. And we can take what we like from the attic. And most of the food at the supper has to be made from eggs,' she added, and both girls started to laugh. Hens were their standby. Dozens of them wandered around the beech woods and their eggs were plentiful even in wintertime.

Mrs Pearson was eventually tracked down by Rose to Great-Aunt Lizzie's bedroom. As they climbed the stairs, they could hear her scolding the maids.

'Nora, haven't you finished Lady Violet's room yet? Dorothy has cleaned three bedrooms while you were lingering here. And Maud, hurry up, child, for goodness sake. There are ten more fireplaces for you to do.' Mrs Pearson could never get used to having only three maids under her.

'Don't be cross, Mrs Pearson; we've come to you for some advice.' Daisy knew that Mrs Pearson had a soft spot for good gossip and she led the housekeeper into Violet's bedroom. 'Poppy and I were thinking about having a birthday party for Violet next week; Great-Aunt says that we may, but we're not sure what to do about it.

You remember the old days, don't you, when there were parties all the time?'

Mrs Pearson began to smile. 'Well, of course, there were only two boys at Beech Grove Manor when I first became housekeeper, but then of course . . . later on, when . . . when your mother came here . . . But I suppose you know all about that.'

'A bit,' said Daisy, frowning at Poppy who, she guessed, was going to bring Mrs Pearson back to the point. It was better to let the old lady have her reminiscences and gently steer her back to practicalities. 'Was Mother pretty?'

'Very!' Mrs Pearson sighed. 'They were . . . Yes, she was lovely. Well, no good talking about the past,' she said, to the girls' relief. 'You were asking about parties and I can tell you we had plenty of them the year your mother came here.'

'Sit here, Mrs Pearson.' Violet pushed forward the shabby old chair. It had originally been covered in velvet, but most of the silky nap had been worn off so the chair had been moved out of the library to the bedroom. 'Tell us all about it.'

Violet, Daisy was glad to see, gave her a beautiful smile and began to look as happy as a girl whose future lies ahead of her. She was an imaginative person and it was easy for her to lose herself in a dream. The trouble came when she had to face reality.

'Did they use the ballroom?' asked Rose.

'Of course they did! And musicians hired from

London.' Mrs Pearson sank into the still-comfortable ancient chair. The four Derrington girls arranged themselves in a row on the bed.

'There was more staff then: four scullery maids to do all the fires, three parlourmaids and six chambermaids – and, of course, your mother's lady's maid.' Old Mrs Pearson smiled at the memory. 'And Mrs Beaton had a couple of useful girls to help her with the cooking – training them she was, of course.'

'Of course,' echoed Daisy, trying to visualize possibilities for useful-young-girls-to-help-in-the-kitchen from among the inhabitants of the village beyond Beech Grove Manor on the day of Violet's party and then rejecting the idea. Even girls from the village school would want to be paid.

'Of course lots and lots of visitors used to come to stay. Every room in the house filled, for sure,' went on Mrs Pearson. 'And all those beautiful young ladies and fine young men! And our own ladies . . . lady . . . the most beautiful and the cleverest of them all. And the sweetest by a long shot. This was before the war, of course. Everything was different then.'

'We could never do that nowadays, of course. But we wondered about just having a small party for Violet's eighteenth birthday.' Daisy decided to take a chance and lead the conversation back to the present.

Mrs Pearson had been shaking her head sadly but at Daisy's last words, she stiffened. A light of battle came into her old eyes.

'I don't see why we shouldn't,' she said. 'It doesn't seem right that an eighteenth birthday shouldn't be marked. I remember when your father was eighteen, the celebrations – nothing to when he was twenty-one, of course. They were roasting whole deer out in the park for the tenants then and the house was full of young people.'

'And my Uncle Robert?' asked Daisy. What she wanted was an account of a smaller party.

'He was dead, poor fellow, before he ever reached the age of twenty-one. That nasty old Boer War.' A tear came into the old lady's eye. She sighed heavily and then said hastily as she got to her feet, 'We could do a small party for you, Lady Violet. Mrs Beaton would make some nice little cakes and we could have a trifle I dare say. Custard is no problem; the hens are still laying well and, of course, there's always cream from the Jersey cow. That would be nice. You have a little chat with Mrs Beaton and I'm sure that she'll come up with some good ideas.'

'Now for the attic!' said Poppy as soon as Mrs Pearson had gone

The trunk marked with the label LADY MARY DERRINGTON, BEECH GROVE MANOR, KENT, ENGLAND was still there. Daisy threw back the lid and started to pull out dresses, wraps, petticoats, and pretty gloves, stockings and shoes.

But there was a shock.

As each dress was shaken and held up to the light of the roof window the awful truth was revealed.

They had all been attacked by moths.

Thousands of tiny holes showed like pinpricks against the light and then the fabric began to split and rends appeared. Garment after garment was taken out until only an old photograph album was left at the bottom of the trunk. But it was no good – they were all ruined. A musty smell set them all coughing and sneezing.

Poppy's eyes met Daisy's with dismay.

'It's us,' she said, half laughing, half ashamed. 'We probably left the lid open when we used to dress up years ago.'

'Look, a photograph album,' said Rose, picking out the pockmarked velvet-covered book. 'Oh, how sweet! Look, it says POPPY AGED ONE MONTH. What a dear little girl. *Beautiful Baby Grows Up to Be Ugly Duckling!*'

'Just Poppy? Where am I?' wondered Daisy.

'Perhaps you were camera-shy,' suggested Rose.

'I can't believe it,' muttered Violet. 'Everything always goes wrong. We can't use any of these – they'll probably fall apart on the dance floor.'

She got up and wandered irritably around the attic and then stopped beside a trunk labelled LORD ROBERT DERRINGTON. 'Perhaps we could make it a fancy dress party,' she said. 'This will have his uniform from the Boer War. Father's probably got his Indian Army stuff somewhere as well.'

Daisy thought of her father's fury if they meddled with his uniforms. 'Wouldn't suit you,' she said hastily. 'You're not one of those girls that look good in men's clothing. You're the Lady of Shalott type.'

'Here you are, Daisy,' said Poppy, who had now got hold of the photograph album. 'Here we are, both of us: "POPPY AND DAISY ON BOARD SHIP". This must have been going back to England after the news came about grandfather's death.'

'You look more advanced than I do,' said Daisy, peering over her shoulder. 'I seem to be all floppy-headed and you're holding your head up and looking all around you.'

'LADY ELAINE CARRUTHERS,' read Rose, who had been kicking noisily at a jammed cupboard door in another room of the attic and had just managed to get it open. And then she repeated in excited tones: 'Elaine Carruthers! Come quick, everyone – I've found another trunk in this cupboard. Who's Lady Elaine Carruthers?'

There was a clatter of feet as her sisters followed her, Daisy hastily replacing the photograph album.

'Carruthers? But that's Great-Aunt Lizzie's name.'

'And Mother's – she was Great-Aunt Lizzie's niece.'

'This Elaine must have been related to Mother.'

'Wonder what her clothes are like?'

'I seem to remember,' said Daisy, 'that when Father was talking once to Great-Aunt about the entail and how Dastardly Denis would get the lot because the estate is entailed to a male, she sniffed and said: "Nothing like that in our family – the two girls inherited everything! No nonsense about having to have a brother."'

'So perhaps Elaine was Mother's sister,' said Poppy.

'But why haven't we heard anything about her? Why the secret? Perhaps she murdered someone and died on the scaffold.' Rose was enraptured.

'Probably she and Great-Aunt Lizzie had a quarrel. You know what she's like.' Daisy pulled at the upended trunk, pushing it around so that the handle could be found.

'Bet she had some good clothes – Mother's family were very rich. I think, from something that Great-Aunt Lizzie said, that was how Father financed the diamond mine out in India,' said Violet happily. 'Wonder if Elaine looked like me? After all, if she was Mother's sister she would have been our aunt.'

'Do you know, this is the funny thing,' said Daisy. 'I don't think that I've seen a photograph of her. I must have a look in the gallery.'

'It's locked; the trunk is locked,' announced Rose, holding a stout padlock in her hand and then letting it fall. The sisters looked at each other.

'Well,' said Daisy, 'Great-Aunt Lizzie did say that we could use anything from the attic. Poppy, see if you can find Morgan.'

Poppy was gone almost before the last word fell from Daisy's lips. The remaining three girls looked carefully at the label on the trunk. 'That's Mrs Pearson's handwriting,' said Violet after a moment. 'I know the way that she makes a "E". I've seen it often enough on the pots of elderberry jam.'

'Perhaps Elaine Carruthers went out to India with Mother and Father. Mrs Pearson must have packed away all the clothes that Elaine didn't take with her,' said Daisy. 'Perhaps she got married out in India and never turned up to claim her clothes. Let's hope that she left behind a few decent dresses.' And then something caught her attention and she bent over the trunk. 'It's been sealed with wax,' she said with awe. 'Good old Mrs P – no moths here.'

'Hope there's something for me,' said Rose wistfully. 'It's sad to be the sister who is always ignored and left out of things.'

'Don't worry, you're as tall as Daisy and these days no one needs a figure,' said Violet kindly. 'We'll find something for you if we can get the trunk open.'

Funny the way that no one suggests asking Great-Aunt Lizzie for a key, thought Daisy. We're probably right though. There's something odd about this Elaine. Why haven't we heard about her before? Perhaps it was true that she went out to India with Mother and Father and left behind the clothes she wasn't taking with her. But why has she never been mentioned by either Great-Aunt Lizzie or Father? She made a resolution to hunt for a photograph of the long-vanished Elaine and went to the door to wait for Morgan.

When Poppy reappeared though, she was followed by the tall figure of Justin.

'Morgan's not back from the village yet; Mrs Beaton went with him so they may be ages. I've brought Justin. I've told him about the party and about us looking for dresses. Oh, and Rose, Great-Aunt Lizzie is looking for you everywhere. You'd better fly.'

Daisy could see a struggle in Violet's face as horror at Poppy's outspokenness fought with the desire to see what was in the trunk. She won't worry too much, thought Daisy, watching her elder sister with interest as she shrugged her shoulders. He's a younger son; he has no money, no house, no estate. She could almost see the words 'Why should I care about him?' form on her sister's lovely lips before she smiled and said graciously, 'It's very kind of you to come all the way up here.'

'On the contrary, you're doing me a favour. I've been carrying around this ridiculous penknife with forty blades in it since the days when I was a Boy Scout,' he said with a smile that deepened the dimple on his chin. 'Let's drag the trunk over under the light. Now, I wonder, how does one pick a lock? You read these things in books, don't you? They always sound so easy. Let's try the blade for getting stones out of a horse's hoof. That's the only one that I've ever used.'

'Never mind,' said Violet kindly after a good ten minutes had passed and Justin had risen to his feet, staring in a frustrated way at the lock which remained stubbornly fastened. 'You did your best . . .'

'I suppose you've tried this key already,' said Justin. He reached over to the top of a worm-eaten tallboy standing in the corner of the room and took down a small key, blowing the dust off it before handing it to Violet. Daisy could see her sister's hand tremble as she fitted it into the lock and the click seemed very loud as she turned it.

'Well, we never thought of looking for a key up there,'

said Poppy. 'Good job you're so tall.'

'I'm so sorry that we troubled you.' Violet had gone back to her society manner, modelled on Great-Aunt Lizzie.

'Not at all,' Justin responded with equal politeness. 'In fact, you have probably done me a great service. Now that my inability to pick locks has been so clearly demonstrated I will give up all thoughts of entering the housebreaking trade and will devote myself to the law.'

'You could put your knife to use in breaking the wax seal,' pointed out Daisy. She had decided that she rather liked Justin. What a pity he was a younger son, she thought. Either he would have to marry a rich girl or he would have to wait for years until he made enough money to support someone as poor as Violet. The Earl's estate, of course, would go to Justin's eldest brother – entailed also, of course. Life was good to eldest sons. One of the blades on the Boy Scout knife sliced neatly through the solid wax seal, but Violet did not move to open the lid.

'We're most grateful to you,' she said, standing up in imitation of Great-Aunt Lizzie when she felt that a morning visit by a neighbour had gone on long enough.

Justin took the hint. 'Not at all,' he murmured. 'Now, if you'll excuse me, I'll go back to my fishing rod. Your father has very kindly invited me to cast a line into your lake whenever I want.'

'You could have at least asked him to lunch,' said

Daisy once Justin's firm footsteps on the attic staircase had died away.

'Bread and cheese,' said Violet with scorn.

Daisy said no more. The important thing now was what was in this carefully sealed trunk.

'Go on, open it,' she said. 'Let's see what she has there. I bet she did go out to India with Mother and Father.'

'You realize how long ago,' said Violet. 'All the stuff will be those awful Edwardian tight waists and long trains. I hope you don't think we'll look good in that.' She had a half-cross, half-excited look.

'Well, we'll take the scissors to it,' said Daisy cheerfully.

With trembling hands Violet opened the lid and gasped. Inside was a rainbow of soft colours; fabrics that glowed and shimmered in the dim light of the attic.

One by one they took the clothes out – all smelling deliciously of lavender and cedar-wood shavings. On the top were elegant silk blouses, then came soft cashmere jumpers with short sleeves and fitted waists and small fitted linen jackets, and lastly packets of silk stockings and doeskin gloves still as white as lime and trimmed with fluffy pieces of swansdown.

And then they came to the bottom of the top tray of the trunk.

'Lift it out.' Violet's voice was just a croak.

Underneath this was another tray smothered in sheet after sheet of tissue paper. No one said anything – they just pulled it away frantically, scattering the attic floor with crumpled pieces.

And there on the top lay the most beautiful dress. It was made from pink satin, glossy and gleaming as though it were new and trimmed with snowy white lace. Violet bent down, picked it up and held it against Daisy.

'This would be just right for you if it weren't in such a ridiculous shape with that pinched-in waist and trailing skirt.' She gazed at it for a moment and then nodded her head.

'I'll be able to do something with that,' she said, sounding quite unlike the Lady of Shalott and more like a competent dressmaker.

Daisy took the dress. The colour would be perfect for her, she thought, wishing there was a mirror up here in the attic.

'I say, I'd quite like that white silk and that little jacket with the black beads on it,' said Poppy. 'Black and white is what all the jazz players wear. Put that aside for me, Daisy. I have to go now. Baz and George will be in Morgan's cottage already. Hope he's back. Why does he have to keep going on ridiculous errands for Great-Aunt Lizzie when he has much more important things to do?'

And then she was gone.

'Like playing jazz,' commented Daisy with a grin. Poppy's inability to see anything except from her own point of view always amused her. She picked up the elegantly waisted white silk dress and shook it.

'There are yards and yards of material in this,' she said. 'I suppose it would have had a bustle under the train, just like all those old-fashioned photographs of Mother. Can't think how they could have worn such clothes, can you? They look so ridiculous nowadays.'

'Cut on the bias, and really short . . .' began Violet and then screamed with delight. 'Look at this! I didn't know they had colours like this in Edwardian times.'

The dress that Violet had taken out was in a box marked 'Worth of Paris' and it was still wrapped in reams and reams of soft tissue paper. It had probably never been worn, thought Daisy. If this mysterious Elaine had had the same colouring as her, a dress of that colour would probably have been too vivid to suit her.

Violet unwrapped it reverentially, but one glance had been enough to show her that it was what she was looking for. It was the same colour as the dragonflies that darted around the lake in summer months – a gorgeous shade of shimmering green-blue silk sewn with thousands of tiny electric-blue beads. As Violet held it up to the light from the overhead window the dress glittered and the colour deepened and intensified the extraordinary shade of her eyes.

'Let's go down to my bedroom,' she said. 'I've got the most space.'

'You go on down,' said Daisy. 'I'll find something for Rose. She and Poppy can always change it later on if they don't like it.' Violet had a better eye than her for what suited her sisters, but she knew that all of Violet's attention would now be on the beautiful shimmering blue dress and it would be useless to try to divert her.

When Daisy came down from the attic with a velvet dress in a dusky-red colour for Rose, the white silk for Poppy and the pink for herself, Violet was examining herself in the looking glass.

'If only I could bob my hair,' she said wistfully. 'Long hair is so old-fashioned.'

Lying open on the bed was a fashion magazine – Violet spent all of her pocket money on these magazines while Daisy spent hers on film and chemicals to develop the film and Poppy on sheets of jazz music. Rose was deemed too young by Great-Aunt Lizzie to have any pocket money so Violet shared her magazines with her youngest sister. It had a page of fashionable hairstyles and now Violet was looking longingly at them.

Leaving her sister intent on comparing her own image in the looking glass with the pictures in her magazine, Daisy ran up to the schoolroom, passing through the gallery where all the photographs and not-so-valuable family portraits covered almost every inch of the wall. She dawdled there for a while listening to Great-Aunt Lizzie's voice explaining compound interest to Rose, but most of her mind was on her search for a photo or a painting of Elaine.

Even distant cousins were there – all neatly labelled. On wet days she and Poppy used to play games making up stories about all of them, but there was definitely no one who could be Elaine. Suddenly Daisy was intensely curious about her.

She went on to the schoolroom door.

'Excuse me, Great-Aunt Lizzie,' she said, having tapped politely on the door before opening it. 'We have found some dresses that should suit. They'll need quite a bit of sewing to alter them, but Violet thinks that we can do it.'

Daisy laid a slight emphasis on the word 'sewing'. Great-Aunt Lizzie was a wonderful needlewoman, forever embroidering useless cushion covers. She loved to see her nieces stitching.

'Let's go and see the dresses you have chosen,' said Great-Aunt Lizzie graciously. 'Perhaps we should finish for today, Rose. Then your sisters can have the schoolroom for their sewing, if they wish.' She unlocked the big cupboard and took out her pride and joy, an old-fashioned sewing machine that she had bought to help with the war effort almost ten years ago. Many a man fighting in the trenches of Belgium had received one of the shirts sewn in Beech Grove Manor. Even though almost ten years old now, it would be a great help, thought Daisy. Judging by the pictures in Violet's magazines, there would be a lot of hems to be taken up.

Great-Aunt Lizzie was silent for a moment when she saw the costumes laid out on Violet's bed. 'Where did you get these?' she asked eventually. There was an odd note in her voice and Rose looked at her with puzzlement.

'They were from one of the trunks,' explained Violet. 'It was marked "Elaine Carruthers". Was she a cousin or something? We thought that she wouldn't want them again, as they're so old-fashioned. That pink will be just right for Daisy, won't it?'

'Just right,' said Great-Aunt Lizzie huskily as Violet held up the dress against Daisy. 'That will hardly need any alteration. You are the image of her at your age. Perhaps a few tucks . . .'

'Perhaps,' said Violet hastily. 'Don't you worry about it, Great-Aunt Lizzie; you will have enough to do. We'll do all the stitching.'

'And what about you, Violet dear?'

'Well, I thought about this.' Hesitantly Violet opened the cardboard box and slowly unfolded the dragonfly-blue dress from its swathes of tissue paper.

There was a moment's silence in the room, a silence full of tension.

'I gave that to Elaine.' The words seemed to be jerked out from Great-Aunt Lizzie's lips. She gazed broodingly at the glorious colour, her lips pressed together.

'It's never been worn, has it?' Daisy waited for a rebuff, but Great-Aunt Lizzie said nothing for a few seconds and when she did speak her voice was hesitant. 'No, it was too . . . no, it didn't fit,' she ended.

Odd, thought Daisy. The dress looked the same size as the others. Even if it were slightly too tight, or too loose, surely it could have been altered or exchanged. She wanted to ask her aunt a million questions, but knew her well enough not to bombard her.

'It should be perfect on you, Violet dear.' The old lady had regained her usual brisk tone and was turning away. 'I'd better go and have a word with Mrs Pearson,' she said.

'You can manage then, girls, can you?' Without waiting for an answer she went through the door with the air of one who is glad to leave a room full of reminders of the past.

When she had gone, Daisy turned to Violet.

'You're not going to wear it like that, Vi, are you?' she asked, looking at the narrow-waisted dress with its huge train.

'You must be joking,' said Violet, an ethereal smile lighting up her beautiful face. 'Great-Aunt Lizzie is going to get a bit of shock next week.'

Chapter Six

❁

The telegrams arrived on the afternoon of Violet's birthday. The telegraph boy from the village post office cycled up the avenue and appeared at the back door just as Daisy and Rose were bringing in the last sheaves of beech leaves to decorate the Chinese vases in the hall.

'Two telegrams, my lady,' he said, taking them from the basket in front of his bicycle and handing them to Daisy.

'Two!' exclaimed Rose.

'One for Violet,' said Daisy as she smiled her thanks at the boy and told him to wait a minute in case there was an answer. 'And the other for Great-Aunt Lizzie. Quick, Rose – run and get Violet and bring her down to the dining room.' She cast a quick glance into the kitchen. Mrs Beaton was hard at work. Justin had caught a huge pike which he had presented as his offering to the party and Mrs Beaton was busy turning it into hundreds of tiny fishcakes deliciously flavoured with fresh basil.

Up in the dining room Great-Aunt Lizzie was drawing an enormous linen tablecloth from the depths of a tomb-like oak chest.

'Lazarus rises from the dead!' said Rose, coming in with Violet who was flushed and breathless from her run down the stairs. She gazed at the tablecloth and added reverentially, '*And he that was dead came forth, bound hand and foot with graveclothes.*'

'Rose!'

'Telegrams,' intervened Daisy quickly, presenting them to Great-Aunt Lizzie, who handed Violet's to her and turned towards a window for light to read her own.

'It's from the Duchess, wishing me a happy birthday,' said Violet, her blue eyes shining.

A gasp from the window made them all swing round. 'She's coming here!' exclaimed Aunt Lizzie. The telegram fell from her fingers.

Daisy picked it up. There, stuck on to the tan-coloured paper, were the words: ON WAY TO FRANCE STOP WILL CALL AT SIX PM TODAY TO SEE VIOLET.

'On way to France stop,' said Rose, savouring the words on her tongue. Daisy could foresee that most of her sister's remarks were now going to be made in telegraphic form. However, her attention was on her aunt. The old lady had turned almost grey.

'She won't be coming to stay, Great-Aunt,' she said reassuringly. 'She's bound to have booked her passage on the boat. She probably got a present for Violet after she received the photograph and she didn't have time to post it. Sir Guy will be here to keep father company, and Morgan's brought in a huge amount of wood for the fires downstairs and in the ballroom. And everything looks nice by candlelight.' And all the shabbiness and the cobwebs are hidden, she added silently.

'I must finish the dresses.' Violet sprinted out of the

room and ran lightly up the stairs, singing the latest Bessie Smith song.

'I must reply.' Great-Aunt Lizzie made a visible effort to pull herself together.

'Oh please, let me do it,' begged Rose. 'I know just what to say: COME STOP EAT STOP BUT DON'T STOP STOP.'

'Rose, there's Justin with a load of wood; ask him if he could possibly bring it up to the ballroom,' said Daisy hurriedly. Justin had been getting a bit of exercise helping Morgan to chop wood and had arrived each morning carrying an axe as well as a fishing rod. He had turned out to be rather fun, entering into all the plans for the party – only turning stiff and pompous when Violet tried to be the grand lady. Daisy liked him more and more each day. Now she gave him a quick wave through the window and then turned to the elderly woman. 'Her Grace won't stay the night, I'm sure she won't, but it might work out very well for her to visit here. You know what Violet is like when she's excited and in a good mood. And she'll be wearing that gorgeous dress. She'll look beautiful. I'm sure that the Duchess will offer to present her when she sees her. This room is lovely at night.' Pity about the torn curtains, she thought, and said hastily, 'Luckily we have all those candles that Maud found in the basement. I always think that candle flames look awfully nice reflected on dark glass.'

'That's your artistic nature, Daisy,' said the old lady graciously. She had begun to recover. 'Bring me a pencil and some paper and I'll draft a telegram. Is the boy still in the kitchen?'

'I told him to wait,' said Daisy. Morgan could fetch the Duchess and then return her to the station for the next train, she decided. Mrs Beaton had made a splendid cake. Violet and her three sisters would all be dressed in party clothes. There would be hot fires and artistic arrangements of candles and leaves everywhere. Her eye went to the windowsills – some holly from the woodland, she thought, visualizing pinpricks of light reflected on polished green leaves.

Sir Guy Beresford arrived at Beech Grove Manor at five o'clock. As usual he was impeccably dressed and as usual he came with a parcel in his hands. He had got into the film industry about fourteen years earlier and it had made him very rich. With no children of his own he tended to spoil Daisy, his goddaughter, and he seldom arrived without some present for her.

Morgan drove him to the door and Daisy, who had been watching from an upstairs window, came flying down to meet him.

'How's my very favourite godfather?' she asked as the bulky figure struggled out of the back of the Humber, leaning heavily on Morgan's outstretched arm.

'You've only got one,' grunted Sir Guy. 'You want something out of me, Daisy; don't think I don't know what you're like.' His arms enveloped her in a bear-like hug and she hugged him back.

'Come up to your bedroom,' she said, tugging at his arm as they went into the house. 'Bateman will say that you're having tea upstairs. Here's Father. Great-Aunt Lizzie says that he can't take the dogs through the woods in case the Duchess arrives early. She's fussing terribly about the party.'

'Am I the first? Hallo, Michael!' said Sir Guy, delving into his pocket and handing a small, flat, wrapped box to Daisy. 'What's this about a duchess?'

'Some of this nonsense about Violet being presented,' grunted the Earl. 'How are you, Guy? Looking forward to a chinwag with you – got a drag hunt coming up in a few days if you care to stay on for that.' He was always in a good humour when Sir Guy arrived and a drag hunt was his favourite form of amusement.

'Excuse me, my lord.' Bateman approached. 'Morgan wishes to know if you need the car at the moment, or if he may –' Bateman coughed – 'attend to his duties upstairs until we hear about the Duchess's train.'

Daisy smothered a giggle. Bateman sounded as though playing the drums was some obscure form of chauffeuring.

'No, tell him to carry on,' said the Earl, sounding a little more cheerful. 'What do you think about that, Guy? My chauffeur has a jazz band. Sign of the times, eh? Jolly good they are too.' He liked Morgan and was amused at the idea that his chauffeur had formed a jazz band from the neighbouring young people and one of his daughters. 'They've been practising for most of the afternoon,' he added. 'You should hear Poppy play that clarinet. You'd think she was a professional.' Poppy, in her father's eyes, could do no wrong.

Daisy unpeeled the wrapping from the box – probably sweets, she thought. Although Sir Guy showered her with presents, he generally treated her as though she was about eight years old.

But there was an inner wrapping. And this time it was an expensive-looking embossed paper with a silver sheen. Daisy took that off more carefully and then opened the lid of the box and there, coiled on a bed of pale pink velvet, was a rope of shimmering pearls.

'Your father said that you were all getting dressed up for Violet's party,' grunted Sir Guy.

For a moment Daisy said nothing. The pearls were exquisite – and the string was very, very long. They would be just perfect with her short pink silk dress. There was a picture of someone wearing a rope of pearls just like that in one of Violet's magazines. She flung her arms around Sir Guy and kissed his wrinkled old cheek.

'I'll never be able to thank you enough.'

'Very generous of you, Guy, old man,' said the Earl. He had a look of regret on his face and Daisy guessed that he was thinking of Violet. She should have been the first to have pearls. If only he had not put so much of his money in that unlucky diamond mine in India. Daisy could see from the way his face darkened and the lines around his mouth tightened that he was thinking of that unlucky investment.

'Better get back in the library,' he said reluctantly. 'Aunt Lizzie is like a cat on hot bricks. We've had a telegram from Violet's godmother, the Duchess of Denton. She's on her way to France, but she will stop off to give Violet her birthday present. Lizzie, of course, has got it into her head that if everything goes well the Duchess will take up Violet and present her at court or something like that. Stupid idea – can't stand the woman.'

'Excuse me, my lord.' Bateman had appeared again. 'That was the stationmaster on the phone. He says that the London train left on time and we should expect Her Grace to be at the village station in just over an hour.'

'Better have a quick brandy before she descends on us.' The Earl shot back into the library and Daisy grabbed Sir Guy's sleeve.

'Quick,' she said. 'Let's go and hide, or else Great-Aunt Lizzie will think that you should be standing around ready to be polite to the Duchess a good hour before she arrives.'

She took him upstairs and into the blue bedroom. She had been in and out of this room during the afternoon and everything was ready. The fire was burning well, she noticed and on a small table beside the comfortable old armchair she had placed a decanter with some of her father's favourite brandy in it. She took her godfather's coat from him and hung it up in the wardrobe and watched solicitously as he sank into the chair. He was looking quite tired, she thought, as he gave a sigh of relief. Her father had been talking about how ridiculous it was for a wealthy man like Sir Guy to be working so hard at the film industry, but Daisy understood that fascination. It wasn't just a matter of making money, she guessed. He was part of a new and fascinating world – the world of the cinema – and she envied him.

'Have a drink while you're waiting for your tea,' she said, pouring the brandy carefully. 'I'll pop down and get it.'

The jazz band was playing loudly and vigorously, the music almost seeming to rock the old house, as Daisy ran down the back staircase. No chance of meeting the Duchess or Great-Aunt Lizzie on this uncarpeted realm of the servants. The tray had been prepared by her earlier on – all of Sir Guy's favourites were on it, including Marmite sandwiches made from thinly cut bread: lots of butter and a faint skim of Marmite spread over the top.

'I see you are all ready for me.' Sir Guy was sipping his brandy when she returned. He had a grin on his face as he pointed to the screen that Morgan had made for her which now hung between the door and the wardrobe, and the projector standing on the bedside table.

'It's very short – only five minutes,' said Daisy firmly. 'It will give you something to do while you are drinking your tea and eating your sandwiches. I cut the bread myself so it's just the way you like it.'

Quickly she drew the curtains and then turned off the overhead lamp, leaving just the small lamp behind his chair. That would give him light enough to eat by.

It was Violet who was the making of the film, she

thought as she watched it critically. The story was sweet and the horses were great and the way that she had captured Justin, that day by the lake looking at Violet, made him appear quite handsome – though he was no actor and some of the subsequent film showed him a bit wooden. However, the leading lady was what everyone would remember. The story needed to be stronger the next time, she thought. A murder mystery perhaps, she thought as she waited for Sir Guy's verdict.

'Very, very promising,' he said as soon as he had swallowed his tea. 'I think I could sell that. It would make a very good little short before a main film about a horse or something like that. How much do you want for it?'

'How much is it worth?' asked Daisy. 'Be honest, now,' she added.

'I'll take a chance on it.' He took out his pocketbook and handed her a crisp ten-pound note.

Daisy stared at it. She longed to take it. It was enough to buy a dress for Violet. However, she forced herself to shake her head. She had to be fair and she wanted to be considered a professional. 'Sell it first,' she said firmly. 'I'll wait for the money.'

'I'll sell it,' he said confidently. 'It's just the sort of thing that people want. Make them feel good. You have a clever eye for the right sort of thing, and a good, steady hand. I must bring you a tripod the next time I come. Go on, take it. Ten pounds is nothing. I paid a hundred pounds the other day for a film by someone I had never heard of. And he just took his story from a book. I tell you what, Daisy, you could do a lot of filming tonight. Young people having a party – that's the sort of thing that cinema-goers like to see. You can always make up a story to go with it – nothing complicated. Complicated stories don't work on film.'

'I'd like to do something longer – something with more of a story in it,' said Daisy. 'Of course, Rose is complaining that I cut out a lot of hers – it was a sort of back story, all about the heroine having a jealous stepmother and about the stepbrother being favoured. It was very good, especially considering she is only twelve, but I didn't think that all that sort of stuff could be shown in a film.'

'You're quite right,' said Sir Guy. 'What you want in a film is action – something that can be conveyed by the expressions on the faces and then just summarized in the storyboards. One of these days someone will invent a camera that can record sound at the same time as filming but until that happens, you have to work inside the limitations of your medium. Do you understand what I mean by that?'

Daisy nodded. 'That's the way I think,' she said. 'I find myself reading books like that these days – often you could do a chapter with just one shot and a caption. I was reading *Wuthering Heights* the other day and I was thinking of how I could film it. The trouble is that I have no actors! Violet looks good, but she can't act.'

'Use what you've got,' advised Sir Guy. 'If I were you I would film people doing what they do naturally, then pick out good shots and try to fit a story around them. Use the house, the lake, the woods – everything. This party now – if you film that, you will probably come up with a story to fit it. And remember, no one worries about having an original plot. Good heavens, the number of versions of "Anna the Adventuress" that I've seen during the last three years!'

Chapter Seven

Poppy and Daisy shared one of the biggest bedrooms in the house. When they were babies, the yellow room, as it was called, had been turned into a night nursery with a bed for the nurse as well as cots for the two little girls. It was a lovely room with five big windows, three of them facing south and the other two catching the early morning sun from the east. The wallpaper was a design of soft yellow primroses and the curtains matched in colour. Both were now faded but the place was still pretty with a yellow-painted dressing room attached to the main room, attractive white-painted storage cupboards and wardrobes, and a white marble fireplace.

Normally the room was stone cold, but tonight the four sisters were determined to be warm and a huge fire of beech logs burned brightly. The luxury was so great that Daisy had earlier decided to spend part of each day picking up twigs and fallen branches from the woods around the house and saving them for a fire – at least for an hour or so in the evenings.

But now she could think of little other than the four dresses.

'If ever this mysterious Elaine turns up there are plenty of bits of material from her dresses left over. Look – I've filled the sewing basket with them just in case we need any last-minute touches.' Violet was in an excited, giggly mood. The relief of having the four dresses ready on time overwhelmed her. 'I've just done the hems on the sewing machine,' she added, holding up Rose's dress. 'Great-Aunt Lizzie will have a fit when she sees them – she thinks a hem should be invisibly slip-stitched, but I saw a dress in one of the fashion magazines where the hems were tiny and you could see the stitching on them.'

Poppy was already getting into her dress. She was the one who had shown the least interest during the making of them, but now her face was flushed with excitement.

'Thank you, dear Elaine, for the stockings!' She addressed the eastern windows and then pulled on the white silk stockings. None of the sisters had ever possessed a pair of silk stockings before. Rose had dabbed their sensible tan-coloured shoes with a tennis shoe whitening liquid so at least they would not look too bad early on in the evening.

Poppy's dress was the simplest of all. It was very straight and short, with a high neckline in front and cut low at the back, right down to her shoulder blades, But the sheen and gloss of the white satin, coupled with Poppy's extraordinarily beautiful flame-coloured hair, made her look like a society beauty. She stared at herself in the mirror and nodded her head firmly.

'Daisy, you will just have to bob my hair. The dress is good, but with that hair streaming around my shoulders I look like one of the Victorian paintings by that fellow

75

Burne-Jones.' She removed the dress with a determined air and handed Daisy a comb and scissors.

'Excuse me, your ladyships, I've brought more wood for the fire.' Maud must have knocked while they were all exclaiming loudly over Poppy's dress and now she stood there with the wood basket in her hands, looking intently at Poppy, surveying her with her head to one side.

'I wouldn't bob your hair, my lady, if I were you.' Maud addressed Poppy in the rather forthright style she used to Rose when none of the adults were around. She dumped the basket of wood on the floor and then went over to Poppy. 'There's some good styles in those magazines . . . Excuse me, my lady,' she said to Violet. 'I can't help noticing your magazines sometimes and I've seen a style that would suit you, Lady Poppy.'

'Maud used to do hairstyles for all the girls in the orphanage when they were in their dormitory at night,' Rose informed them.

'What would you do with all of this, Maud?' asked Poppy, clutching handfuls of her hair. Violet looked shocked at her sister talking to a scullery maid in such a friendly fashion, but Poppy never cared about things like that.

'You need something for a headband, my lady.' Maud picked a long strip of beaded sash out of Violet's sewing basket. It was cut from the dress that had formed Poppy's short jacket. Daisy guessed that the scullery maid had been looking through the pieces of material earlier on when the basket had been up in the schoolroom as she had selected the sash without hesitation. She watched with interest as Maud quickly swept back the heavy mass of red hair, brushed it carefully, tucked it behind Poppy's ears, and then wound the beaded sash around her head, letting it sit like a crown over her sister's eyebrows. Daisy held her breath.

'Jazzy,' said Poppy after a long moment.

And it was perfect. The effect was completely up-to-date and very flattering without spoiling the impact of Poppy's beautiful hair. Daisy knew that it would break her father's heart if she cut the hair that was so like his wife's.

'Could you do my hair like that?' asked Rose.

'There are plenty of sashes in the sewing basket,' said Violet. She gazed at Poppy's hair, a slight struggle showing in her face. Then she made up her mind. Violet rarely spent long trying to decide about anything – she just went with her first instinct. Immediately she began to get dressed.

Violet had made her own dress short, with a hemline that fell to above her knee on one side and dipped heavily on the other. Apart from this, the dress was simply made, cut fairly low in the front and back, sleeveless, but the gorgeous shade of shimmering green-blue silk sewn with thousands of tiny electric-blue beads needed no extra embellishments. She looked wonderful in it, the dress glittering and her violet-coloured eyes glowing. She gazed at her reflection in the looking glass and then turned to Maud.

'What do you think, Maud?' she asked, sitting down in front of the dressing table. 'Would the same style as Poppy suit me?'

Maud didn't answer, just picked up the silky hair and cupped it in her hand, looking at the glass over Violet's shoulder. Then she dropped it and reached for a jar of enormous old-fashioned hairpins, presented to Poppy by Great-Aunt Lizzie with advice about keeping her hair tidy. Maud wove Violet's long hair into one very loose plait, then tucked it under and pinned it at the nape of her neck, loosening the strands near her face. The effect was a sleek, bell-like bob that curved around Violet's ears and below her chin. When Maud was satisfied she went across to the sewing box and took out the other half of the beaded sash and tired it round Violet's head like an Alice band, knotting the ends at the nape of the neck to secure the plait in place, and then cutting off the spare material with a decisive snip of the scissors.

'Perfect,' breathed Violet, smiling at her reflection.

'What about Daisy?' asked Rose.

'I think I'd like the same as Violet,' said Daisy. 'We won't look like twins or anything because I have blonde curly hair and she has dark straight hair. Wait a minute, Maud; wait till you see my dress.'

She began to dress hurriedly. Violet had surpassed herself with this costume, she thought gratefully. The pale pink silk, though a colour that suited her very well, might have looked a little insipid, but Violet had an inspiration and decided to make it with a stunning hemline, dipping down below the knees on both sides and swooping up above them in the centre. The curved line was enhanced with deep flounces of ruffled lace machine-sewn to the dress so that the stitching line did not show. To go with it was a pink stole, wound once around Daisy's neck and then hanging down in front, looking very modern and the height of fashion.

'Quite short hair for you, my lady,' said Maud as decisively as if she were an experienced lady's maid. She gazed intently at Daisy's face, feeling the spring of the tight curls between finger and thumb. 'No hairband, I think,' she added, almost to herself.

Working rapidly, Maud pinned up Daisy's curly hair, halving the length as she went, and by the time she had finished, even Daisy herself felt that she looked as though she had had it bobbed. Her hair was even shorter than Violet's and somehow made her look years older – rather like a young lady about town. She gazed at herself for a moment with immense satisfaction. Yes, the effect was quite different from Violet's and she was glad of that. She wanted to be herself, not a poor relation in loveliness to her two sisters. 'Bang up-to-date,' she murmured and then turned to her youngest sister.

'Come on, Rosie, let's get you dressed, and don't ask to have your hair put up or Great-Aunt Lizzie will send you back to your bedroom. Hold up your arms. Now then, look at that! Isn't she gorgeous, Maud?'

Rose's soft crimson velvet dress was cleverly done – short enough to show off her long legs, cut on the bias and yet with quite a youthful swing to it. Short puffed sleeves covered the top of her childishly thin arms and there was a neat ruff around her neck. Yes, thought Daisy, Great-Aunt Lizzie will have to approve of this frock. Maud ignored the others and got Rose to sit at the dressing table. She spent a long time brushing the soft brown hair until it shone like silk and then picked out a strip of rose-coloured velvet from the sewing box, folded it expertly and bound it around Rose's forehead, passing it behind the ears and lastly tying it at the nape of the neck under the curtain of hair. Suddenly Rose looked years older.

Quickly Daisy fetched her camera. She would have to trust Maud to press the button but she was determined to have a photograph of herself and her sisters together just before their very first grown-up party.

'Line up,' she said. 'Poppy next to Violet, then leave a space for me and then you, Rose.'

She peered at them for a moment and then handed the camera to Maud and took her place between her sisters.

'*Derrington Sisters Take the Fashionable World by Storm*,' said Rose.

The stage is set, thought Daisy an hour later. It was one minute to six and everyone was gathered in the transformed dining room.

The telephone had been busy. Bateman's friend the stationmaster had rung the house when the Duchess's train was within ten minutes of the station and again when Morgan had left with Her Grace, so they knew almost to the minute what time she would arrive at the house. Daisy had arranged everybody in the dining room – young men in a group where candlelight fell on their starched snowy shirts, Great-Aunt Lizzie in an upright chair looking splendidly Victorian and sparkling with diamonds, Rose in her short velvet dress on a rug by her feet, Poppy on a chair by the window, her magnificent sheaf of bronze hair spread over the white silk and distracting attention from the frayed curtains, the table with colourful food spread on Lazarus's winding sheet and Violet, all by herself, standing beside the branched chandelier whose light gleamed on her black hair while the firelight made her blue-green dress sparkle as if the beads were precious stones.

Encouraged by Sir Guy's words, Daisy moved around the room, photographing the groups, keeping everyone in position until the big moment arrived.

'Her Grace, the Duchess of Denton,' announced Bateman and Great-Aunt Lizzie turned and smiled with such pure pleasure and slight surprise that Daisy thought she might be the best actor in the family.

'Your Grace.' Great-Aunt Lizzie got to her feet gracefully and Michael Derrington moved forward, just one step behind her.

'So kind of you to allow to me to break my journey here.' The Duchess was a small fat woman with an enormous bosom. She pecked the air somewhere in the vicinity of her hostess's left cheek and announced, 'I must say that I loathe staying in those hotels at

Dover. Full of all sorts of riff-raff.'

Great-Aunt Lizzie did not blanch. Daisy's eyes met the butler's and he gave a tiny nod. He and Mrs Pearson could be relied on to have a fire lit in the purple room and clean sheets and bedding would be produced from the linen cupboard. In a moment, thought Daisy, I'll slip out and help, but in the meantime she wanted to see the impression made by Violet who was just being introduced playfully as 'the birthday girl'.

'But my dear, you are so lovely.' The Duchess craned up to kiss Violet's cheeks, murmuring about how the years had passed and presenting her with a tiny box which Violet opened to reveal a small oval-shaped brooch . It was a pallid affair with a row of seed pearls interspersed with a few tiny chips of diamonds.

'I must get to know you, my dear,' she said graciously. 'Goodness, I can't believe that you are eighteen years old already. Tell me, what are the plans for your debut?'

'What do you think?' Rose whispered to Daisy with her eyes fixed discreetly on the floor and her hands clasped demurely in front of her. Daisy did not need to ask her sister what she meant. There was only one question in the minds of all of the Derrington females: would the Duchess sponsor Violet through the debutante season and the presentation at Buckingham Palace?

The whole of the staff at Beech Grove Manor waited at table when the party sat down to the birthday supper. 'A small, informal affair for the children,' Great-Aunt Lizzie informed the Duchess. Even Maud the scullery maid had been fitted out with a snowy white apron and cap and drilled by Mrs Pearson in the correct way to hand and remove dishes. Morgan had removed his chauffeur's uniform and, wearing a ten-year-old suit of the Earl's – too tight for its owner – proved to be very useful as a footman, pouring wine and serving the Duchess with an elaborate flourish which made the butler look at him with alarm.

Daisy leaned over and rescued her camera from under the chair.

'Daisy, dear, do put away your camera,' said Great-Aunt Lizzie, but not before the flashbulb had gone off three times.

'Just a few birthday photographs, Great-Aunt,' said Daisy. 'Excuse me, Your Grace; I should have asked first, I know, but I didn't want anyone posing.'

The Duchess smiled forgivingly at Daisy. 'What a very pretty dress, my dear – that pink so suits you. And what lovely pearls. I must say that you have four very beautiful daughters, my lord – all so unalike, aren't they? My two girls are like peas in a pod except that Catherine is eighteen and Paula is sixteen. No, no more, thank you.' She put down her knife and fork and ranged them side by side in a determined gesture, turning to Baz with a sweet smile. 'I hear you young people are going to have a little dance afterwards,' she said. 'Your chauffeur told me on the way from the station.' Her glance ranged over the servants standing stiffly to attention at the side of the room and passed over Morgan without recognition.

Next the Duchess whispered to Simon, who had been

sitting next to her, and he started to his feet, his fair-skinned face slightly flushing, and went up to Violet, politely pulling out her chair and escorting her to his place beside the Duchess.

Daisy stole a look at Great-Aunt Lizzie, who had looked slightly affronted at first to see her dinner arrangements upset but then smiled with satisfaction as she saw the Duchess plying Violet with questions.

Simon and Justin stared at each other with mutual annoyance.

'All those boys are in love with Violet,' Sir Guy remarked to Daisy. Great-Aunt Lizzie was talking so loudly to Justin and Poppy was laughing so much over Baz's jokes, which seemed to be aiming at getting Morgan to laugh too, that Sir Guy's quietly spoken comments only reached her ear.

'Not Baz,' pointed out Daisy. 'He and Poppy have been friends since they were little and when they're together they talk nothing but jazz. Anyway, none of those boys have a chance with Vi. You know she will settle for nothing less than a duke.'

'What about you, Daisy?' asked Sir Guy. 'Got anyone in mind?'

'Not really,' she said. 'I just don't meet anyone except the jazz band boys and they seem a bit silly and young to me.'

He chuckled. 'Your father and I were exactly the same when we were their age – racing around the corridors of this place getting into all sorts of scrapes.'

'Did you meet Elaine Carruthers when you used to stay here?' Daisy asked casually.

Sir Guy was eating devilled eggs when the question came. His fork slipped from his grasp and fell to the floor. Instantly Morgan was at his side proffering a clean one on a silver tray.

'Thank you, Morgan,' said Sir Guy solemnly.

'Sir,' said Morgan stiffly, and Daisy saw the butler give an approving glance from the corner of his eye.

'He's doing quite a good impression of a real footman,' said Sir Guy, as the chauffeur withdrew. 'You should use him in a film, Daisy. If he can act like that he would be a wonderful asset to you.'

Aware that he was trying to distract her, she tried again. 'What did Elaine look like?'

Sir Guy shot her an uneasy glance.

'Who's been talking to you about Elaine?'

'No one,' said Daisy with perfect truth. 'That's why I am asking you. You know what Father is like.' She glanced over her shoulder, but Michael Derrington was consulting with the butler about a port that he fancied might still be down in the cellar. The wine at supper had done him good. He face was slightly flushed and his eyes had lost that deep look of sadness that they normally wore. And now that the Duchess's attention was fastened on Violet he was quite happy. 'You know what he's like,' she repeated in low tones. 'He hates to be reminded of Mother.'

'Yes, yes, I know,' said Sir Guy. 'Well, to be honest,

I don't know much about Elaine. I know that there was some sort of row, but I don't know the details. Elaine was so much younger than your mother that no one would have taken them to be sisters. She was just a child when I used to visit here, before your parents went out to India.'

So she *was* her mother's sister.

'How many years were between them?' asked Daisy casually, selecting one of the pike fishcakes and sending a smile across the table at Justin as she bit into it.

'Let me see . . . she must have been a child of four or five when your mother was married. That's the last time that I saw her, I think.' He paused, obviously considering how much he should divulge. 'That's right, a little blonde girl. Never saw her again,' he added. 'Went out to India when she was about seventeen or eighteen, I think.'

'That's right,' said Daisy. It was time to change the conversation. 'What about Great-Aunt Lizzie, Sir Guy? How would she do in a film? Has she got an interesting face?'

'She'll do better when the talking films come in. Her voice is good and she can put a chap down very easily. I could see a role in the right sort of film, but only as a background in these silent films. Look at her face – it doesn't show much. She's a lady who keeps her thoughts to herself.'

She certainly does, thought Daisy. What could possibly have happened to make the family pretend that Elaine had never existed?

Chapter Eight

The ballroom looked wonderful. It was a long room, stretching from the front to the back of the house, with two windows at each end and two fireplaces made from fine white marble. Normally it seemed bare and rather dismal, but tonight, filled with dancing couples, it looked like something out of a painting. The colourful dresses worn by the girls, the rich splendour of the Duchess and even Great-Aunt Lizzie's finery showed up well against the black and white evening dress of the men. The original chandeliers that had been put in over a hundred years before had been carefully cleaned by Daisy and Nora under the supervision of Great-Aunt Lizzie and they glittered wonderfully. Morgan had spent much of the day carrying logs upstairs and feeding the fires in the two fireplaces so by now the long room was quite warm. The tall vases of daffodils and fluffy pussy willow catkins were in the coolest corners of the room well away from the fires. Rose had collected cushions from every room in the house and heaped them on to the four windowsills, which would do for seats when people got tired. Two of the jazz band had carried an old spindly-legged sofa down from the attic as well. Disguised with a gold-tasselled bedspread from the linen cupboard, it made an acceptable seat for a duchess.

*

Daisy was dancing with Justin. She had not imagined that he would ask her to dance while Violet was in the room, but he had. He had walked straight past Violet and come over to her and taken her hand saying, 'Can you foxtrot?'

'A bit,' she answered, her eyes sliding over towards Violet who was pretending to gaze into the fire, leaning on the marble fireplace and looking pensive.

'That's a bit more than I can,' he assured her, but they managed passably well. Although only Morgan and George were playing at the moment, the music was fast and the beat was strong. Poppy danced with Baz, and Simon, having been rejected by Violet, asked Great Aunt-Lizzie to dance. Michael Derrington did his best with the Duchess, and Rose, who was the best dancer in the family, danced Edwin into the ground, leaving him breathless. Justin laughed and blew Rose a kiss and Violet glared at him.

Daisy wondered if Violet would be nicer to Justin if she were able to inherit Beech Grove Manor and didn't have to worry about marrying someone rich – he was awfully attractive.

'Justin,' she said, 'you've studied law. Explain to me about this entail business. If ever I ask Father he just gets all upset and says I wouldn't understand. Why can't Violet inherit?'

'Entail?' He had been gazing at Violet and now looked at Daisy, startled.

'Yes, entail. You must know what entail means. You've been studying the law for years.'

'Oh, entail,' said Justin vaguely. 'Sorry, I didn't quite catch what you said. Yes, entail. It's actually called fee tail, which comes from the Latin *feodum talliatum* and—'

'Oh, for goodness sake, Justin,' broke in Daisy impatiently, 'I don't want a lecture. Just explain in words of one syllable about the entail, or fee tail, or any other kind of tail, on the Beech Grove Estate.'

Justin took his eyes from Violet and looked down at Daisy with a glimmer of interest in his eyes. 'Strictly speaking, that's fee tail male.'

'Yes, I know,' said Daisy. 'Come on, Justin. A lawyer should be able to explain things to an ordinary person like myself.'

'You've obviously never been in court,' said Justin with a grin.

'Well, anyway,' said Daisy, 'pretend you're not a lawyer. Pretend you're a teacher. Just explain.'

'Look,' said Justin, 'I can't think straight while you are doing all those flips and shakes and twirls around. You're making me dizzy. Let's go and sit on the windowsill and then I'll explain everything to you. It's actually quite an interesting case, Beech Grove Manor, come to think of it.'

'Oh good,' said Daisy. She felt somewhat annoyed that Justin could not think and dance at the same time; she adored dancing and they had all been practising the latest dances just for this one splendid evening. Still, she did want to understand the position about Denis and about Violet. The sacrifices I make for that girl, she thought. Most of her time these days seemed to be spent in planning a brilliant future for Violet.

'As I say, it's an interesting case,' Justin continued. 'I remember looking it up when I was a student at Gray's Inn in London. It has been going on for a long time, the estate mostly transferring from father to son until the time of your grandfather who decided to put a stop to it. He and your father agreed – and you do always need the heir's agreement to something like this – well, they agreed that the entail would only last through two more generations: your father and his heir.'

'Except that Father didn't have a son . . .'

Justin nodded. 'Exactly,' he said. 'He didn't have a son so now the estate will be for this very distant relation – I believe they had to go right back through the family tree in order to find him.'

'So after Father's death Denis will inherit; and not only will there not be a penny for us, we won't even have anywhere to live.' Daisy sighed. 'I see. Now let's go back and finish the dance.'

'You and your sisters don't go to school, do you?' asked Justin as they took their places again on the well-polished floor. For years, on wet days, the four girls had been skating on this floor with pads of sheepskin tied to their shoes – one of Great-Aunt Lizzie's more imaginative ideas – and it had only needed a quick burnishing to get it right for the party.

'No, thank goodness,' said Daisy fervently. 'Though Rose should. She is the clever one of the family.'

'Oh, I don't know – waste of time, school. Better than those dreary governesses though, I suppose.'

'We didn't even have one of these – not even when we had more money.' She added in an undertone and with a quick glance over her shoulder, 'Great-Aunt Lizzie fancies herself as a teacher – mainly because she was once told that she had the most beautiful handwriting in the world.'

'I loathed Harrow,' said Justin haughtily. 'It was the wrong place for me. There was never any interest in boys who had original ideas.'

'Tell me about it,' Daisy said. She was enjoying this party; she had visualized it completely as a setting for Violet, but Poppy and Rose also seemed to be having a very good time.

'Harrow was just a bore,' said Justin disdainfully. 'Of course I tried to have as much fun as I could. I'm really good at annoying people when I want to and all the masters used to get into fearful bates with me. I nearly got thrown out, once. Myself and another boy went through all of the books in the library and every time we came across one that said in the Foreword: "*This should be obligatory for all young people*" – or something like that, well, we just used to write in the margin: "*'Tis his only chance of selling a boring book like this.*" We were sent up before the beak and were nearly sacked, but I argued that a school like Harrow existed to encourage independent thought in its pupils and this so confused him that in the end we both got off with having to write a hundred lines.'

'Perhaps that's why you decided to become a lawyer – you found arguing suited you,' said Daisy, hoping this dance would go on a bit longer. If he asked her again she would have to turn him in the direction of Violet. It was, after all, Violet's party and they could not risk the Duchess thinking that she was a wallflower. The jazz band was playing fairly quietly – she had told Morgan that while the Duchess was there the music had to be kept fairly soft.

'Don't think so,' he said, frowning. 'Actually, I just wanted to make money. I have three elder brothers and there was nothing left for me by the time I got to be eighteen. I could have gone to Oxford,' he added, 'but I decided that the sooner I got to be in a position to earn money the better it would be.'

'And are you?' Perhaps he might do for Violet after all.

'I shortly hope to be offered a very well-paid position,' he said loftily and then laughed quite suddenly. 'As a matter of fact, Daisy, I'm down to my last fifty pounds in the bank and am going on a tour of relations so that I no longer have to pay for my lodgings. I'm doing quite well at it. In fact, the Duchess has just asked me to her house party in London in two weeks' time. That should be good – high living, and I'll be on the spot if there are any jobs going in the big London law firms.'

'Why on earth did the Duchess ask you to a house party? She's never met you before, has she?'

'Charm, my dear Daisy, just charm. I can't help it, you know. It oozes out of me.'

'You sound so conceited when you say things like that,' said Daisy.

Justin laughed. 'To be honest with you,' he said, 'she's probably short of men for her house party. All those mamas find it quite hard to get enough young men to stay when it's a question of house parties in London. Different in the country when hunting is thrown in and some decent horses are provided for riding. Anyway, Daisy, advise me. What will I do after the house party if I'm not snapped up by then? Must I starve?'

'You're quite good-looking,' said Daisy earnestly. She hoped that she wasn't blushing and added hastily, 'I mean from the point of view of a film-maker. Perhaps you should speculate your last fifty pounds in going to Hollywood. You could always hang around giving free advice to film stars about their contracts and perhaps one of them would get you a small part in a film. It would be like Douglas Fairbanks – he started in very small roles and now look at him!'

'And what about you?' he asked kindly. 'I suppose you are looking forward to a season in a couple of years' time – every girl's dream, isn't it?'

'Certainly not,' said Daisy indignantly. 'My dream is to set up a film studio in London and have my films bought by all of those cinemas – even Hollywood, perhaps. Now go and ask Violet for the next dance – that's why you were invited. I'm going down to the kitchen to talk to Mrs Beaton about snacks – that supper wasn't very substantial.'

To Daisy's annoyance, Justin swept the Duchess a playful bow and took her hand for the next dance rather than Violet, who was now short of a partner.

Oh well, thought Daisy as she went out of the end door of the ballroom and down the back stairs, I've done my best. Violet can't go around being so haughty if she wants to attract men.

Daisy tiptoed past the housekeeper's room and went into the kitchen – she wanted to know more about the mysterious Elaine and it was much easier to get information from Mrs Beaton than from Mrs Pearson.

'Dear, dear Beaty, I'm so hungry. I was so busy upstairs being polite to everybody at supper that I didn't think to take enough for myself.'

Mrs Beaton was taking a tray of bakes out of the oven. They were golden brown and smelled delicious.

'Now my lady, don't burn your fingers. These are hot!'

'Hazelnut bakes! Beaty, you're a genius. Everyone will love these. I'm glad we collected so many nuts this autumn.'

'I thought that they might be good up in the ballroom. Those boys are always hungry. Where's Maud? Maud, put these on to that wicker tray and take them up. Put a napkin under them, girl. And put your cap straight! I don't know! Girls nowadays! Nora, you get that blackberry and crab apple punch ready. No alcohol, his lordship said, my lady,' Mrs Beaton lowered her voice, 'but I put a little brandy in it. Spices it up, you know.'

'I suppose in the old days when Lady Elaine was making her debut there were great feasts prepared,' said Daisy as Maud and Nora took their trays and departed up to the ballroom.

There was a silence. Daisy munched thoughtfully into the crunchy hazelnut bake and averted her eyes. Mrs Beaton loved a gossip and she hoped she would be unable to resist temptation.

'Funny to think that I've never even met her,' she added nonchalantly. 'Anyway, tell me about the feasts.'

'Great feasts!' echoed Mrs Beaton, sounding relieved. 'Of course there was plenty of help in the kitchen then – not like nowadays with those ignorant girls from the village.'

'Yes, that's what I meant,' said Daisy rapidly. 'I suppose it was all very stylish and very expensive. Mmm, this is so tasty. How clever you are. What made you think of putting hazelnuts into bakes? The jazz band boys will love these.' She paused for a moment and then said casually, 'Funny the way that Elaine disappeared, wasn't it? Why does she never come to visit?'

'Well, it's a long way, isn't it?' said Mrs Beaton.

Daisy registered that Mrs Beaton was agreeing about the length of the journey. So, Sir Guy was right about Elaine going to India and presumably she was still out there. But why no letters? There was only one answer to that.

'What was the row about then?' she asked, biting into yet another hazelnut bake. She wouldn't be able to dance if she ate any more but she was determined to find out the truth about this mysterious Elaine.

'Well, you know what Lady Elizabeth is like,' said Mrs Beaton confidentially. 'And of course the old Earl, your grandfather, he had a terrible temper. Now, my lady, you'd better be getting back upstairs. You enjoy yourself, now, and send Nora or Maud down if you need anything more to eat or drink. Lovely to see a bit of company in the house and you all dressed up so beautifully. That's the way it should be all the time.'

'Pity Father lost his money in those diamond mines,' said Daisy with sigh. 'Still, we've got the most wonderful cook in the world so we're a lucky family.'

'Go on with you! None of your flannel now,' said Mrs Beaton with high good humour as Daisy blew her a kiss from the door.

The rhythmic beat of the tango was making the old timbers creak as Daisy went back up the servants' staircase again. She opened the door into the ballroom and stood for a moment.

The whole of the jazz band was playing. The Earl and Sir Guy were sitting on one of the windowsills chatting together. Great-Aunt Lizzie, stiff as a ramrod, was standing behind the draped sofa. Rose was on the sofa with the Duchess, showing her precious scrapbook about the royal family.

There was only one couple dancing.

There in the middle of the ballroom were two figures doing an energetic tango. One of them was her beautiful sister, Violet. And the other was Justin.

Daisy remembered Sir Guy's advice. Lots of thoughts had gone through her head when she came into the ballroom and saw Violet and Justin together, chiefly surprise that Violet had stopped glaring at Justin long enough to dance with him. However, all those thoughts were submerged by the urgent necessity to get the expression on Violet's face on to film – she knew she could build a story around it. Instantly she went to the corner of the room and grabbed her camera. She lifted it to her eyes and began filming.

It was perfect. *'Oh, how I love him!'* was the title that sprang to her mind. Rose would, of course, think of a better one, but this fitted the expression on Violet's face. Her enormous purple-blue eyes were fixed on the dark eyes of her partner. No wonder everyone clapped when the dance finished. Justin and Violet moved together as if they had practised with each other for weeks. As if they had been in love with each other for an eternity. No one would have believed that an hour ago they had been ignoring each other. Daisy supposed they must both have been trying to impress the Duchess. So they *could* act!

As an afterthought she moved the camera in the Duchess's direction and saw with amusement how Her Grace preened herself slightly, fixing an artificial smile on her face. Still, her diamonds were wonderful and they would glint beautifully in the black and white film so Daisy allowed the camera to roll while Justin approached the sofa and said blandly, 'Next big thing in Hollywood, this young lady, Your Grace. I have it on impeccable authority. Sir Guy Beresford thinks that Daisy will be famous one of these days.'

Daisy lowered the camera, feeling embarrassed, but there was a calculating look on the Duchess's face.

'Daisy, dear, I wonder whether you would come to a little house party that I am having – as a guest, of course, but it would be so wonderful if you would film the occasion. Such a lovely record. I loathe and abominate those people who give the Press free access, but a few posed photographs – now, that's a different matter. As I said to Catherine, these people have to earn their living, but as to having them in the house . . .' The Duchess gave an exaggerated shiver and then turned back to practicalities. 'But I'm sure that you would enjoy doing something like that, Daisy, dear. It would be a great experience for you. I would provide you with all that you need. What do you think, Sir Guy?'

'I'll get one of my workers to bring over whatever Daisy needs to develop the film, Your Grace,' said Sir Guy gravely. 'Of course, you'll have to have Rose along too. She does all the title cards – she's essential. A lovely turn of phrase, and very artistic too. I'm thinking of employing her myself. She's as good as that fellow who works for Paramount – what's his name? Alfred Hitchcock, I think.'

'Of course we must have dear Rose,' said the Duchess graciously. She looked around. 'Michael, you simply must lend me your four lovely daughters for a few days. They can bring their maid and be quite comfortable together. I hope they will enjoy the company of other young folk. What do you say, Lady Elizabeth?'

Daisy held her breath. Great-Aunt Lizzie would be thrilled for Violet to be invited to the house party and she might be happy for Daisy and Poppy to accompany her, but twelve-year-old Rose! A house party!

There was a long moment. Michael Derrington looked at his wife's aunt and then at his daughters' faces. He took one step backwards as though to distance himself from the decision. Great-Aunt Lizzie smiled graciously, her wrinkled old face creasing and her hooded eyes glinting.

'What a lovely idea,' she exclaimed. 'Thank Her Grace, girls.'

Chapter Nine

❧

'I just can't believe it.' It was the third time Violet had said that and Daisy was getting tired of it.

'Well, you'd better believe it,' she said, 'because we have less than two weeks to go and we all have to have the right sort of clothes for a house party.'

'*Poverty-Stricken Girls Rifle Through Old Trunks,*' said Rose.

'Exactly,' said Daisy. 'There's plenty of stuff in Elaine's trunk. We just need to get to work on it.'

'All four of us going has complicated everything,' complained Violet. She looked around at her younger sisters, and added, 'Don't think I'm being selfish, but it would have been best if I had been the only one asked. Things would have been much simpler then. Perhaps Father could have found some money for my clothes, but he'll never agree to buying clothes for us all.' A note of grievance crept into her voice.

'You will need your sisters by your side,' said Rose wisely. 'We don't want you to make a mess of everything.'

'Let's go up and have a look at the trunk,' said Daisy hastily, seeing a flush of temper stain the cheek of her leading lady.

'I must go. Baz is coming over this morning,' said Poppy. She had little interest in clothes and was not that keen on going to the Duchess's house party. If Daisy had not told her that her refusal would spoil Violet's chances she would have declined the invitation.

Rose was in seventh heaven at the idea of taking part in a house party. Her scrapbooks were full of cuttings from ancient issues of *Tatler* and other society magazines and she had thoroughly enoyed her chat with the Duchess the evening before. Her Grace had stories to tell about most of the slightly faded figures on the dance floor at the Queen Charlotte's Ball, posing for debutante photographs, on horseback or watching horse racing at Epsom.

'Whatever we can't get from the trunk,' said Daisy, 'I'll be able to buy with the money Sir Guy gave me. Don't worry, Violet. We'll manage.'

'What about this lady's maid idea?' asked Poppy in a muffled voice as she pulled on an extra jumper before setting off through the woods to Morgan's cottage. It was a baggy old fishing pullover, something Poppy had begged from her father who had bought it in Scotland twenty years earlier, but its rich brown suited her and it was extremely warm. 'Great-Aunt Lizzie didn't say anything, did she?' she said as her head emerged. 'I say, do you think she is going to hire a maid for us?'

'No need,' said Rose. 'We take Maud.'

'Don't be ridiculous,' cried Violet. 'Maud's only a scullery maid.'

'She may be as well born as you or I,' said Rose mysteriously.

'What on earth are you talking about?' Violet was in

a het-up, nervy state of mind. Daisy felt a little sorry for her. Violet had her future mapped out so clearly in her mind and things kept going wrong for her.

'I think Maud would work out quite well,' she said aloud, watching Poppy impatiently braid her hair into a loose untidy plait that hung down her back. 'She did our hair really nicely for Violet's party and, dressed up properly, who's to tell that she's not really a lady's maid? It will be useful to have her, Violet,' she said in a warning tone of voice. 'We don't want the Duchess to think you are too poor to have a maid, do we? Father could never spare the money to engage a proper lady's maid. They would cost about fifty pounds a year at least. What do you think, Poppy?'

'I like Maud,' declared Poppy. 'I don't know what you are talking about anyway, Violet. Who cares whether she is or isn't a lady's maid? She can do Rose's sums and our hair. That's more than you can do, Vi.' She cast a quick look around at her sisters and said, 'Must fly. We're going to practise that dance tune again.' A moment later they heard her footsteps clattering down the uncarpeted staircase to the back door.

Violet shrugged her shoulders. 'Have it your own way,' she said with a martyred air. 'If she's unmasked, on your head be it, Daisy.'

'I say,' said Rose. 'Talking of being unmasked, haven't you shown her the letter, Daisy? Daisy found a letter from someone in 1906 who thinks she's expecting a baby. And we think the baby was Maud. She says that . . . what was it, Daisy? *They'll have to allow us to get married. They can't say that we're too young now.* Daisy, should we tell her, do you think?' At Daisy's look of horror, she continued, 'No, you're quite right, not until we're sure. How sad it sounds! It's like Romeo and Juliet, isn't it, Violet?'

'Sounds like nonsense to me,' said Violet. 'Why on earth should it be anything to do with Maud? Anyway, it was probably written by some housemaid who got herself in trouble.' She sounded impatient and completely uninterested and reverted immediately to the subject that was on her mind.

'All right,' she said with a sigh, 'let's go up to the attic again, Daisy, and see whether any of that stuff of Elaine's will do. Stop it, Rose – I don't want to hear any more of your stories. You read too much rubbish and your mind is full of nonsense.'

'You shock me,' said Rose. 'I thought you would not be able to wait to hear the whole story. I see I was mistaken in you. *Romantic Girl Unmasked As Fraud. "I Just Want to Marry Money," Says Earl's Daughter,*' she murmured. Nevertheless she followed her two older sisters up to the attic.

'I thought as much,' said Violet in despairing tones after a long scrutiny of the top layer of Elaine's clothes. 'These jumpers and cardigans might be good quality, but they just have such an old-fashioned look – and I can't chop up knitted stuff. And the blouses too. People are going to laugh at us if we arrive wearing these. I want to be stylish.' She mused for a moment and then went quickly across to the trunk marked ROBERT DERRINGTON and flung it open.

It was at that moment Daisy heard a heavy footstep on the stairs. 'Shut it, Violet,' she hissed. 'Father is coming. You don't want him to see you taking things out of his brother's trunk.'

However, it was not the Earl but Justin who came in, ducking his dark head below the small, low doorway.

'Any use for a man with a handy knife?' he enquired as he saw Violet on her knees in front of the trunk. A ray of sunshine coming in through the attic window lit a smile on his face.

'No, thank you.' Violet's voice was curt and she did not look at him, but frowned to herself as she pulled out shirt after folded shirt.

The smile faded from Justin's face, but then it came back as he turned to Daisy. 'How did the filming go?' he asked with an air of genuine interest.

It seemed that the truce the two had called during the tango was over. 'Haven't had the time to do anything with it yet. We've been wondering what to wear when we visit the Duchess. Have you ever been to one of those house parties, Justin?' Daisy was determined that Violet wasn't going to boss her. She would talk to Justin if she wanted to.

'I've been to a couple. Can't think what the girls wore, though. Dresses, I suppose,' he said unhelpfully and went to sit on the low window seat. The little attic window jutted out from the roof and the sun was pouring through it now, making the seat a warm and comfortable place to be. He looked as though he were determined to stay so Violet gave a shrug and turned back to her sisters.

'I've just had an idea,' she said, wearing that intent look which always came over her face when she was talking about clothes. 'It was seeing Poppy in that old pullover of Father's. I've always thought it was ridiculous, but looking at it this morning, I suddenly thought that she looked rather good in it.'

She bent down and started to rifle through the trunk, discarding evening clothes, army khaki and army dress uniform, until at the bottom she came across what she was looking for. Carefully packed in a bag, heavily impregnated with lavender and cedar shavings, were the jumpers.

Daisy could see at glance that there was going to be nothing there to suit her. Robert had obviously had the Derrington colouring – he appeared to be a dark-haired, dark-eyed young man in all the photographs and who-ever selected his jumpers had done it with an eye to what would look good on him. There were heather green and moss green jumpers, three of each, and then one russet one which would look good on Poppy and a couple of blues and one soft black cashmere.

'What I was thinking,' said Violet, flushing with ex-citement, 'was that Elaine has got all those lovely tweed skirts – really dowdy now, of course, because they must have been nearly down to the ankles, but they're made from heavenly tweed. If I cut them so that they are above the knee – straight skirts, quite short, like the ones shown at Coco Chanel's last fashion show – well, the oversize jumpers over these short skirts could look rather smart and just the thing for morning wear. Let me see. That blue one should do you, Rose – pull it on.'

The jumper almost came to Rose's knees, but the clear blue suited her and Violet gave a satisfied nod. 'Looks good with the riding breeches,' she remarked, 'but I'd say that in London you'd have no excuse to wear them. It will have to be skirts.'

She picked up a soft moss green, put it aside with an appraising look, and then took the black jumper from the pile.

'Try it on, Daisy,' she urged.

'It will make me look ridiculous, as if I'm in mourning,' objected Daisy, but it was easier to give in to her sister so she pulled it over her head. It felt incredibly soft, and warm as a blanket.

'Looks good,' said Justin from the windowsill. 'Makes you look very grown-up. Shows up your hair too. Makes it a lovely silvery blonde. And makes your skin seem very white.'

Daisy felt herself blush and hoped that Violet would not notice, or if she did that she would not make any comment.

'Come down and you can see yourself in the looking glass,' suggested Violet, but Daisy shook her head.

'No, I can't, Vi. I'll help you carry down the stuff but I need to work on my film. Rose, why don't you do your schoolwork now and then when I've finished developing we can plan the film together and you can do some title cards for the frames we select.'

When Daisy reached the basement she was surprised to see Sir Guy coming in the back door, followed by Morgan carrying something large, wrapped in brown paper, in his arms.

'Ah, my favourite goddaughter,' said Sir Guy, looking a little embarrassed.

'I'm your only one,' responded Daisy mechanically, wondering what on earth Morgan was carrying. Sir Guy had volunteered, to everyone's surprise, to escort the Duchess to the station at Maidstone and had gone off, after an early breakfast, sitting beside Her Grace in the squashy back seat of the ancient Humber.

'Just go out and see if I left my newspaper in the car, would you, Daisy?' said Sir Guy and she went out of the back door, shivering a little as she crossed over towards the stables. She was half sorry that she hadn't grabbed one of the discarded jumpers from Robert's trunk. Even if that dark green was quite unbecoming on her, it would have been warm. Today, with the frost still silver in the shadowy parts of the stable yard, was definitely a three-jumper day – especially in the icy darkness of her dairy. In a while I'll have a hot mug of cocoa, thought Daisy. It will warm my hands as well as my insides. She would take another out to Justin, she decided. Even if the sun was on the bridge it would be cold work fishing on a day like today.

There was no newspaper on the seat of the Humber and none in its capacious boot. In the distance Daisy could see her father riding slowly down the back avenue – he had come home earlier than usual from his morning ride. He would be worried about the house party and would be racking his brains to think how he could get money to buy new clothes for his daughters. His instinct would be to refuse permission to allow the visit and that would solve all his problems. As long as he could shut away the outside world he could avoid confronting his financial problems. But first of all he had to justify himself and Daisy was the one he usually chose in order to unburden himself of guilt.

I'm not going to tell him that turning down this visit is the right thing to do, thought Daisy. Not this time. This is too important for Violet. She has a right to have her chance.

There were voices inside the open door to her darkroom as she came in and she stopped short.

There was a smell of oil in the room, but that was not all.

Standing in the corner of the dairy pantry, well fenced in with an ancient fireguard, was an upright oil heater, painted black and with the word PERFECTION stamped on it. It had a screened window to view the flame and a small brass fuel-level indicator to show how much oil was in it. Already a wave of delicious warmth was filling the tiny room. Daisy gasped. Her eyes began to fill with tears. Her voice shook as she said uncertainly, 'That's not for me!'

Daisy was not used to being given treats. It was so seldom that anyone had time to think of her. She was sensible enough to know that Poppy needed to be treated carefully and that her music lessons were essential, that Rose was a delicate child who needed extra care, that life at Beech Grove Manor was harder on Violet than on anyone else, but sometimes she felt that it would be nice to think someone was concerned about her.

'No, no, no.' Sir Guy sounded shocked. 'Not for you at all, m'dear. I'm just worried about the film. Isn't that right, Morgan?'

Morgan gave a grin. 'That's right, Sir Guy. Expensive stuff, films. Cold and damp must be very bad for them. I feel the same about my drums. Never let the fire in the range die down too far.'

'There you are then,' said Sir Guy happily. He accepted Daisy's kiss, but said hurriedly, 'Now get working, Miss Daisy. I'm looking forward to seeing this film. Remember, tell a story and tell it through the pictures. Don't say this to Rose, but the fewer the title cards, the better your film will be and the more your audience in the cinema will lose themselves in the story.'

'And don't move that heater from that safe corner, or fill it yourself,' added Morgan. 'Sir Guy has bought a barrelful of oil that will be delivered later. I'll keep it in my workshop in the stables and I'll light the burner and check the level every morning. Don't you touch it, my lady! If anything is wrong with it come and fetch me.'

'That's right,' agreed her godfather. 'Film is dangerous

stuff. Will burst into flames as easy as anything. Always happening in studios! These young lads insist on smoking and one spark and the place goes up in flames. I make my youngsters go outside to smoke. Can't stand the smell of their cheap cigarettes either.'

Talking fast to cover Daisy's thanks, he went out and Morgan, giving her a smile, went after him.

Two hours later, Daisy sat back and thought. The reel of film had been developed and pegged on to the little line to dry. Then she had taken out her scissors and cut out promising sequences. Normally she rushed in and out, doing one job at a time, but today, in this delicious warmth, she just sat and thought. What did she want to achieve with this film? A movie that had substance . . . that would have the audience sitting on the edges of their seats . . . a story that would bring gasps of horror – even the odd tear.

What had she got so far?

Well, lots and lots of wonderful background shots. Violet's first sight of Justin that day by the lake; Justin looking up at Violet as she sat on her horse and looked demurely down at him. A few interesting close-up frames – Justin and Violet dancing together, their eyes locked, every fibre of their being showing how attracted they were to each other. Daisy gazed for a long time at these frames. It was such a shame that they were just pretending. Justin was exactly the sort of man she wanted for her eldest sister – someone who had some spark. But it was impossible – Justin had made no secret of the fact that he was as poor as they were, living by his wits at the moment. He would be on the lookout to marry a rich heiress, not someone like Violet without a penny to her name, a girl from an almost bankrupt estate that would descend to a hostile heir. Denis Derrington had no interest in the family, no desire to do anything that would make their life more bearable, and that fact was unalterable. Violet had to marry money. And, thought Daisy wisely, she would be happiest if she married a man with a country estate and a grand house. Unlike her younger sisters she had never become reconciled to their poverty.

Still, her professional side told her that the frames were excellent. There were other good ones: Rose listening to the Duchess with bated breath; Baz and Poppy laughing together; Great-Aunt Lizzie with a look of satisfaction in her gimlet eyes; Maud serving demurely at table; Bateman bending over her father offering him wine with a look of such affection, such concern on his old face; Violet crying hopelessly (but still looking pretty) sitting on the windowsill of her bedroom . . .

Not enough drama, she thought. She got to her feet, leaving her prize frames on the table. She would walk around and think, she decided. Perhaps being so warm was robbing her of ideas. Almost automatically she took her camera, loaded a new spool of film into it and went out into the stable yard. Morgan was out there, a workbench spread with nuts and bolts from the ancient Humber in front of him.

Morgan seemed to be having trouble with one of the nuts on a bolt. She heard him swear as he desperately twisted the wrench, but nothing seemed to happen. He stood back, took a long breath, his chest swelling under the tight singlet that he wore. Immediately Daisy raised the camera. A look of fury was on his face as he eyed the nut – more than fury, a look of intense hatred, a look such as she had never seen him wear before. He was so immersed that he did not look towards her and did not hear the camera whirring. He swung the sledgehammer and brought it crashing down on the bolt.

Then he looked over at Daisy, surprised to see her. She lowered the camera and eyed him appraisingly.

'It's all right,' he said. 'Don't worry. I always imagine that I am hitting the man who killed my best friend when we were in the trenches. There's nothing like good honest hatred. Gives you that extra bit of strength. There's always a way around things, isn't there?'

'That's probably very true,' said Daisy gravely. Yes, she thought as she walked back to her darkroom. There is always a solution if you juggle ideas enough.

She knew now how to handle her film.

Morgan would be the murderer, she thought as the gong went for lunch.

Chapter Ten

'I have a brilliant idea,' said Rose next day. She was studying the frames laid out on the table and stretching her thin hands appreciatively towards the lovely warmth coming from the oil heater. She picked up the ones that showed Morgan brandishing the sledgehammer and smiled.

Daisy waited. Her youngest sister had a wonderful imagination.

'Murder in the Dark,' said Rose.

'You mean for a title?'

'No, the game.'

'Oh, the game.' Daisy was beginning to guess. Right through the winter months the Derrington girls and the jazz band boys played the game Murder in the Dark, an elaborate and much more thrilling form of hide and seek. 'Yes, we play Murder in the Dark, you film it – now, wait a minute, let me think . . . Yes, I've got it.' Rose took a deep breath and shut her eyes.

Daisy watched her with amusement. Rose could be very dramatic.

'The film,' began Rose in her story-telling voice, 'all takes place at a house-party weekend. The heroine, a beautiful girl (Violet), is madly in love with a handsome young man (Justin). Her father—'

'Sir Guy,' interrupted Daisy. She was beginning to guess. 'He said that he wanted to be a victim,' she added.

'Her father,' continued Rose, 'refuses to allow them to marry. So during a game of Murder in the Dark, he is actually murdered.'

'But not by Justin,' stated Daisy.

'Of course not. The hero is never the murderer,' said Rose wisely. 'The murderer has to be Morgan with that great shot you took of him.'

'So who will Morgan be, then?' asked Daisy.

'Morgan will be the chauffeur. That's easy to set up – just shoot a couple of frames of him with the car. Anyway, for years he has nursed a hopeless passion for Vi. A bit like the Hunchback of Notre-Dame. When he hears her father deny his daughter her last chance of happiness – well, he thinks he will willingly go to the scaffold in order to give his beloved her heart's desire. *It is a far, far better thing that I do, than I have ever done,*' she added dramatically. Rose was a great fan of the works of Charles Dickens and had read them all before she was ten years old.

'I think that would work,' said Daisy slowly, seeing the story in dramatic black and white unfold in her mind's eye.

'While the young people are playing the game of Murder in the Dark during a house party,' resumed Rose, 'he listens at the window, then steals into the house, finds Sir Guy and hits him over the head.'

'That's very good,' said Daisy admiringly. 'But I need some more shots, don't I – as well as the Murder in the

Dark ones, of course. I need to have Justin quarrelling with Sir Guy. I think I might have an idea about that,' she went on thoughtfully, 'but the difficulty will be to have Morgan gazing longingly at Violet.'

'Excuse me, your ladyship, Lady Elizabeth is looking everywhere for you.' Maud tapped on the door and then put her head inside and gave Rose a quick smile.

'I'll slip out the back door,' said Rose rapidly. 'Tell her I have gone for a health-giving walk.'

'Take my spare jumper – I don't need it. I'm really warm here.' When Rose had disappeared, Daisy eyed Maud. There seemed to be no way of asking the question tactfully so she came straight out with it, explaining Rose's idea for a film and showing the picture of Morgan and his sledgehammer. 'I just want one of him looking longingly, lovingly at someone,' she finished, looking hopefully at Maud.

'Not seen him do that, my lady,' said Maud briskly. 'You'd best be asking Lady Poppy. She'd know him better, I reckon.'

So there was no love interest between Morgan and Maud – or if there were, she was not willing to divulge it. She would have to ask Poppy. Perhaps he looked lovingly and longingly at his drums. That would be quite a bonus, thought Daisy, and then switched her mind to Sir Guy. He had told her firmly that he couldn't act, but he was happy to be a body. However, she had an idea and now was the time to put it into practice.

Now for Justin, thought Daisy. She needed his

co-operation, so first of all she made two mugs of hot cocoa and carried them out to the bridge over the lake.

'Drink it quickly while it's still hot,' she ordered. He didn't look too happy, she thought and the fishing basket was empty of fish. All to the good – he might be more willing to fall in with her suggestion.

'Do you remember telling me that you were very good at annoying people?' she began, omitting to point out that he had a chocolate moustache around his mouth. He had a touchy sense of his own dignity and she wanted to get his agreement to her plan. 'When you were at school, at Harrow,' she added.

'Oh, that!' He began to laugh. 'I could tell you some funny stories.'

'How did you do it though?' she asked, trying to sound meek and admiring.

'Well,' he said, 'it's easy when you understand psychology. Once you can put your finger on someone's weak spot, you can always needle them.'

Daisy nodded admiringly. 'That's very clever,' she said. 'So if you wanted to annoy Sir Guy, you would criticize one of his films.'

'Never seen any, to my knowledge,' he said promptly. 'Anyway, why do you want me to annoy him? He seems a nice fellow.'

'It's for my film and I've got an idea. He and my father have gone over to Brampton to see about the drag hunt; they'll be back soon – you could meet him in the yard. I'll ask Rose to get Father out of the way. Try to make Sir Guy stop just outside the hen house. I'll be inside, with the camera on the windowsill, and the clucking of the hens will stop him hearing the whirring sound as I'm filming. I only need a minute or so.'

'So what am I going to say?' To her relief, Justin sounded amused.

'Just tell him that you hear he's going to make a film of *A Tale of Two Cities*, and as a lover of Dickens—'

'Can't stand his books – too long-winded,' interrupted Justin, 'but I get your point.' A mischievous smile curved his lips. Daisy could not resist and reached up with her handkerchief to wipe the chocolate foam from around his mouth.

'Stop behaving like my nanny,' he said, but he was still smiling. 'Trust me. I think I can annoy anyone when I put my mind to it – sheer jealousy of a superior mind, of course. That always does the trick.'

There was a very good view of the avenue from the front windows of the ballroom and Daisy waited there until she saw her father and Sir Guy come riding slowly through the large iron gates. They stopped then, and after a minute's conversation the Earl turned off towards the farm manager's cottage, leaving Sir Guy to ride on alone. This was an unexpected piece of luck. No need to get Rose to separate her father from his friend. She ran downstairs, grabbed her camera and was safely in the hen house by the time Sir Guy rode past towards the stable yard.

Justin gave him a few minutes and then sauntered up,

loitering around the cobbled yard, nudging with his boot at hens that came running up in the hope of being fed.

'Ah, Sir Guy.' His tone of voice was condescending and Daisy smiled to herself as she saw the slightly offended look on her godfather's face.

But that was nothing to the look that dawned when Justin went into a passionate tirade about the sacredness of Charles Dickens's work and the idiocy – Justin repeated the word with satisfaction – of expecting to be able to convey the depths of the novelist's genius through such a trumpery medium as cinema. There was a lot more like that. Justin liked the sound of his own voice and began to be carried away by his own artistic pretensions. Not only did he give his opinions in a way that was quite unlike any young man of his age, continually interrupting Sir Guy's attempts at justifying his project, but he poured such scorn on it and made it sound so ridiculous that Daisy, safely hidden within the hen house, had to bite her lip hard to stop giggling and risk jerking the camera.

The fury on Sir Guy's face was wonderful. Daisy kept the camera going, shooting frame after frame. Justin was good too. Blank astonishment, rising anger, and then, as the older man's fury erupted, head hanging, backing away. Sir Guy shouted after him that he did not know the first thing about cinema, that cinema was an art form . . .

And then Daisy emerged, picking feathers from her hair and holding out the camera.

'And cut,' she said, bursting out laughing at his expression.

'What! You little monkey.' Her godfather began to laugh. 'You put him up to it, didn't you?'

'Come into my office and I'll tell you all about it,' she said grandly. 'You come, too, Justin. You might have some ideas for me.'

'Yes, I'm sure that I will. But it'll be a bit of a squash in there. Let's go up to the schoolroom,' said Justin, taking charge without any show of false modesty. 'Violet might have some ideas too.'

I doubt it, thought Daisy, but she didn't like to say what was in her mind. More to the point, Rose would probably be in the schoolroom, struggling with some mathematical problems. She had already produced some cleverly phrased dramatic title cards and would be eager to get on with the story behind the film. Rose was always so creative and by now probably had another forty ideas to propose.

'On the top floor,' groaned Sir Guy.

'It will get you fit in time for the hunt,' said Daisy unsympathetically, but she took his arm and slowed her steps to his, making sure that Justin followed behind as they went up the narrow back staircase to the third floor.

Sounds of music, interspersed with the rattle of the treadle sewing machine, came down to them as they climbed the last flight of steps. Poppy was playing some jazz on the clarinet, Rose accompanying her on the schoolroom piano. Just as they reached the top step, the clarinet ceased and Poppy's exasperated voice shouted, 'Oh, for heaven's sake, Violet, do you have to make such an awful noise with that machine?'

'Well, I like that—' Violet stopped in mid-sentence as they came in. Her eyes went to Justin immediately. She smiled graciously, but there was a flush of annoyance on her face.

'Didn't know that you were musical, Rose,' Sir Guy observed tactfully. 'I thought Poppy was the only one.'

'Rose is very musical too, but she's never had lessons,' said Daisy. Rose was neglected, she thought. It seemed as though once she had been slotted into the pigeonhole of delicacy, her father was uninterested in the talents of his youngest child.

'Not enough money,' said Rose cheerfully. '*Talented Girl Neglected. Musical Genius Left to Starve in the Garret. Blues Singer Begs for Guitar, but is Repulsed by Unfeeling Family*.' She played a chord on the piano and began to sing 'The St Louis Blues' in the low, slightly croaky voice that she affected when singing jazz and Poppy lifted her clarinet and accompanied her, while Violet started to run her sewing machine again.

'It's not just the machine, it's that you deliberately put it on top of that loose board,' shouted Poppy, breaking off in mid-phrase. She was always quite uninhibited and Daisy was not surprised that she took no notice of either Sir Guy or Justin.

'You could go somewhere else,' pointed out Violet, trying to smile sweetly. 'As for loose floorboards, well, I have to have this machine here; it's the only part of the room where there is enough light for me to see what I'm doing. Why don't you go down to Morgan's cottage or something?'

'No, we can't; Rose has to do her maths,' snapped Poppy. Sir Guy grinned at the discarded books on the table and Rose giggled.

'Why don't I have a look at that loose floorboard?' said Justin. 'My Boy Scout pocket-knife makes a good screw-driver, even if it failed the test as a lock-picker.'

'What are you sewing, Violet?' asked Sir Guy at the same moment.

Both of them were keen to bring a smile back to the leading lady's beautiful face, thought Daisy. It did seem to her that Violet was making an unnecessary noise with that sewing machine. She continually refused offers of help with the clothes, but then wore a martyred air that she was left with all the sewing.

Justin lifted the sewing machine as if it were feather-light, then knelt down on the boards with his knife in his hand. There was no doubt that this particular floorboard seemed to fit badly. First he tried tightening the screws, but then shook his head with annoyance. Daisy watched as he loosened all the screws again, lifting the board from its place.

'It just doesn't seem to fit . . .' he began at the same moment as Violet said in alarmed tones, 'Don't get dust on our skirts.' The other two stopped playing.

'There's a box under there,' said Daisy, bending down.

'*Long-lost Treasure Uncovered from its Centuries-Old Hiding Place.*' Rose came out from behind the piano.

'No wonder that floorboard didn't fit. I knew there was something wrong as soon as I put my trusty knife on to it.' Justin dusted his hands with satisfaction and bent down, taking out the box. Daisy took it from him and carried it over to the window. The schoolroom was tucked into the north-eastern corner at the top of the house, and the light was poor there for most of the day.

The box was made from a thin, fine wood with a hinged lid. That was not what Daisy looked at though. There, on the outside of the box, scrawled in large, uneven, childish capital letters, was the name ELAINE CARRUTHERS.

'The mysterious Elaine again,' said Violet, peering over her shoulder. 'She's apparently an aunt of ours,' she added to Justin.

'We imagine that she had some huge row with Great-Aunt Lizzie so her name must never again be breathed within the sacred portals of Beech Grove Manor,' explained Rose.

'Open it, Daisy,' said Poppy.

'Hope it's jewellery,' said Violet. 'I could just do with a string of pearls like Daisy's.' Then she blushed and gave Sir Guy an embarrassed look.

'You shall have one as soon as I am snapped up by one of the top London law firms – at a top salary, of course,' promised Justin, and Violet glared at him.

'I hardly think that will be necessary once I am married to a duke,' she said airily. Justin made a show of being shot in the heart and falling down dead and she laughed.

'Look, everyone – it's a doll!' exclaimed Rose.

The box was narrow and deep. On the top of it lay the most beautiful doll. She was a baby doll, her wax face so delicately made and so skilfully tinted that she almost looked real. She had pink cheeks, blue eyes and blonde curls made from real hair. She was dressed in an elaborately flowing gown of palest pink satin with a lace bodice, a frilled hem and a long sash of pink velvet.

'What's underneath?' asked Rose. 'Oh pray, let me hold her and imagine what it would be like to be young again.'

Daisy handed the doll to her sister. 'It's like a little bed,' she said as she lifted out the tray where the doll had lain. It was covered in a tiny patchwork quilt with a small satin pillow. Underneath was a linen sheet, and beneath that a miniature mattress. 'Oh, it's a wardrobe!'

The rest of the box was designed like a child's wardrobe, painted white with tiny primroses stencilled between the decorative scrolls. It had a hinged door. Daisy set it on end and opened it.

Hanging on the rail were more dresses and fur cloaks, even a muff the size of a stamp to keep the baby's hands warm. Beside the hanging space was a row of drawers, each with a little brass knob. The top drawer was full of nappies and safety pins, the second had caps of all descriptions – lace caps, cotton caps and knitted wool caps – and the third held aprons.

Daisy pulled out the top apron and then she had a shock.

The apron, like all the clothes, was exquisitely made,

but the embroidery on it was obviously done by a young child. In large, unsteady, uneven stitches was the word DAISY. The other aprons also bore that name.

'She's called after you,' said Rose. 'She must be your doll from another life.'

'No, she's Elaine's doll,' said Daisy. For a moment she had been puzzled by the name, but then she found an explanation. 'I suppose when I was born I looked like Elaine's doll – I was blonde and blue-eyed so Mother decided to call me Daisy – anyway, it went well with Poppy and Violet,' she added briskly. For a moment she hesitated and then spoke out. 'Don't let's say anything about this,' she said with a glance at Justin and Sir Guy.

'Or Great-Aunt Lizzie will sell it.' Rose nodded wisely. 'It's a sad thing to watch one so old becoming so mercenary,' she added.

'Let's talk about the film,' said Daisy hurriedly. 'Justin, can you put back the floorboard? Give me the doll, Rose. I'll just take it down and hide it in my wardrobe.'

By the time she came back Poppy had disappeared but the others were busily discussing the film – or at least Justin was giving his views and everyone else was listening: Sir Guy with a good-humoured expression on his face, Violet with bated breath, needle in hand, and Rose drawing spiders inside glass boxes on the back page of her mathematics book.

'What we've decided is the best plan, Daisy,' said Justin with authority, 'is for you to film me and Violet in all sorts of outdoor locations: near the stables – it could be me and Violet about to ride together, sitting on our horses, with Morgan watching over the hood of the car, of course – and then there could be Violet feeding the hens with me watching her, showing love and admiration on my face, and then . . . and then,' he said with a sidelong glance at Violet, 'there could be a scene where Morgan goes for a walk through the garden and comes upon me and Violet kissing under the archway . . .'

'Certainly not,' said Violet, but she said it with a smile and Daisy noticed Sir Guy look appraisingly from her face to Justin's.

'*Quelle histoire ennuyeuse*,' said Rose with a yawn. Aunt Lizzie had taught her from the battered copy of *French for Young Ladies* that she had used when teaching the older girls, but that was not enough for Rose so now she was teaching herself French by means of the books of Victor Hugo and a dictionary and liked to sprinkle her conversation with French phrases. Justin looked annoyed and Sir Guy amused.

'Some good ideas there,' said Daisy briskly, trying to banish speculations about the doll from her mind. 'I'll talk to Morgan,' she said. 'Now let's plan what I need to film during the hunt and during the Murder in the Dark game.'

Chapter Eleven

The day of the hunt started off gloomily but once breakfast was over the fine rain had begun to cease and the sun had appeared through the trees by the time the first of the neighbours trotted up the avenue. The Beech Grove Manor drag hunts were famous and people came from miles around to attend them. Traditionally everyone brought their own sandwiches and their own flask, whether of coffee or something stronger, so this was one of the few social events that the Derrington family could afford to keep up.

Daisy and Poppy had made up six packages of sandwiches for the house party the night before, sitting cosily in front of the kitchen stove wrapping them in greaseproof paper and filling flasks of coffee and tea. Lunch would be eaten at The Folly, an eighteenth-century copy of a Roman temple built by an ancestor on top of a hill in order to give a good view of the whole estate and its woods. The Folly, though open at the sides, was furnished with a cast iron table and a dozen chairs. Morgan had found pieces of an iron stove out in the stables which he had carried out and reassembled inside the stately building. Now everyone would be warm as well as sheltered while they ate their lunch.

The scene outside the stables was very colourful with

black, brown, white and palomino horses and orange and white harrier hounds. Some of the neighbours were in hunting pink, although most, like the Earl himself, just wore their usual tweed jackets.

One by one everyone mounted, until only a single horse was left without a rider. Eventually Sir Guy appeared and looked without favour at the huge animal being held by the stableman.

'What's his name?' he asked dubiously.

'Morning Cloud, sir.' The stableman moved the horse a little nearer to the mounting block.

'Are you sure it's not Brute?' muttered Sir Guy as the horse backed and tossed its head.

'C'mon, Guy,' said Michael Derrington. 'You're always saying that you would like to experience a hunt. Well, now's your chance. Anyway, that's the only horse in the stable that will bear your weight, old man.'

Daisy eyed her father with a grin. She was a little sorry for her godfather, but on the other hand it was lovely to see her father so cheerful. She hoped that the day would go well for him. It would take a lot to disturb his mood this morning with the prospect of a good run through the beech woods ahead of him. He loved dogs, he loved horses, and above all he loved the woods and fields of the estate that had been owned by his family for hundreds of years.

'Keep to the rear when we get into the woods, Sir Guy,' she advised. 'You'll be all right with him. He's an old horse. He won't be too interested in trying to keep up with youngsters.'

'Tell him that, not me,' grumbled Sir Guy.

'*Lifeless Body of Well-known Film Magnate Dragged Through Historic Woods,*' chanted Rose as they walked their horses down the avenue behind the whirling, tail-wagging medley of white and orange dogs.

'*"Nothing to do with me," says Earl. "The man just did not know how to ride",*' chimed in Baz.

'*"Gave him the best horse in my stables",*' said Edwin from the other side of Poppy.

'*Ugly Rumours in the Neighbourhood,*' went on Rose happily.

'You can mock,' said Sir Guy, 'but I've got a huge Fuller's walnut cake, sent down by train yesterday, for my lunch; I'm warning you now that only sympathetic and understanding young people will get a slice of it.'

'They've picked up the scent!' yelled Baz. 'Hold on to your hats, you guys and dolls. Can you take that hedge, Poppy?'

'You betcha,' said Poppy. She jumped and they heard Baz yell 'Jeepers creepers!' as her horse almost tumbled, righting itself at the last moment.

'Come on, Justin,' shouted Violet.

But Justin had reined back his horse, watching Violet. It was not a good angle for her but she cleared the hedge magnificently.

'I'm going around by the gate,' Daisy heard him say as she herself cleared the hedge a little further down, but by then Violet was almost out of sight.

I should check on Sir Guy, thought Daisy, but she couldn't make herself slow down or stop. Ahead were the dogs, screaming with excitement. Their noses were to the ground where a bag of aniseed had been trailed across the wet earth earlier this morning which still gave off a pungent, exciting smell. These were dogs bred to hunt and this was what they lived for: the rushing through trees, the scrambling up hillsides, the splashing through puddles, the swimming through streams, the agony of losing the trail, the ecstasy of finding it again.

There was nothing in the world as exciting as drag hunting, thought Daisy, who had never quite accepted the idea of hunting a living, breathing animal. She should have been filming, she knew, but she could not resist the first run of the day. Morgan had promised to bring her camera when he came out to light the fire at The Folly and she would sacrifice the second run for the sake of her film.

After two and a half hours of hectic riding, the hounds eventually found the bag of aniseed in a disused chalk quarry at the foot of Folly Hill. The dog cart was there already and the stableman had a bag of treats for the dogs to distract them from the aniseed, which was quickly packed away to be kept for another day. Wearily everyone dismounted. The horses were rubbed down and allowed to drink from the river before they could have their own lunch.

'Why didn't you wait for me?' said Justin in aggrieved tones to Violet as they climbed the steep hill ahead of

Daisy. 'After all, you were the one who invited me to go on this hunt. Pretty rude to go off without your guest, wasn't it?'

Violet turned to face him, her colour high. She never could bear criticism.

'Well,' she said with a shrug, 'come to that, why were you such a coward? Why couldn't you jump that little hedge instead of going all the way around? I hate not being in the front of the hunt. I wouldn't have mentioned it,' she added loftily, 'if you hadn't been so rude. Well, go on then, why didn't you stay with me?'

'Didn't want to get myself killed.' Justin's voice was cold.

'Don't be ridiculous,' said Violet impatiently. 'Who gets killed jumping a little hedge?'

My Uncle Clifford did,' said Justin. 'I saw him break his neck – not a very nice sight. I was about five years old at the time – on my first pony – he was seventeen – it made quite an impression on me – rather put me off all this hunting stuff, I'm afraid.'

And with that he almost elbowed Violet out of the way and strode at a fast pace up the hill. Violet raced after him, but when Daisy got there they were apart – Violet greeting their guests, a little red in the face, and Justin sitting alone, gazing with a set expression into the flames of the lovely fire that Morgan had lit in the old stove. He did not even approach the table when Rose shrieked with delight at the sight of the magic name of F & M on the label of a large, handsome wicker basket.

'Fortnum and Mason hamper! Oh I say, old boy, that's very generous of you,' said the Earl as Sir Guy came staggering in.

'Pour me a glass of brandy and no one speak to me until I have swallowed it,' said Sir Guy, limping over to a chair and sitting down stiffly. 'Daisy, I shall accompany you and your camera this afternoon. Nothing would ever persuade me to get up on that brute again.'

'Take you back to the house in the dog cart, sir, if his lordship is agreeable to that,' said Morgan. 'You could have a bit of a rest.' He grinned at the stableman. 'Tom here will lead back the two horses, won't you, Tom?'

'A nice sleep on my bed until all you lively people come back . . . well that sounds just right,' said Sir Guy, beginning to revive a little after finishing his brandy. He leaned forward with interest as Rose untied the red silken ribbon and pushed back the wicker lid. 'They told me that it is a hunting hamper, but I made them add a Fuller's walnut special. C'mon, m'dear, find something for a dying man. And who knows,' he added, 'I might just last until I am murdered in the dark tonight.'

Surveying with satisfaction the astonished glances from the neighbouring hunting squires and their offspring, Sir Guy seized the knife from the hamper, sliced off a neat segment from the large iced walnut cake and offered it to Daisy.

Rose nudged her and inclined her head towards Justin, who was still gazing broodily at the fire. '*Childhood Trauma Causes Lovers' Tiff*,' she intoned.

Daisy grinned but then the smile faded as she glanced at Violet. Her sister's eyes were wet with tears as she looked under her eyelashes at Justin. Slowly she got up, walked across and knelt on the floor beside him, pretending to hold her hands out to the flames. He sat stiffly, but Daisy saw the expression on his face change and soften. After a minute, Violet put her hand on his arm. He didn't look at her, but he lifted his own hand and covered hers. They sat very close, almost as though they were on an island of their own in the midst of a sea of laughing, joking people.

Chapter Twelve

❀

'Yes, yes, of course I'll play,' said the Earl impatiently. 'I was the one who invented the game. Guy will too, won't you, old man? Many's the game we played when we were young. We start in the library after dinner,' he explained to Justin, the only one present who, he thought, did not know about the famous Murder in the Dark games at Beech Grove Manor. 'There's one victim, and the rest of us are murderers. The victim declares himself and then has five minutes to hide before the hunt is after him. The detective does not stir from the library until the murder is announced by Bateman. He'll sound the dinner gong, so when you hear that everyone comes back to the library and the detective has to guess who committed the dastardly crime.'

'And Bateman will sound the gong after one hour if the victim manages to escape the murderers.'

'Sounds fun,' said Justin amiably. 'So we all go off and hide in dark places. How is the victim chosen?'

'We draw lots,' said the Earl.

'And when you're murdered you must count to ten and then scream,' Rose told him.

'And the victim, whoever it is, has to be dumb after that one scream,' put in Daisy. 'You're not allowed to say who murdered you, even if you know.'

'And you can hide anywhere?'

'Anywhere in the house,' said the Earl. It was understood by all those who had played the game before that the servants' quarters were not intruded upon. Daisy was counting on that.

'Come on, then – hand out the cards, Daisy. Let's know our fate.' The Earl was eager to get on with the game.

'You do it, Justin; I'm still stiff after hunting first and then dancing.' Daisy had given the pack of cards to Justin earlier and wasn't too sure what he had done with them. He had laughed off her concern that the right card might not go to the chosen victim, Sir Guy, and on hearing how much the Earl fancied himself as a Sherlock Holmes, had promised to make sure that her father would be detective.

'Easy to tell that you haven't been to school,' he had said. 'That was one of the first things I learned when I went to Harrow. I can guarantee to give any card I choose to anyone.'

'Ladies and gentlemen, you will each get a card,' intoned the Earl. 'If you get an ordinary card, then you are a potential murderer, the Joker goes to the victim and the ace of spades is the detective. These are the only picture cards. Have you counted them out, Daisy?'

'Yes,' said Daisy. She hoped everything would go well. Justin was making a great pantomime out of shuffling and reshuffling the cards, then cutting the pack and asking Rose to cut it again. At last he advanced upon the guests, all seated around the table in the library.

'The victim has to declare themselves immediately; the detective keeps quiet. Once everyone has their card, Bateman turns out the lights.' The Earl was impatient to get on with the game. Daisy tensed. Justin was overplaying his part and her father was getting irritated with his continual shuffling of the cards. He pressed the bell and Bateman appeared almost instantly, just as if he were standing in the back hallway awaiting the summons.

'Just going to play Murder in the Dark, Bateman. Have you been told all about it?'

'Yes, my lord,' said Bateman respectfully. 'The usual candles are placed on landings of the stairways so that no one stumbles. Otherwise the house will be in complete darkness. I have warned the kitchen staff.'

'So here goes,' said Justin. 'One last cut and shuffle for luck and now you take the top card, please.' He went around the circle. Each person took a card, glanced at it and held it concealed. Justin himself took the last card and then looked around.

'Poker faces,' he said. 'Someone must have received the Joker. Come on, now, admit it.'

'I did,' said Sir Guy dramatically after a couple of moments. 'Well, there you are. I had a presentiment today, when I was being hurtled through the woods by that brute, that this would be the day when I would see my last sundown.'

'Except that you were asleep for sundown – what a shame,' said Rose sweetly.

'Well, that's a bit of luck for you,' said the Earl heartily.

'Being chosen as victim, I mean. It's ever so jolly lying there in the dark and waiting for someone to come and murder you.'

'I'm sure,' said Sir Guy resignedly.

'Get the scarf, Rose. You have to tie this white silk scarf around your neck, Guy, so that you can be identified as the victim.'

'The sacrificial lamb,' said Rose with satisfaction.

The scarf, a present to the Earl by an elderly cousin about ten years ago, had never been worn by him on the grounds that it was too flashy, but it was ideal for the game. Even the slightest glimmer of light made it shine out like a beacon.

'Knot it so that it can't fall off. Let me do it.' The Earl tied the scarf in a noose-like fashion around his friend's neck.

'Well, there we are then. Right, Bateman, the fuse box, if you please. Off you go, Guy.'

'Sprint as though you are the fox and the hounds are after you,' Baz could not help advising, adding with his amiable smile, 'Sorry, sir; just a joke, sir.'

'Tarantara!' Edwin blew an imaginary hunting horn and Sir Guy, his white scarf gleaming, cast one look of exaggerated indignation over his shoulder as he strode out of the room at a stately pace.

'All ready for the filming?' whispered Justin in Daisy's ear and she nodded. The camera was upstairs. It had been put carefully into position, ready for action. She hoped that no one had heard him. She wanted expressions to be natural.

'Three more minutes to go,' said her father, watch in hand.

And then it was two more minutes. Daisy began to feel a tingle of excitement. This was what the hounds felt on drag-hunting mornings.

'One more minute,' said the Earl. He began to count aloud. This was also part of the tradition and somehow it heightened the tension as those measured digits came forward one after the other.

'Fifty-five, fifty-six, fifty-seven, fifty-eight, fifty-nine, sixty!' And just as the last number was called the gong in the hall began to sound. Bateman was enjoying himself.

And then there was the sound of the door to the servants' passageway being opened and shut softly. Presumably Bateman had retired to the kitchen. The whole company turned to face each other.

'Look for one last time on the face of a murderer,' intoned Baz.

'Prepare to meet thy doom, Sir Guy Beresford,' said Rose dramatically.

'And there she goes,' shouted Baz as the room was suddenly plunged from brightly lit solidity to darkness. It was odd how darkness disorientated people, thought Daisy as she groped her way to the door. It didn't do that to animals, just people. Once, when the Earl was the victim, she and Poppy, for a joke, had fetched her father's favourite hunting dog from the stables. He found his master instantly and their father was furious and said he would never allow them to play again. He did, of course – his bark was always worse than his bite – but she and Poppy kept out of his way for a while and were extremely well-behaved until he forgot about it.

Daisy wished that she had a dog with her now. Everything seemed fluid: furniture was in odd places as she groped her way to the door

As usually happened everyone made instantly for the doorway to the staircase, stumbling over each other. Once that was opened a faint gleam of light came down from the large window in the landing above. No chance of a hiding place in the gallery – that had only two upright chairs and hundreds of paintings and photographs. The bedrooms were the usual places to hide and for the murderous throng to seek the victim – though Daisy had overheard Great-Aunt Lizzie, who was away for the weekend visiting a friend, telling the chambermaid to lock her bedroom door so that the hunting party would not go stumbling around, knocking over her bottles of scent and things like that.

Soon just she and Justin were left standing by the library door. 'You managed that very well,' she whispered, smiling in the darkness.

'Pity your father always fancies the part of the detective,' he whispered back. 'I've given it to him, but I rather fancied doing that myself. Perhaps I'll reveal myself as a detective sent down from Scotland Yard to keep an eye on old Sherlock Holmes.'

'Follow me,' she whispered back. 'I know a place where you can keep an eye on all the comings and goings and then you can slip down to the basement once they've all had a bit of a hunt around.' She hoped that she could get a few shots of him with Violet later on, but since the quarrel earlier in the day they were avoiding each other.

Daisy's eyes were now getting accustomed to the dark. Quickly she led Justin through the door to the servants' passageway and then up the servants' stairs. She herself had planned the placing of the candles, and the small light in the old-fashioned bedroom lamp gleamed from a windowsill at the top of the uncarpeted stairs.

'Where are you going?' said Justin in her ear.

'The linen cupboard,' she whispered back. 'You open the door to the gallery. Hook it back so that no one closes it.'

The linen cupboard, or hot press, as Mrs Pearson always called it, stood opposite to the door from the servants' stairway to the gallery. Daisy took her camera from the windowsill near the candlestick, then opened the doors, allowing out a rush of hot air and the delicious smell of ironed linen. The shelves were much emptier of sheets and bedclothes than usual – she and Poppy had made up five extra beds on the top floor so that Justin and the jazz band boys could stay the night. Daisy climbed the slatted shelves easily until she was about halfway up, then she propped open the two top doors.

'Pull the bottom doors shut once you're up here,' she whispered. Now the two of them were on the top shelf, looking down. The hot press couldn't be better placed. From the shelf it commanded a view of the servants' staircase, the main staircase, the gallery and the six doors leading to the bedrooms on that floor. Dark shadows darted in and out. Daisy arranged a pile of pillowcases in front of her, building them up to eye level, placed the camera on them, opened the shutter, detonated the percussive cap in the trough of flashlight powder and pressed the button.

'There was a scream when the first flash came –Violet by the sound of it, thought Daisy. A slim figure looked around fearfully – yes, it was Violet. Daisy thought she would spot her and Justin in the hot press, but she went towards the staircase leading down to the ground floor and Daisy could hear the sound of her shoes tapping on the oak boards.

'Any luck, Baz?' That was Edwin. Daisy had the camera in position as they both came out of Sir Guy's bedroom. She ignited the flash once more and giggled silently as Edwin said: 'What was that? A touch of lightning. I say, that will be fun.'

'I'm going to try the back hallway – thought I heard the door go to the servants' quarters when he left the library.'

'That was probably just Bateman – I'm going to have a go at the front attics, Baz. Obvious place really – full of old junk up there. Probably find him in an old trunk.'

And then there was a figure that came slowly and cautiously up the back stairs – a heavy figure, moving slowly, unlike the others, who were galloping exuberantly, leaping from stair to stair, rushing into rooms.

'This is getting a bit boring,' said Justin in Daisy's ear.

'I think I'll be off. Pity I can't do a real murder. I must say that I feel like it,' he added as he slid down.

Probably fed up about Violet, thought Daisy. He, too, must have thought that Violet had seen him and then turned her back and walked away. She would give him a minute and then follow. It was time for her to play her part before anyone decided to try the basement.

She leaned over, pushed open the lower doors of the hot press and climbed down, reaching up for her camera when she was near the bottom.

'And now for the wash-house,' said Daisy aloud.

The wash-house at Beech Grove Manor was a small suite of rooms. There was the drying room with its enormous clothes horse suspended on ropes from the ceiling, its solid pine table and its heavily blackleaded stove in the corner with a set of Victorian flat irons and box irons neatly ranged in size on top. The next room was the mangling pantry where the water was squeezed from the clothes by a huge old mangle. Daisy put a candle on the floor in front of it – the wheel made an interesting shadow on the wall and she filmed that before passing through into the inner room, the wash-house itself with its pump and washboard and its set of enormous tubs for soaking and washing clothes.

She entered the large room to to see a figure slumped on a chair with his head on the pine table. Only the back of the head was visible but by the candlelight she could see the red stain that smeared and clotted the white hair.

Daisy ran outside into the stone-flagged passageway

and screamed 'Murder!' at the top of her voice.

And then there was a moment's silence. Daisy shivered but waited until she heard the first sounds: doors being opened, light and heavy footsteps running down the grand staircase, exclamations, and then the first footsteps sounding on the servants' passageway. They would all be here in a moment. She stepped back until half-hidden by the shadow of the door and began to film, turning the camera first to the dead body, sweeping it in a large arc around the whitewashed walls and then coming back to the table again.

Justin was the first one through the door. Daisy filmed him frantically, praying that she had caught that first moment of shock in his eyes, that slackening of his jaw.

And then the others came – Baz and Poppy giggling together and then stopping abruptly; the Earl frowning, taken aback by the silent figure slumped against the table; Edwin, Simon and then Rose, who screamed loudly and with great drama. Daisy carried on filming – great expressions, she thought exultantly: the stunned disbelief, horror, shock, fear and dread seemed to flit from one face to the other as people in the room moved and shifted from pools of light into dark shadows, their unease and dismay translating into these abrupt changes of position.

And that was the moment when Violet came in. Thinking about it afterwards, Daisy realized that Violet was tired and very strained these days. As soon as she saw Sir Guy she started violently, then burst into tears, sobbing hysterically. Justin's arm went around her immediately and Sir Guy, hearing genuine sobs, sat up and said jovially: '*"Reports of my death are greatly exaggerated."* I've always envied Mark Twain the opportunity to say that wonderful line,' he added.

'Oh, bother,' said Daisy. 'You could have stayed dead for another few minutes – still, I think I have some good footage.'

'You'll have to forgive us the trick we played on you all,' said Sir Guy. 'It was Daisy's idea. Dry your eyes, Violet. When you are a film star earning millions in Hollywood, you will look back at this film as the first step on the ladder of fame. Get that film developed as soon as possible, Daisy. I'm really looking forward to seeing myself in a starring role.'

'I'll never forgive you,' said Violet, but she said it with a smile. Justin's arm was still around her, noticed Daisy. They seemed to have forgotten their quarrel at the hunt earlier in the day.

'Let's go and have a brandy, Guy,' said the Earl when his friend had finished vigorously towelling the sparse remains of his hair.

'I say,' said Baz when the two men had departed in search of the library fire, 'let's have a party. I don't want to go to bed – bit tame after all that fun.'

'Our dresses are already packed away,' said Violet, but she sounded tempted.

'A pyjama party,' said Baz. 'Just pyjamas and dressing gowns. It's all the thing in London these days –

my brother tells me all about them.'

'Jazzy!' Poppy did a little twirl on the tiled floor then kissed Basil's cheek as sign of her approval of his genius.

'A pyjama party,' echoed George. 'That would be the bee's knees! Edwin and I will go and get Morgan and bring back the drums and the double bass from his cottage.'

'And I'll be able to stay up all night as Great-Aunt Lizzie is away,' said Rose and then added, predictably: *'Deprived Child has Glimpse of Paradise.'*

'Violet looks cold; she's had a shock. Should we light a fire in the ballroom?' asked Simon. He was so shy and quiet normally that Daisy looked at him with surprise.

'Wonderful idea!' Violet beamed at him. 'Thank you, Simon.'

'I'll help you.' Justin squared his shoulders, giving Simon a cold look. 'Where's that axe?'

'There's chopped wood in the timber store,' said Daisy. 'Take a basket each. Poppy, you go and have a quick word with Father. Promise to keep the music low.'

'But I don't like low music,' declared Poppy with a note of surprise in her voice.

'Just say it,' said Daisy firmly.

'Let's go and talk to Mrs Beaton, Daise,' said Baz. 'I bet she has a few goodies hidden.'

'No, don't,' said Daisy. She didn't want the elderly cook to be disturbed and there was little to spare in their cupboards, except eggs, of course. She and Rose had collected a large basketful yesterday.

'Eggs,' she said aloud. 'I have a wonderful idea. Let's make a Spanish omelette. Come on, everyone – you can all help. Basil, you do the eggs – Poppy can help you when she comes back. Two for each person and two for the pan – oh, just put in a couple of dozen. Violet, will you do the potatoes? Rose, help her while I find that huge old frying pan.'

The old frying pan was eventually discovered on a high shelf in one of the back pantries. Daisy came into the kitchen staggering under its weight. Her eyes went immediately to her elder sister's face, but to her relief Violet seemed to have shed her ill humour and was laughing happily as she chopped up some dried thyme. She waved a large bottle of olive oil, saying triumphantly, 'Look what I've found!'

She had managed to unload the dirty job of washing and scrubbing potatoes to Maud and Rose, but Daisy was so relieved to see her change of mood that she made no comment on this.

'Great,' she said, pouring the oil in after giving the pan a quick rinse.

'It's as big as a cartwheel,' said Rose admiringly. 'I don't think I've ever seen it before.'

'Let me riddle the fire, my lady,' said Maud. 'I understand that stove and its moods.'

The girl seemed quite at home with the young people, very different from the silent scullery maid who flattened herself against the wall with lowered eyes whenever a member of the family passed. She was laughing now at

Basil and Poppy, who were both endeavouring to beat the eggs in the frenetic style of a drummer.

'I'll put on a second pan as well for the potatoes,' said Daisy. 'They should be soft, I think, but not browned. Chop them small, you two.'

'Fires are lit,' said Justin, coming in. 'Oh, I say, what are you making?'

'Spanish omelette,' said Daisy. 'We need help with the potatoes, so you and Simon get to work on them.'

'We've taken all the mattresses from our beds into the ballroom and put them by the fire with pillows piled on them – the rooms are stone cold on the top floor.' Justin began to scrub some more of the home-grown potatoes enthusiastically. 'Don't bother taking the skins off,' he said. 'The Spaniards don't!'

'Let's eat down here,' Daisy said impulsively when the egg mixture was poured over the softened potatoes. 'The omelette will be cold by the time we all trudge upstairs. And we're bound to forget something.' This was true, but knew that she wanted both Maud and Morgan to have their share of the impromptu feast. 'Morgan, you keep shaking this pan while Rose and I lay the table. Let's see, there are eleven of us . . . That's right, isn't it?'

'Does it get tossed?' asked Baz. 'Bags I do it.'

'And then we'll all get down on the floor and lap it up,' said Violet tartly. 'Don't let him, Daisy.'

'I rather fancy it nice and creamy on the top,' said Daisy. Violet was right; that frying pan was hugely heavy and the omelette was enormous. She needn't have bitten the boy's head off like that, but it was good to have her attention on scolding Poppy and Baz – it distracted from the eleven places laid around the table and made sure that she did not comment and embarrass Maud. Daisy decided she would ensure that everyone was seated around the table before Violet noticed.

Violet Derrington, the most beautiful and most popular debutante of the season – she had found that on a piece of paper written in Violet's elegant script lying on top of her sister's dressing table, no doubt inspired by a headline from one of her fashion magazines.

Debutantes, of course, could never, ever have makeshift meals eaten with spoons from a frying pan placed on a kitchen table in company with a scullery maid and a chauffeur.

On the other hand, high-earning film directors and women of the world, like her sister Daisy, could please themselves.

Chapter Thirteen

The fortnight between the Duchess's invitation and the day of their departure for London passed in what seemed to Daisy like a flash.

Violet, in a panic at the amount of sewing she had undertaken, passed over the turning up of hems and other simple tasks to her and sometimes between that and work on her film Daisy did not get to bed until midnight.

Great-Aunt Lizzie, though she had to be kept in the dark about the length of the skirts and dresses, was unexpectedly helpful about adding new collars and lace edges to various blouses and eventually the work was done. Violet fitted Maud up with one of Elaine's old-fashioned dresses before broaching the subject of taking her with them as a lady's maid, and to their relief the old lady agreed immediately that the scullery maid could fill the role.

'I'm nervous,' said Violet suddenly when the car had left Maidstone and they were rolling smoothly along the road to London.

'Why?' Poppy sounded amazed. 'You can't be wondering how to behave when we are staying at the Duchess's place,' she added. 'Great-Aunt Lizzie has been telling us all what to do and what not to do for the last fortnight.'

'I'm thinking of writing a book about it,' said Rose

dreamily. 'It will be called *The Debutante's Dream* and it will be full of useful hints for young gels embarking on their season. It will be an indispensable guide.'

She stopped for a minute, looking from face to face.

'Ah,' she said. 'You need stronger meat. Let's turn it into a melodrama. A young girl, tired of her great-aunt's lectures, decides to do everything that she should not do. She allows herself to be abducted by a notorious rake, but she proves more than a match for him . . . In fact, I must inform you, my dearest sisters,' she went on earnestly, 'I've finally made up my mind as to what my destiny is in life. I shall be an author – like Charles Dickens, but with more interesting girls. My girls will be full of spirit and will do what they want to do and not hang around repeating all the nice things that people say of them – like that boring Esther in *Bleak House*. My girls are more likely to carry a gun than a bunch of keys. I think I will have a heroine like Poppy. She always does what she wants and says what she feels like saying. Violet and Daisy worry too much.'

'Don't be ridiculous, Rose, and don't interrupt; I wasn't talking to you.' Violet's irritation and nerves were threatening to make the journey unpleasant so Daisy said to her consolingly, 'Well, at least Justin will be there. I bet he will ask you to dance at the ball tomorrow.' And me, perhaps, she thought silently, but decided not to mention partners for Poppy and herself.

Even Rose was going to be allowed to attend the ball. The Duchess had written to Great-Aunt Lizzie asking that the girls bring their 'charming gowns' for the 'little dance' that she was holding for her daughter. 'Some young boy cousins have been invited,' she wrote, 'so in that way my Paula and your three girls may have their own little young people's dance at the end of the room.'

'And that means "Hands off the Debs' Delights",' interpreted Rose after Great-Aunt Lizzie had gone off with her letter and a worried frown on her face.

'What are Debs' Delights?' asked Poppy vaguely but didn't wait for an answer before clattering down the stairs. These days she seemed to be escaping from the house even more than usual. Daisy had seen her wandering hand in hand with Baz in the woods, and had wondered about her sister.

'Are you and Baz in love?' she had asked the previous night when they were both in bed.

'I suppose so,' was all that Poppy would say, and then she began to sing 'Love Will Find a Way' in her rich, smooth voice. Daisy had waited. It never worked to push Poppy. She would speak when she was ready.

Daisy was almost asleep when Poppy's voice roused her.

'Baz has got his own house, you know,' she said.

'What!' Instantly Daisy was wide awake.

'It's his grandfather – his mother's father,' explained Poppy. 'He died last week and left most of his money to his eldest grandson, but he left Baz a little mews house in a place called Belgravia. Baz and I have plans. We're going to turn it into jazz club downstairs and we can sleep upstairs. We won't bother about a kitchen – Baz says that you never need to cook in London. There are places everywhere selling cheap food and cups of coffee.'

'But Baz is only sixteen,' said Daisy. 'He can't inherit a house when he's only sixteen. I mean he can, but his father must be looking after it for him, or one of his older brothers.' Baz was the youngest of a large family.

'I suppose so,' said Poppy vaguely. 'We thought that when we are married they will have to hand it over.'

And with that she had turned on her side, throwing her pillow to the bottom of the bed to warm her toes, and soon she was snoring gently.

Perhaps they really did intend to get married. They were constantly in each other's company. Perhaps that was why Poppy was so openly bored with the idea of the staying in the Duchess's town house.

Rose, on the other hand, was fizzing with delight at the prospect. During the car journey she kept poking Maud in the back and pointing out various landmarks as they went through the Kent countryside. By the time they entered central London she was ecstatic as they glimpsed names familiar to her from reading the novels of Charles Dickens, gasping dramatically at the sight of Westminster, the Strand, Trafalgar Square and Piccadilly Circus.

'Coming into Mayfair now, your ladyships,' said Morgan as he manoeuvred the big car expertly along Regent Street. The road was crowded – Daisy could see at least a dozen cars as well as an open-topped bus full of men and women standing on its top storey.

'Mayfair,' breathed Rose in ecstasy. 'Oh, I say! Lady Tippins! Mrs Gowan! Lord Verisopht! The Honourable Bob Stables! Mrs Sparsit, whose husband was a Powler! The Tite Barnacles! Nupkins! Oh, pinch me, someone!'

'I will if you don't sit still. We're squashed enough as it is,' said Violet. Daisy, looking sideways at her, saw that her face was quite white with apprehension.

'Will you be going to listen to jazz while we're in this boring place, Morgan?' asked Poppy.

'I was thinking of going to a few Dixieland sessions, my lady,' he admitted. 'His lordship has given leave for me to stay in London for the few days.'

Father should pay for his lodgings, thought Daisy. Morgan is probably staying for the sake of the ancient car. Four journeys like that might put a finish to what Morgan called 'an old lady held together with a few pieces of wire and a prayer'. However, he would enjoy his jazz sessions.

'Wish I could go,' muttered Poppy disconsolately and Morgan laughed.

'No one under twenty-one,' he said.

'Liar,' said Poppy. 'Baz has been to one. His grandfather took him the last time he was in London.'

'Is this it?' asked Violet, her voice full of tension, as the car slowed and came to a stop.

The house at Grosvenor Square was very tall and narrow. A flight of stone steps led from the pavement to the front door with its shining brass knocker. There was no sign of anyone to welcome them – we're not considered to be very important guests, thought Daisy.

'Now what happens at these sorts of places?' Morgan looked over his shoulder enquiringly.

Violet gave an impatient click of her tongue. Rose suggested blowing the horn but Morgan turned down that notion, slipped out from behind the wheel, walked with stiffly erect back up the stone steps and knocked on the door.

A footman with a superior expression opened the door and accompanied Morgan back down to the car, opening the door politely and assisting Violet out. Two of the girls followed her hastily, Rose shaking with suppressed giggles and Poppy quite at ease. Daisy waited for a second and then tapped Maud on the shoulder and whispered in her ear, 'Go to the back door.'

The whole procedure had been gone through several times with Great-Aunt Lizzie, who had lamented daily for the previous fortnight that the Duchess had not invited her and that her nieces would be on their own for their very first opportunity to join a house party.

'Oh, my dears,' said the Duchess in her gushing manner when they were ushered into the drawing room. 'Have you had a terrible journey? Are you cold? What was the traffic like on the way up? Terrible the amount of cars on the road these days, isn't it? You didn't witness any nasty accident, did you?' Without waiting for an answer to any of her questions, she said abruptly to the footman, 'Robert, fetch the young ladies – oh, and MacDonald, Robert.'

'MacDonald is my maid.' She turned back to the girls

after Robert had bowed and backed out of her presence. 'She'll look after you and show your own maid where to find everything. Did you have a good journey, my dears? Do come a little nearer the fire. We've had the happy idea of putting you all in together. We thought you would be more comfortable like that. Violet, dear, how pretty you look!'

'Thank you, Your Grace.' Violet's voice was clear and self-possessed but a touch of colour warmed her cheeks. This first meeting was always going to be the worst hurdle. Try as she might, there was no way around the fact that their coats, run up by the village dressmaker from a bolt of cheap tweed, were old-fashioned and shabby.

'Ah, here comes MacDonald! On second thoughts, my dears, perhaps you would like to wash and change after your journey before you meet Catherine and Paula and the other young people. Yes, that will be best. MacDonald?' The Duchess suddenly ran out of words and looked appealingly at her maid.

'Yes, Your Grace. Come with me, your ladyships.'

In a moment the lady's maid had whisked the girls out from under her ladyship's nose as if they were some piece of mess that had to be cleaned away quickly before it caused offence. Violet's colour was high and she stared haughtily at Rose with an expression that said clearly *I dare you to utter any of your headlines*.

Daisy exchanged a grin with Poppy as they followed meekly in Violet's footsteps. Daisy hoped that Violet would enjoy the next few days, but she herself was glad that she had come. London seemed such a busy, bustling place, full of noise and life – of crowds crossing roads, riding on buses, driving cars, shouting across streets, greeting others – that she was sure she would love it. And Sir Guy had promised to call the following morning with a letter of introduction from their father, and take her to see his film studio, packed with young men who smoked cheap cigarettes and argued about films. She couldn't wait.

'You're in here, your ladyships,' said MacDonald after they had toiled up three flights of stairs. She had a slightly disparaging tone in her voice as she opened the door to a suite of rooms on the top floor and showed them around. Daisy wondered whether it had formerly been the nursery suite. It had two bedrooms, a small room like a dressing room, where Maud would sleep, and a bathroom, all of which opened off a small, dark lobby.

But the wonderful thing was that each room was as warm as toast with a large coal fire burning in the fireplace. There was even a fire in the bathroom, with lovely thick, soft towels draped over a clothes stand and one huge towel over the wicker armchair.

As they peered into it from the lobby, a door from the back stairs opened and Maud came puffing in, carrying two suitcases.

'Ah, here's your ladyships' maid,' said MacDonald. 'Tea is in the drawing room from four o'clock onwards.' She gave another look around, nodded her head at Maud and then withdrew, shutting the door with practised care.

'Spiffing!' said Daisy, borrowing one of Poppy's expressions. She went to the window and looked down at the street. A young woman, wearing a fashionable cloche hat fitting closely to her head and a stylish wrap-around lemon-coloured coat, came out of a house across the road. She ran lightly down the steps, climbed into a bright blue car, slammed the door and took off. Daisy wondered whether Morgan would teach her how to drive. She would need a car when she became a film producer and it was getting very old-fashioned to rely on a chauffeur.

'And we're all in together,' Poppy was saying with satisfaction. 'Bags you and me this room, Daise; Violet and Rose can share the other one. What's your room like, Maud? I say, that's a bit small and dark, isn't it?' she remarked as she peered into the dressing room.

'It's fine,' said Maud hurriedly. She began to unpack, competently storing things on hangers or in drawers. Rose went to help her while Poppy joined Daisy at the window. Maud's room was probably better than the one she had back in Beech Grove Manor, where she shared a freezing cold room with Nora, thought Daisy.

'Better than sharing with that stuck-up MacDonald,' said Rose. 'MacDonald! What a name!'

Daisy had already noticed that the Duchess's lady's maid was called by her surname. That must be the custom for lady's maids, and she hoped they had not forgotten a vital rule of Great-Aunt Lizzie's etiquette. Still, she realized, she didn't know what Maud's surname was so she couldn't very well use it anyway.

*

'Rose, dear,' said Violet after all the unpacking was finished, 'could you possibly go into Daisy and Poppy's room for a moment? I would like to have a little time to think about what I am going to wear. Rose, are you listening to me? Rose, put down those old newspapers – they must have been left there by mistake. All my drawers are lined with scented paper.'

Daisy looked back and to her amusement saw that Rose was pulling out sheets of newspaper that had been lining the drawers of an old tallboy in the corner. She was scanning the headlines and chuckling with glee. '*Scandal at Westminster. Ancient Name Besmirched*,' she read before Violet snatched them from her and stuffed them back into the tallboy. She faced her three younger sisters nervously.

'It's not that I want to outshine anyone or anything like that,' she said. 'It's just that for all our sakes I want to make a good impression and . . .' she hesitated.

'And a brilliant match,' put in Poppy with a yawn.

'It's for your sakes as well as mine,' said Violet defensively. 'I keep telling you: once I am married with a home of my own I can have you all to stay and throw parties, give balls, present you at court – but it all depends,' she lowered her voice and glanced at the door, 'it all depends on the Duchess offering to present me, to give me a season. Stuck down in Beech Grove Manor I'll never meet anyone. I want to be a debutante, to have a little fun for the first time in my life.'

'C'mon, Rose.' Poppy was getting sick of Violet's intensity. 'Let's get changed.'

'Wait.' Violet pulled out three identical pinafore dresses made by the village dressmaker earlier in the year. Daisy stared at them with surprise. She had not realized they had been packed.

'Wear them with those Peter Pan collared blouses,' ordered Violet.

'What are you going to wear?' Daisy reviewed in her mind her sister's outfits. 'Should you send Maud to ask MacDonald what the other girls are wearing?' she suggested helpfully.

'Certainly not,' snapped Violet. 'I want to be a leader of fashion, not a follower. Maud, come and do my hair.'

'What about our hair?' asked Poppy.

'Just braid it,' said Violet hurriedly. 'Don't you see?' she went on in despairing tones. 'I want to look my age, not one of the children, like you three.'

With that she grabbed Maud and closed the door behind them firmly. Poppy grinned. 'Wish they'd bring tea up here as if we were in the nursery,' she said. 'The Duchess is a bore.'

'How can you say such a thing, Poppy? Don't you know that the Duchess has a wonderful flow of witty conversation?' Rose mimicked Violet's intensity with the rebuke, and then her voice changed into a high-pitched trill: ' "Have you had a terrible journey? Are you cold? What was the traffic like on the way up? Terrible the amount of cars on the road these days, isn't it? You didn't witness any nasty accident, did you?" Admit! What a feast of reason and flow of soul!'

'What do we care anyway?' Poppy began to pull on the Peter Pan blouse and the baggy pinafore dress.

But I care, thought Daisy. I don't want to look like a child either. Nevertheless, Violet had a point. If she married well then the grinding poverty of their existence at Beech Grove Manor would be at an end for her sisters. Somehow or other she would have to have her chance.

'I suppose it might look better if I seem like a schoolroom miss when I'm filming – people won't take too much notice of me then. Let me braid your hair, Poppy. You can wear it loose for the ball tomorrow night.' She said the words as cheerfully as she could and went into the bathroom to wash her face and hands.

When Violet emerged from the bedroom she was transformed. She wore a short tweed skirt in a blue/purple heather shade. Over it the outsize blue jumper, taken from the Robert Derrington trunk, reached well below her hips and was belted with a narrow leather belt – also taken from the trunk. The effect was to make her look incredibly slim. Daisy's ten pounds from Sir Guy had gone on buying new shoes for them all and Violet was wearing a pair of pointy-toed shoes with a very high heel.

'You're wearing make-up! Where did you get that?'

'I bought a lipstick in the village when I was collecting my magazine,' said Violet, surveying herself in the looking glass with satisfaction. 'And I've brought along one of those charcoal sticks that Great-Aunt Lizzie used to plague us with for doing tasteful sketches. Look!' She fluttered her eyelashes enticingly to show her eyelids smudged with the dark powder and then surveyed her sisters critically.

'Oh, Rose, darling,' she gushed in an excess of sisterly feeling. 'How sweet you look. That little Peter Pan collar suits you so much; you look like Alice in Wonderland.'

'You're beginning to sound like the Duchess,' said Rose grumpily, but nothing could alter Violet's good humour and she smiled happily, saying, 'Perhaps that's a good omen; perhaps I'll marry a duke.'

'It's a shame that the son of the Duke of Devonshire got married a few years ago – he would have been quite right for you,' observed Rose after a minute. Her eyes were thoughtful and she bore the look of one scanning through lists for a suitable suitor.

'Her Grace sent me up to fetch you down.' MacDonald knocked perfunctorily on the door and then came in. Her eyes went to Violet immediately and a grudging look of admiration came into them. She glanced at the three younger girls without interest and said over her shoulder, 'Tea in the kitchen,' in Maud's direction.

'Catherine, my dear, come and meet my goddaughter. Here's dear Violet and her little sisters,' trilled the Duchess when MacDonald had pushed open the drawing-room door. Violet advanced as nonchalantly as she could, while balancing carefully on her first pair of high-heeled shoes. Daisy felt heavy and ugly in comparison to her sister.

Catherine smiled sweetly at Violet and more cordially at the other three, turning to summon her sister Paula for what Rose had muttered was *the nursery party*. They were alike, the two sisters – both plump, pale-faced and with an abundance of light, fair hair. Daisy was glad that she had refused to braid her hair when she saw that Paula wore hers loose on her shoulders.

'Such a crowd,' said Catherine to Violet. 'It must be horrid for you. You live very quietly in the country, Mama says.'

'Oh, but I love crowds,' said Violet so loudly that lots of heads turned. 'Oh Catherine, please introduce me to everyone.' Violet, in her short skirt and hip-length jumper, seemed to have totally forgotten all of Great-Aunt Lizzie's advice and was now acting just like one of the flappers in the film that Sir Guy had taken them all to see a few months ago. Daisy would not have been surprised to see her take out a cigarette holder from her handbag.

'Violet!' Justin pushed through the cluster of girls and took her hand. 'You're looking lovely,' he said gazing at her with great admiration. There was a slight stir in the drawing room – there were mainly girls present, Daisy noticed. Justin was probably right about the lack of men available for house parties in London; certainly all female eyes were on him and he did, she had to admit, look very handsome with his black hair flicked back from his forehead.

'Let's go over here,' said Paula to the three younger Derrington girls. 'I'd like to introduce you to my cousins who are in London for the week.'

Daisy took one look at the group of shy, rather spotty-faced youngsters clustered around the potted palms beside the grand piano – all brothers, she reckoned by the resemblances – and produced her camera from the bag hanging over her arm.

'You go on,' she said with an amiable smile at Paula. 'Your mother wants me to make a film of the weekend and I think it would best to get people used to me and my camera, don't you?'

'Do you play the piano?' Poppy was asking Paula as they moved away. Daisy hoped that she would not suggest a 'jam session'. Poppy, of course, had brought her treasured clarinet, carefully packed among her clothes in her suitcase.

A camera was like a cloak that made you invisible, Daisy thought as she moved around filming. After a while the girls ceased to look at her and returned to chattering among themselves. There were several comments on Violet – rather begrudging, thought Daisy – and there were many whispers about Justin – the dimple on his chin, his smile, the colour of his eyes, the width of his shoulders. These went on even after the arrival of several young men – Debs' Delights, she supposed.

But then the fatal words were spoken, uttered by a tall, thin young lady with a triple row of pearls dangling down her chiffon dress.

'My dear,' she whispered to a girl who swooning over Justin's dark Byronic looks, 'don't you know,' and she spoke the next words with great emphasis, '*he's only a younger son.*'

And then Catherine and all her friends turned their back on Justin, leaving him with Violet, and started to busy themselves in clusters around the few young men who had arrived.

No debutante worth her salt would get entangled with a younger son so early in the season.

Chapter Fourteen

Once dinner was over, Daisy escaped upstairs to her temporary darkroom. Everything was just perfect there. Sir Guy had sent over just what she needed. There was even a red light so that she did not have to work in darkness once she loaded the film into the developing tank. There were a few interesting shots, she thought, as she hung the film on the little line to drip-dry. Two in particular, of Catherine looking jealously at Violet who was standing chatting to a group of men, Justin in the foreground, and then turning to whisper something to her neighbour, would have made a very good sequence in a film.

'If I were you, Vi,' she said when they were all getting ready for bed, 'I wouldn't try to outshine Catherine tomorrow. After all, it is her ball and her season and—'

'When I want your advice I'll ask for it.' Violet's bright, chatty facade seemed to disappear once the door was closed behind them. 'Run my bath, please, Maud.' Her tone was abrupt.

'Have it your own way,' said Daisy. 'You always do,' she couldn't help adding.

Violet's only answer to that was to go into the far bedroom and slam the door behind her.

'*Spoilt by success,*' quoted Rose sadly and Maud's lips twitched as she went in to run the bath.

'What are they like downstairs, Maud?' Daisy followed her into the bathroom.

Maud considered this question gravely. 'Not very friendly, my lady,' she said after a while. 'Of course, I'm not used to a big staff like that. Back home it's just myself and Nora and the cook mainly. Mrs Pearson and Mr Bateman are not too bad either. That MacDonald is very haughty. I think she guesses that I'm not really a lady's maid.'

'Thank you, Maud.' Violet came out of her room wrapped in her dressing gown. 'Could you kindly get out of the bathroom while I bathe, Daisy, if it's not too much trouble?'

'Very haughty,' said Rose with a grin as the bathroom door lock clicked.

'Hope she leaves us some hot water,' said Poppy. She took out her clarinet and blew softly into it and Daisy couldn't be bothered stopping her. She was too tired of Violet's moods.

'Hope tomorrow is more fun than today,' she said as she began to undress. Violet, she noticed, had left her clothes on the floor – and Maud was busy picking things up and hanging them in the wardrobe. Mrs Pearson had given her a package of washing soap so that the girls' underclothes and blouses could be laundered by her. Privately, Daisy guessed, Great-Aunt Lizzie was ashamed of their shabbiness and Daisy had decided that the money Sir Guy had given her was better spent on shoes, which would be seen, than on knickers and liberty bodices which would not be seen.

*

Daisy was first up in the morning. She had slept with the little alarm clock beneath her pillow and roused herself at its first chime. She got sleepily out of bed, noticing that someone had been into the bedroom and had seen to the fire. Maud was already up and was in the bathroom checking on the underclothes that she had draped around the room to dry overnight. She smiled when Daisy came in. 'This is lovely, my lady, isn't it?' she said. 'The scullery maid came in and made up the fires about half an hour ago so the bathroom is nice and warm for your bath. Shall I run it, my lady?'

'Yes, please,' said Daisy. It would be so wonderfully luxurious to wallow in a hot bath compared to the horrors of the stone cold water at home. She went to the window and peered out from underneath the drawn blind. The scene outside was busy – people walking briskly with rolled umbrellas, men and some women also, carrying attaché cases, all on their way to work.

'Would you like to live and work in London, Maud? I would,' she said as Maud joined her.

'I'm not sure, my lady,' Maud said hesitantly.

'Why don't you go and have a walk around London this morning?' said Daisy. 'It looks a very interesting place.' It would do no harm, she thought. Violet was due to take coffee in Harrods with Catherine and her house guests, the Duchess had fixed up for Rose and Poppy to accompany her three nephews and Paula on a trip to the British Museum and she, Daisy – she hugged herself at the thought – was going to visit Sir Guy's studios in his company. It had been arranged that he would collect her at eleven o'clock, the Duchess had told her last night. She had looked disapproving but Daisy was too excited by the news to care.

'Would you know where Somerset House is, my lady?' said Maud from behind her.

'Somerset House?' Daisy turned to face her. 'I've never heard of Somerset House,' she said. 'Why do you want to go there?'

'They keep birth certificates for everyone there, my lady. Morgan told me that when I said that I didn't know when my birthday was. He told me that the orphanage would have registered me at Somerset House even if my mother didn't. And for seven-and-sixpence I'd get a copy of the birth certificate. I got Mrs Pearson to give me some of my wages. Normally she keeps them for me and just doles them out when I ask for them.'

'I'll tell you what we'll do,' said Daisy decisively. 'Sir Guy is calling for me with a cab soon after breakfast. I'll tell the Duchess that I will be taking my maid with me – she'll like that. Then we can get the cab driver to drop you off at Somerset House, wherever it is.'

This would clear up the mystery of the letter once and for all.

When Daisy had finished her bath she went into the bedroom and took her tweed skirt and the black cashmere jumper out of the wardrobe. A pair of black silk stockings and her new black pumps would complete the outfit nicely.

Violet, Daisy had to admit, had a wonderful eye for clothes. That soft black really suited her and as for the skirt – well, it was just gorgeous. Woven from a mixture of white and carmine strands of wool, the finished result was a clear sharp pink which enhanced the soft depths of the black jumper. The overlong sleeves had been sewn with rows of elastic so that they could be pushed up from the wrists and allowed to balloon becomingly over her arms. She took out Sir Guy's necklace and fastened it behind her neck, admiring how the black set off the shimmering pinkish-white of the pearls.

By the time Daisy had finished dressing, there were sounds of Violet rousing Rose. Poppy was now awake, humming softly to herself, luxuriating in the warmth of the glowing coal fire. Daisy went to the dressing table and sat down in front of the looking glass.

'Maud, would you put up my hair for me?'

'I thought we agreed that we would only do that for the ball,' said Violet, coming through the door. The night's sleep had not done much for her humour and she had dark shadows under her eyes.

'You said that was what you were going to do,' said Daisy calmly. 'Oh good, you've found the hair clips, Maud; here's the comb.'

'I was going to wear the jumper and skirt today, and now I can't since you are,' complained Violet.

'Try a pinafore – you can borrow Poppy's if you forgot to bring your own,' said Daisy sweetly, but then she felt a little sorry. After all, this visit was all about Violet's dream of becoming a debutante and making a splash in London society.

'Why don't you wear that green jersey dress – you know, the one where you sewed the narrow fur stole to the hem? That looks very smart and you don't want to be wearing the same thing all the time, do you?' she said consolingly.

Violet cheered up at that and when they went down to breakfast all four were dressed differently. Poppy was in a short pleated burgundy-coloured fine wool skirt with a white blouse, her hair tied loosely at the nape of her neck and brushed out over her shoulders by Maud. Rose, to her huge delight, was allowed to wear a pale blue tweed suit.

'Elaine must have been really small, mustn't she?' Daisy remarked, observing with interest how the shoulders of the jacket fitted her sister's shoulders. Rose, after all, was only twelve and though tall, she was very thin. Violet had taken up the skirt, of course, but nothing else needed to be done.

Breakfast was a revelation. Daisy blushed at the thought of the Duchess having breakfast at Beech Grove Manor where she would have been given a choice of boiled eggs, fried eggs or scrambled eggs. Here every inch of the sideboard was crowded with silver dishes sitting on top of small spirit lamps and each one had its cover. Two footmen were in attendance and the atmosphere was so starchy that for a moment Daisy found herself envying Maud. Breakfast in the kitchen would have been more fun, she thought, though apparently Her Grace the Duchess was breakfasting in bed. That was one relief.

'Morning!' Justin was behind her in the queue, saying in her ear, 'May I help your ladyship to a piece of burned Spanish omelette?'

'Certainly not,' said Daisy emphatically. 'I've never eaten such a thing in my life. The last Spanish omelette that I ate was perfectly cooked.'

'Thank you, Robert. Just a little kedgeree and some coffee and toast for me,' said Violet in a stately manner.

'What's this about Spanish omelettes?' asked one of Justin's admirers.

'Well,' said Justin, 'wait till I get a bite to eat before telling you the story of Daisy's omelette. Let me lift a few lids first – I'm a great lifter of lids at breakfast time.' After giving the other footman a huge order for almost everything under the silver covers he came over and sat down, looking around the table to make sure that he had a responsive audience.

'Well, when I was at a house party at the Derringtons' place, Daisy cooked an omelette in a giant pan – the size of this table.'

'Oh, what fun,' said one of the girls uncertainly and Daisy stole an uneasy glance at Violet.

'It was enormous fun!' To her surprise, Violet had decided to make a dramatic story out of the whole incident. 'We all went down to the kitchen feeling hungry.'

'At the witching hour of midnight,' put in Rose dramatically.

'And Daisy suggested cooking a Spanish omelette,' said Justin. 'Of course, I was the only one who had been to Spain so I was in charge.'

'I'd love to see you in a chef's overall and cap, Justin,' said a girl called Giselle daringly and Catherine, at the head of the table in her mother's absence, looked around nervously. However, the guests were all laughing and animated and every eye was on Violet as she told the story of the omelette and how the boys chopped the potatoes and Poppy and Basil Pattenden had whipped up about three dozen eggs.

'Four dozen,' said Rose, not to be outdone in the matter of exaggeration.

'And there was Daisy with this enormous pan ordering us to put spoons on the kitchen table and eat straight out of it.'

'Oh, I say, what fun! Vi, dear girl, pray do ask me when you have your house party for the season!'

'I love that sort of thing – so modern and up-to-date!'

'Priceless!'

'Gorgeous!'

'Absolutely!'

'These stuffy old parties with chaperones watching our every move and footmen standing around like statues are just so boring,' complained Giselle.

Poppy turned her head and looked at the footmen behind her and then turned back and whispered in

Daisy's ear: 'Didn't move a muscle, either of them.'

'What I want to know,' asked a man called David, 'is what our dear Violet was doing at this famous omelette orgy.'

Everyone screamed with laughter at this – David was obviously the wit of the gathering.

'Me?' said Violet on a rising note of query. She delicately rubbed the tip of her forefinger against her thumb and looked around at the tableful of eyes, smiling sweetly. 'Me, I just crumbled a few herbs.'

Violet had definitely staked her claim to be a leader of fashion, thought Daisy, glancing around at the merry table. Even Catherine was laughing while one of the men choked on a kipper. Breakfast, compared with the boring dinner last night, was certainly going with a swing.

'Well, what a fashionable young lady,' said Sir Guy when Daisy ran down the stairs just as the hall clock chimed the hour of eleven. 'Shouldn't you put on your coat? Won't you be cold?'

'No, I'm fine,' said Daisy hurriedly. 'London is so warm.' The look on the Duchess's face when she had seen their shabby, old-fashioned coats had made her resolve not to wear hers again unless she really had to. She saw him give a questioning glance at Maud but it was only when they were safely in the cab that he had hired that she explained the girl's presence.

'So do you know where Somerset House is, Sir Guy?' she finished.

'Yes, of course, it's in the Strand; we can drop you off there, Maud.' Daisy liked the way that he spoke to Maud, treating her as an equal and showing a calm interest in her story. 'If I were you I'd also ask to have a look at the census of 1901 – before you were born, of course, but you might find your mother. You'll find a census return for every village around, but I would start off at the village where the orphanage is and then work your way through the others. What's your surname?'

'Bucket, sir,' said Maud. She twisted round and smiled slightly over her shoulder at Daisy. 'The girls in the orphanage used to have fun with that.'

Daisy suppressed a giggle. Now she understood why Great-Aunt Lizzie, always such a stickler for correct procedure, had not told them to call Maud by her surname. It would sound too ridiculous to be calling 'Bucket!' or demanding 'Bucket' from one of those aloof footmen.

'Hmm,' said Sir Guy reflectively as the cab made its way around Trafalgar Square. 'That's not a Kent name. In fact, London is the only place that I have heard it. On the other hand, your mother was unlikely to have come all the way from London in order to leave you outside a country orphanage when there is the Thomas Coram place in Bloomsbury. But of course, she might originally have been from London and was working at Beech Grove Manor, or some other place. Or, of course, it might just be a name that the orphanage made up for you. Anyway, here we are now. Good luck to you, Maud, and here's a couple of shillings in case you need them. You can find your way back all right, can you?'

'Yes, sir. Thank you, sir. I've written down the address in this, sir.' Maud produced from her pocket an old copy book formerly belonging to Poppy. Poppy, in the days when Great-Aunt Lizzie still concerned herself with the older girls' education, had done so little work that dozens of those quarter-filled books lay around in the schoolroom at Beech Grove Manor.

'Interesting story – you might make a good film out of her one day,' said Sir Guy, when they had dropped Maud off. 'Interesting face too. Reminds me of someone. Anyway, Daisy, give me your film. I'm going to try a little experiment. I'm going to show it to my team and let them say what they think of it. That's the way we work when I get a submission. We all sit around and argue about it. You won't mind if they criticize, will you? This happens all the time. Sometimes they tear each other's work to shreds.'

'No, I'll like it,' said Daisy earnestly. This was the sort of thing that Poppy and her jazz band boys did – experimenting, suggesting and criticizing. She had often envied her twin sister this companionship and had wished that she were musical too, but now, perhaps, her talents had begun to emerge. 'You're so good to me,' she added. 'Aren't I lucky to have you! Tell me again how you became my godfather.'

'Well,' began Sir Guy, telling the familiar story for the hundredth time, 'I got a wire from your father when he was still on board ship on his way back to England, just after your grandfather's death. He asked me to arrange a hotel for the two of them and the three children to spend the night before going down to Kent and he asked me to be godfather to one of the twins. I remember the telegram well. It was TWO INFANTS STOP TAKE YOUR PICK STOP.'

And you chose me,' said Daisy, tucking her arm into his.

'That's right,' said Sir Guy. 'There was Poppy in your mother's arms, screaming her head off – face as red as her hair – and there were you, curled up in your nurse's arms, sleeping like a little kitten, and I said to your father, 'Michael, old man, I'll have the little blonde one.'

Chapter Fifteen

Sir Guy's studios were in West London. Daisy had expected something grand, but they were just a collection of poorly built concrete sheds erected on the roadside in a stretch of wasteland. There were a few trees clustered in the corner, a murky pond and a concrete road beside a well-mown stretch of grass about ten foot square.

'We can shoot a lot of outdoor stuff here,' said Sir Guy, waving his hand around. 'Woodland, forest – whatever you want, water – we've even got plans to do the Battle of Trafalgar with miniature boats on that, and then we have our lawn for garden parties and this piece of road can be the London-to-Brighton highway.'

Daisy began to laugh. 'I don't think that a garden party would be too convincing on that little square of lawn,' she said.

'Well, we're not all like you – we don't have access to debutante balls and garden parties,' he said good-humouredly. 'You'd be surprised what we can do with this little bit of grass. You have to work within your limits; you know that.'

Daisy nodded. She could see what he meant. When she had shot her hunting sequence it had been in miles and miles of woodland, but when the film was developed all that showed was a few beech trees in the background.

'You're right,' she said.

How is Violet getting on with Her Grace?' he asked with interest and nodded with satisfaction when Daisy told him that Violet was a great success.

'Come and see our sets and don't turn your nose up and say that they are not as good as a duchess's drawing room. This one in here,' he said, pushing open the door of one of the sheds, 'is the throne room at Buckingham Palace. We're planning a film on Queen Victoria. A bit ambitious, but I think we can pull it off.'

'Why is three-quarters of it bare?' asked Daisy, and then answered her own question as she realized that the cameraman and the actors and actresses would have to have their own space. She gazed around and then focused on the throne and a marble bust on a plinth. She went over and touched it. Though pure white it was warm to the touch and a flake of whitewash came off on her finger.

'Made from clay, of course; and the throne was built by one of my lads and then covered with a few yards of material from Petticoat Lane. The illusion is the thing in filming – what do you think of the portraits, by the way?'

'Are they real?' asked Daisy.

Sir Guy chuckled. 'Done by my latest recruit. Anyway, come and meet my lads. You can see the rest of the site later on.'

Sir Guy's studio reminded Daisy of the activity of the hen house at home. Some of the workers were rummaging in untidy piles of film, some were chopping pieces of film with decisive snaps of the scissors, one young man was striding up and down completely lost in thought, another was chatting brightly on the phone with 'darlings' sprinkled into every sentence, and in one corner a very pale young man gilded some swirling scrolls embossed on a clay plaque.

'More decorations for Buckingham Palace,' said Sir Guy. 'How are you today, Fred? Shivers and aches gone?'

The young man called Fred looked up, saw Daisy, and then jumped to his feet. He was staring at her so intently that she was slightly embarrassed. However, a long look in the glass in the Buckingham Palace set had convinced her that she was looking her best so she smiled at him – he was rather handsome.

'Fred is just back from India,' explained Sir Guy after he had introduced them. 'He picked up malaria there and so he keeps running temperatures. He was working in the Corps of Royal Engineers as a draughtsman in the Indian Army, but he had to resign. Their loss: our gain!'

'Did you do those portraits?' asked Daisy eagerly, and when he nodded she said impulsively, 'They're wonderful!'

'Does all our title cards too,' said Sir Guy. 'A great man for borders and lettering. Really distinctive. He can find a font for every mood in the picture. Look at these! Don't think any other studio could beat them.'

As Sir Guy ushered Daisy around the room, introducing her to the cameramen, the film technician, the story writer, the pianist and the set builder, she was conscious that Fred's eyes followed her all the time.

Sir Guy had introduced her as Daisy and after a while she began to feel part of the team, lending a hand here and there, pegging up film, giving her opinions on a choice of cushions to the set builder, suggesting a word to the story writer – and then she sat on the bench and had a go at splicing film, a job that she flattered herself she did neatly. She smiled modestly when Harry, the technician, expressed the opinion that she was a natural.

'It's those dainty little fingers that do it,' he said gallantly, taking care to lower his voice so that Sir Guy did not hear him.

Daisy giggled at the remarks and compliments that were being paid to her. She thought they were all a lot nicer and more fun than the young men she had met at the Duchess's house. By the time they all sat down to a lunch of cold baked beans on toast with cold German sausage chopped into it, she felt as though she had known them all her life. The admiring looks were a nice change, she thought, for a girl who was used to being overshadowed by two spectacularly beautiful sisters.

But while she was scraping out the last of the tin, Fred joined her, cutting off a tiny portion of German sausage. Just an excuse, she felt. He had a slice of toast, heaped with beans and slices of sausage, still untouched on his plate.

'Sorry if I've been staring at you a bit,' he said, clearly embarrassed. 'The thing is that when I was on board the ship coming back from India, I met someone who was the image of you.'

'Of me?' Daisy turned to look at him with her eyebrows raised.

'She was older than you, of course. But as like you as a twin.'

'Funny,' said Daisy. 'I am a twin, but we're not a bit alike.'

'It's just,' said Fred apologetically, 'that this lady was very nice to me. I had run out of quinine and she saw me shivering and gave me some. She told me that her husband had malaria for years and she automatically packed it everywhere she went in case he suddenly became unconscious. In fact, she insisted on giving me all she had. Her husband was dead, she said. She never got malaria herself so she didn't need it.'

'And she looked like me, did she?' Suddenly an idea had come to Daisy. 'What was her name?' she asked. India, she thought. And looking like me . . .

'It was Mrs Coxhead,' said Fred.

'No, I mean her first name.'

'I'm not sure,' said Fred hesitantly. 'I can't really remember. I just wondered whether she was a sister or a cousin of yours.' He seemed a bit embarrassed by her question and began to move away.

'I want my baked beans!' shouted Sir Guy, banging the table with his fork like an overweight toddler.

After lunch they all went into one of the other sheds which was set up like a mini cinema and watched a short film. Instead of the usual hushed silence of a cinema this movie was punctuated with shouts, praise and criticism as the film jerked its way through the story.

'Man's asking fifty pounds for this,' said Sir Guy laconically. 'Now, remember what I told you – I can get four pounds a copy from cinemas. Can we make a profit on this? Don't forget, I have to pay your salaries and buy the baked beans.'

Then there was a heated discussion. Fred did not like it because of the poor and hard-to-read card titles, Tom was for it because of the good camera work, James didn't like the storyline and Daisy found herself saying tentatively, 'The leading lady is not very attractive. I'm not sure that audiences will be that interested in whether she escapes from the villain or not. She's overacting too.'

To her surprise, they all agreed with this immediately and she blushed with the excitement of feeling that her views were been taken seriously.

'Let's have a look at the next one,' said Sir Guy casually as he strolled over to the projector and inserted the film.

The title came up instantly: MURDER IN THE DARK.

The first shot was of the shadow of Morgan seen against the white wall. Heavy, menacing, burly shoulders, strong profile – an ideal silhouette.

'Great!' said Harry with a rising note of enthusiasm. 'That's a really great opening!'

'Can you imagine how that would grab an audience?' said Tom.

'I can just see them coming in, sitting down, getting out their packets of sweets. The credits roll and then that shot appears. It will grab them – I'd lay my life on that.' James was breathless after speaking in a rush.

Daisy glowed. Once they saw Sir Guy as the victim they might guess that the film was made by a friend of his, but nothing could take away from that initial spontaneous reaction.

The appearance of Sir Guy was greeted with less surprise than she had expected. It appeared from the remarks that they often took small roles in films themselves.

'He's different, that young fellow – good face. Not overacting either. You'd imagine they were having a real argument,' said James, and Daisy smothered a giggle, glad that in the darkness no one could see her face.

'I like the leading lady – same one as in the film about the horse, isn't she? That gal's sure got something.'

Most of the comments were favourable and showed how they appreciated the artistic decisions that had been made. However, Fred criticized the amateur quality of the script on the card titles and thought that some of the borders looked childish. Daisy winced a little. Earlier she had been half sorry that she had not brought Rose, but now she was glad. She herself found it hard enough to swallow some of the criticisms, but she tried to be glad for them. After all, these young men had worked on hundreds of films and, from their conversation over lunch, it was clear that they spent most of their free time at the cinema.

'Poor ending though,' said James when the film finished and Harry had switched on the lights.

'Music was good,' said Harry.

'That policeman looked stupid.'

'And that chauffeur was twice his fighting weight. He could have knocked the policeman flying and gone off – would have made a better ending.'

'Looked a bit silly, all that handcuff business.'

'That's right; anyone could see at a glance that he wasn't a real policeman, just some kid dressed up and acting in his first film.'

'Well, he *was* a real policeman,' said Daisy hotly. 'Anyway, I don't agree with you about the ending. You see, what I was trying to do was to show the sacrifice . . .' And then she stopped. Jaws had dropped.

'You mean to say you made that film?'

And then they all rushed to tell her how good it was and picked out all of the best things about it. Her godfather smiled good-naturedly and said nothing. She wanted to ask him his opinion of the ending, but stopped herself. Anything he said now would be suspect as they all knew that she was their employer's goddaughter.

'You're probably right,' she said when she could get a word in. 'But it was a real policeman. He's our village bobby.'

'But he didn't look real,' said Harry.

'And that's what counts in films.'

'But it wasn't just that,' said Fred slowly. 'It just didn't seem a satisfactory ending.'

'You see,' said James earnestly, 'if you think about watching a film . . . You sit there and you live the story if it's a good film. And then the last scene comes up and the lights go on. You stand up, put your coat on, go out in the street. You want to feel satisfied. You want questions to have been answered. You don't want to go away feeling . . .'

'Get the chauffeur to commit suicide,' suggested Harry.

'Hmm,' said James doubtfully.

'Can we put a value on this film?' asked Sir Guy.

'No, no, don't do that,' said Daisy hurriedly. 'I want to work on it and I want to make it as perfect as possible. Let me take it away now and when I go back down to Kent I'll have another go at it.'

'Kent? Do you live in Kent, then?' asked Fred as they went back out of the makeshift cinema and over to the workshop. Without waiting for an answer he went on, 'Yes, I bet that lady on the boat back from India, the one I was telling you about – I bet that she was related to you. I remember her telling me that she was brought up in the depths of rural Kent – that's what she said. She said that she hated the place, so she was going to stay at the Savoy until she could find a house to rent, and live in civilization. She had some business to do with a lawyer – something about the death of her late husband.' He stopped for a minute and stood looking thoughtfully into the middle distance. 'I remember her name now. I heard one of the women call her Elaine.'

Chapter Sixteen

When Daisy arrived back at the Mayfair house, it was already four o'clock in the afternoon. A large furniture van stood outside and men in green baize aprons, supervised by Robert, the footman, were carrying dainty gilded chairs into the house. As she looked out of the cab's back window a caterer's van drew up and a kitchen maid, her cap askew, ran up the basement steps to meet it.

'Of course – it's the ball,' she said. She had almost forgotten about the ball with the interest of the last few hours, but now excitement fizzed in her veins. 'Shame you're not coming,' she said to her godfather affectionately.

'Couldn't imagine anything I would hate more than sitting on those highly uncomfortable chairs for four hours watching all the bright young things cavorting around the dance floor and making conversation with elderly ladies,' he grunted. 'Look at the legs on those chairs! They'd collapse under my weight and I know what you'd do – you'd come up and film the whole thing and then show it to my lads afterwards. How did you like them all, Daisy?' he asked affectionately. 'Had a good time, did you?'

'I had a wonderful time. I can never thank you enough. And I will work on the ending to that film. They were quite right.' Daisy knew that her voice rang with sincerity and he kissed her cheek as Robert came to the door and handed her out of the cab with a polite bow.

'Her Grace said she would like a word with you in the morning room, Lady Daisy, when you come in,' he said, and added, 'Your ladyship's maid has just returned. I sent her straight up to the suite of rooms.'

'Thank you, Robert. Could you just show me where the morning room is?' Daisy was surprised how confident her voice sounded. She was getting used to all of this, she thought. And she nodded intelligently when the Duchess told her the exciting news that a friend had telephoned to ask permission to bring one of the royal princes to the ball that evening.

'Of course, these horrid journalists and photographers from *The Sketch* and *Tatler* will haunt him, no matter who he talks to or what he does – that is what always happens when the young princes attend a party. They follow them everywhere. And often they like to take pictures of their royal highnesses leaving a party and that is always a disaster for the hostess as it looks as though they were bored. I do hope that does not happen tonight, but whatever you do, make sure that you take some good film of him dancing with Catherine,' she finished. 'He's bound to ask her,' she went on with a slight note of doubt in her mind. 'It is, after all, her ball.'

'I'm sure he will,' said Daisy. 'Now if you'll excuse me, Your Grace, I shall go and load a new film in my camera. I want to make certain that everything is right for this evening.'

'Dinner at eight,' said Her Grace. 'Don't use up much film on that – it will just be the house party.'

Poppy was the only member of the family present when Daisy pushed open the door to their rooms. She was standing by the window, playing her clarinet softly – a sad, lonely wail of a tune. When she turned round Daisy was horrified to see marks of tears on her twin sister's cheeks.

'Pops, what's the matter?' she exclaimed.

'I hate this place,' sobbed Poppy. Carefully she put her beloved clarinet back into its case and threw herself on her bed. 'Oh, I wish I'd never come. I want to go home. I had such a boring morning tramping around that endless British Museum with Paula and her governess. Governess! I ask you! And – you won't believe this – she's got a nanny! And she's sixteen years old!'

'You're just missing the jazz band and all the fun with them,' said Daisy wisely. She thought of her day at the film studios and knew that if she got used to that free-and-easy companionship, she would miss it immensely if she had to give it up. 'Where's Rose?' she asked.

A reluctant smile came over Poppy's face. 'Oh, she was having such fun with the governess, asking her difficult questions! She impressed the wretched woman so much that she was hauled off to the schoolroom to see Paula's encyclopaedia when we came back – serve her right! Did you have a nice time, Daisy?'

'I did.' Daisy decided not to go into the details of her conversations with the young film-makers. It might just make Poppy even more homesick. 'Something funny happened though,' she said slowly. 'There was a young man there who does the title cards and the artistic work – he had been working as a draughtsman in India, but he got malaria badly and had to come home – and he told me that on the ship back from India he met a lady who looked just like me. He said she looked like my sister, or even my twin, except that she was lots older.'

Poppy sat up on the bed and stared wide-eyed at Daisy. 'Don't tell me . . .' she began.

Daisy nodded. 'He couldn't remember her name – well, he could, but it was her married name, Mrs Coxhead – but he remembered that she had been brought up in Kent. Well, he was telling me that, and then at the very last moment he suddenly remembered that he had heard one of the other women passengers call her—'

'Not Elaine?'

Daisy nodded but could say no more as there was a knock on the door.

'Excuse me, your ladyships, but this lady is the nanny here – she's been here for twenty-five years. She'd like to meet you both.' Maud had tapped on the door and ushered in a very ancient and very tiny figure wearing a frilly white cap who came in saying, 'And I was Her Grace's nanny before that, when she was a little baby.'

Poppy gave a groan and muttered, 'A nanny!' She jumped off the bed and made for the bathroom, clutching a handkerchief to her lips.

'I'm sorry, my sister is not feeling well,' said Daisy

politely. 'Won't you sit down?'

'I will and welcome. These stairs are a bit much for my old legs these days. I'm eighty years old but I wanted to see you and your sister. I looked after you both when you were young, you know. Your father and mother stayed here for a few days when they came back from India. I didn't have much to do with the older girl – she clung to your mother – but the two babies were in my charge completely.' She peered at Daisy. 'You were the little blonde girl,' she said, and added with a look of surprise, 'You've grown.'

'A bit,' said Daisy, trying to suppress a giggle. She wished that Poppy would come back and they could exchange glances.

'You were the tiniest three-month-old baby I've ever seen in my life and I can tell you I've seen a lot of babies,' went on the old woman. She stared intently at Daisy and then, to Daisy's relief, looked over her shoulder as the door handle turned and Rose came in.

'Well, this is the little one I never met. I'm the nanny here, my dear. Lady Rose, isn't it? I was just telling your sister that I looked after her for a week when she was a baby. She was just so undersized and backward then. The other twin was a beautiful child.'

The old woman nodded her head wisely and then her eyes brightened as Poppy came out of the bathroom. No doubt she had been listening at the door and was amused. She wore a slight smile and all traces of tears had gone.

'Ah, there you are, my dear. Feeling better now, are you? Yes, I remember you were called Poppy and I was ever so proud to take you out in the pram with Lady Paula. Lovely little girl you were. Hair beginning to curl and everything. But the other poor little thing!' Her eyes returned to Daisy. Poppy gave her twin a quick wink, while Rose preserved a face of solemn seriousness and Daisy bit her lip, trying not to giggle.

'I must tell you, my dear,' continued Nanny in a congratulatory voice, turning to Daisy, 'that I'm glad to see you looking so well. I never thought that I would see the day. "Mark my words," I said to Mabel, the nursery maid that we had then – good girl she was, very respectful – "Mark my words," I said to her, "there's something badly wrong with that little blonde one; a three-month-old baby as backward as six-week-old one." Yes, very backward, you were,' she repeated and gazed at Daisy with a puzzled expression.

'She still is, Nanny,' said Rose earnestly. 'We just try to hide it as much as possible. For the sake of the honour of the family, you know.'

'I know what you mean, dear,' said Nanny in a hushed voice. She gave Daisy another look and said encouragingly, 'Still, she looks very well; pity about being so small, but it can't be helped, can it?'

And with that she tottered out on Maud's arm. When she was safely through the door Maud looked back in a slightly worried fashion, but Daisy and Poppy were stretched on the bed, clutching each other and laughing, so she just gave a grin and left them.

'Well, that's done me good!' said Poppy. 'Wasn't she

gorgeous? Baz would have enjoyed that. I must write to him.'

'You'll be back home the day after tomorrow,' pointed out Rose.

'Just pop down to the library and get some writing paper for her, Rose,' said Daisy. And then as Rose made a face, she said coaxingly, 'By the way, the library has a whole table with magazines and newspapers spread out on it. It's got *Tatler* and *The Sketch* and all those kinds of magazines. I saw the footman tidying them when I went out this morning. You could bring a few up here.'

'*Tatler*!' said Rose ecstatically and went off without another word.

'Poppy,' said Daisy when her youngest sister had left the room, 'I think that the mysterious Elaine Carruthers might be in London. At least, of course, she's not Elaine Carruthers now; she's Mrs Elaine Coxhead and she's a widow. The young man I met today who had journeyed back from India on the same ship a few weeks ago said that she talked of being brought up in Kent, but that she wanted to live in London.'

'Could be another Elaine,' said Poppy. 'It's an unusual name, but not that unusual. And Kent is a big place.'

'But you're forgetting that he said she was the image of me. He kept staring at me and then he explained. He said he thought she might be a sister of mine. Remember, she was only about four the year that Father and Mother married. She would be thirty-five or thirty-six now. Not that old.'

'But why didn't she get in touch with Father or Great-Aunt Lizzie if she was coming back from India?'

'I don't know,' said Daisy, 'but this boy, Fred, spoke of Elaine saying she hated Kent. We already know there was some sort of a big row. Perhaps she never wants to see the place again.'

'Now, stop worrying your little head about things that you don't understand,' teased Poppy. She started giggling again. 'It's hard for backward people like you to understand the big grown-up world.'

'That nanny must be in her second childhood,' said Daisy. 'Still, it's quite nice of the Duchess to keep her on. I don't suppose that Paula really wants to have her around. Anyway, wait till you hear – one of the royal princes is coming here tonight.'

'I wonder if he's interested in jazz?' said Poppy, and Daisy laughed.

'I think Vi will say a bit more than that. I say, do you think that if you ring that bell Maud will come?'

'Try it,' said Poppy with an indifferent glance. 'And if someone else comes then you just say, "Send me my maid, please."'

Maud appeared before Daisy made up her mind to touch the bell and Poppy decided to go and get the writing paper herself. She was eager to write to Baz.

'Rose is probably working her way through all the magazines down there,' Poppy said. 'She's obsessed with all this society stuff. Honestly, talk about half-witted. That child! And she could be a really good musician too.

Morgan says she has a great ear and a great sense of timing.'

'I've been dying to know how you got on this morning, Maud,' said Daisy when the door closed behind Poppy, adding hurriedly, 'Don't tell me though, unless you want to.'

'Well, I saw my birth certificate, found my date of birth at least,' said Maud readily. 'It's on or about the eleventh of June 1909, so that means that I'm two years younger than I thought I was. I was registered by the orphanage, but I suppose they got it right. I think I must have been sent to school early so I was always a couple of classes ahead of girls of my own age. I'd say that I thought I was five when really I was only three and it went on from there.'

'So you're only fourteen, not sixteen,' said Daisy, feeling sorry for the girl.

'That's right, my lady. That was about all I found out. I was registered by the orphanage people. Nothing about my mother. And not a word about my father, of course – just a blank space.'

'And you must have been only Rose's age when you started work at Beech Grove Manor.' She tried to imagine what it would be like to go through life not knowing how old you were.

'And there was no trace of my mother or of anyone of the name of Bucket in any villages in 1901, so I suppose she might well have been a housemaid at Beech Grove Manor – Lady Rose thinks so anyway,' she added with a slight smile. 'She had a big story made up about my mother being betrayed by someone in the big house and being driven forth to give birth to an infant in the snow – except that now I find I was born in June.' Daisy thought about the letter that she had found in the old stable. The date on that had been March 1906.

Whoever wrote those anguished words *'They can't say that we're too young now'*, it could not have been Maud's mother if Maud herself was not born until three years later.

So who had written the letter?

Chapter Seventeen

'Look!' Violet was back, wildly excited, her cheeks flushed. She took from her handbag a tiny book tied with a tasselled cord. It had a lily of the valley on the cover and a minute pencil dangled from the cord. She opened it proudly and showed it to her sisters.

'It's a dance programme,' she said. 'Look, all of the dances are listed – see how many of them are booked already.'

'Oh, I say,' said Rose. 'So that's what a dance programme looks like. I hadn't realized they were so small. Who's David? You seem to have him down for lots of dances.'

'He's the eldest son of the Earl of Mulqueen,' said Violet triumphantly. 'And he has his own estate.'

'Ah, an eldest son,' said Rose knowingly.

'How do you find out things like that, Vi?' Poppy looked up from her letter to Baz. 'Do you go around asking every man where he comes in the family? *Excuse me, could you just tell me whether your brothers are older or younger than you – or, Oh joy! Hallelujah! Have you no brothers at all?*' Poppy said the last words in a squeaky, high-pitched tone of voice, and then returned to her letter. Violet cast her a look of annoyance.

'You're too young to understand,' she said irritably.

'Do you want to have a look, Daisy?'

'Yes,' said Daisy. Even to herself her voice sounded uninterested. Nevertheless, she got up and went across and stared at the names on the tiny booklet. She noticed that Justin's name was down a few times, but this eldest son, this David, had far more dances allocated to him. She tried to take an interest – after all, this was what it was all about. If Violet could marry the eldest son of a well-off earl, then surely the money problems of the Derrington family would be at an end.

'And David has asked me to be his partner at dinner,' said Violet triumphantly. 'Wait until you see Catherine's face! She's been trying to make up to him all day. She thinks he's very good-looking.'

Daisy took a deep breath and tried to make her voice sound light-hearted. 'Keep a few spaces empty, Vi,' she advised. 'You haven't heard the news, have you? Prince George is coming to the ball tonight.'

'Prince George!' screamed Rose. 'Oh, the dream of my life! The answer to a maiden's prayer!'

The colour drained completely from Violet's face.

'Prince George,' she said in a whisper.

'But not the Prince of Wales.' Daisy tried to make her voice sound jokey. She was slightly alarmed by Violet's reaction. All this was so intensely important to her elder sister.

'Oh, I wish I had a brand-new dress!' The words came out on a thread of a whisper.

Daisy shook her own thoughts to the back of her head.

This was an emergency. Violet was intensely emotional; she had to be reassured and calmed.

'Don't worry,' she said. 'Keep thinking that the dress you are wearing came from Worth of Paris.'

'Seventeen years ago!' Something between a sob and a laugh came from Violet.

'But the great thing is that it's going to be different from everyone else's dress,' urged Daisy. After a minute she felt reassured. The colour had begun to seep back into Violet's cheeks and her eyes were determined.

'You looked fantastic the night of your birthday dance and you'll look even more fantastic tonight. Let's ring for Maud and you can have the first bath, and then you'll have plenty of time to get ready and have your hair done and everything. Poppy, put a stamp on that letter – remember what Great-Aunt Lizzie said about never asking your hostess for a stamp. She gave me some – they are in my handbag. Are you going to wear your high heels or your pumps, Vi?'

The question of the mysterious Elaine would have to wait; tonight was going to be crucial for Violet and she would need all the help she could get.

'Sit next to me at table, Daisy?' Justin took her arm casually when the four sisters came into the drawing room. He did not look at Violet so Daisy guessed that he knew she was already booked as a dinner partner by this David the Heir, as Rose had named him.

The atmosphere in the drawing room was burning

with anticipation. Pre-dinner drinks – fruit squashes and a few cocktails and other alcoholic drinks – were being served by Robert, under the stern eye of the butler. Daisy saw him smile and shake his head in a paternal fashion when Poppy pointed to a bottle with something of an interesting dark green shade in it.

'Matches my dress,' she pleaded, but he still shook his head and offered her a glass of lemonade. He had his instructions, obviously, that the 'schoolroom party', as the Duchess named them, should not be allowed alcohol.

Poppy was looking magnificent. She was wearing a gown of emerald green silk that made her amber eyes glow with a greenish light. The dress had been beautifully made. It was very simple, cut on the bias with no trimmings, but the asymmetric hem and the shimmer of the silk as Poppy walked made her look like a model straight from Paris. Maud had left the red hair flowing around her shoulders and just confined by a band of emerald green (made from the sash of the dress as it was originally) across her forehead. Daisy had noticed heads turning and eyes settling on Poppy with huge interest when they came in. Violet had made a new dress for herself as well, but Daisy had persuaded her to wear her dragonfly dress.

Violet was a huge success, Daisy thought as she watched the men – except Justin, of course – cluster around her. Daisy looked at her partner with a half-smile. Justin was very proud, she thought. He would not plead with Violet or try to coax himself back into her favour. As soon as she rebuffed him, he walked away in the opposite direction.

'Orange juice, please, Justin – oh, and get one for Rose also, would you?' He had asked her what she wanted to drink. When he came back she entertained him with an account of her morning and of the remarks made by the young film-makers about her film and she pretended not to notice as his eyes strayed towards Violet. 'They didn't like the ending to my film, Justin. I said that I would redo it. I'm going to have to think. I hate changing things but they convinced me that they were right.'

'I'll think about it,' said Justin absent-mindedly. 'Have you got your dance programme, Daisy? May I write my name in it for a few dances?'

'I didn't get one; I don't think that they were given to "the schoolroom party", but—'

'Oh, nonsense! I'll go and fetch you one from the ballroom.' Justin jutted out his chin determinedly and turned towards the door.

'Bring three,' said Daisy. She didn't fancy being left there standing on her own, looking as though she had been deserted, but on the other hand if she stayed where she was she could watch Violet over the rim of her glass.

'What do you think?' Poppy had joined her and was nodding her head in the direction of Violet.

'I'm not sure,' said Daisy, taking care to turn her back on her eldest sister. Violet would be furious at the notion that they were looking at her and whispering about her.

'She's annoying Catherine,' said Poppy. And then

when Daisy looked at her in surprise she said, 'Well, at least that's what Paula says and she should know what her sister is thinking.'

Daisy glanced over towards Catherine. It would be hard to read much from that rather expressionless face, she thought. However, it was true Paula would know her own sister.

'Oh, Marjorie and I are the greatest friends,' Catherine was saying in the rather breathless voice that she always used. 'We used to share a dancing teacher; do you remember, Marjorie? And she started us off practising the proper curtsy to the King when we were five years old.'

'I could do it in my sleep,' said Marjorie. 'Look, everyone!'

And she sank down into a graceful curtsy, saying, 'The secret is to lock your left knee behind your right knee and then you don't wobble or – horrors! – tumble over.'

'What happens if you tumble over, Marjorie?' called out David.

'You are banished into outer darkness for the rest of your natural lifetime,' said Marjorie with a note of mock horror in her voice.

Catherine gave a smile and said softly, 'Oh, but we all learn how to behave in front of royalty as soon as we can walk, so that never happens.' And Daisy saw her eyes rest on Violet.

'Let's see you curtsy, David,' said Violet, picking up the challenge, and David got a huge round of applause as he awkwardly, stiffly, and with an exaggerated wobble sank down in front of Violet, bowing his head to Violet and saying, 'Yes, Your Majesty.'

The sparkle came back into Violet's eyes and she went on talking eagerly, perhaps rather too loudly, teasing David about his lack of grace and sentencing him to six months' attendance at dance classes.

'Here you are,' said Justin, appearing at Daisy's side with the three dance programmes. His eyes went to Violet and then back to her. 'One for each of you. I'll go and give this one to Rose and rescue that footman from her. As far as I could hear as I went through she's endeavouring to get him to teach her how to mix cocktails. She is telling him that she's an author and that she needs the information for a novel. The poor man keeps looking over at the butler for help.'

'Oh, Justin, a dance! Oh, dear, dear, dearest Justin, I never knew that you cared. Oh my poor heart. It is going pit-a-pat.' Rose was by their side, holding her little booklet where Justin had scribbled his name opposite the fifth dance. 'Oh, I must go and show my friend the Duchess. She will be so pleased to know that I am not going to be a wallflower all night. The shame would have killed me.'

And then she was off. She and the Duchess were great friends as they shared an enormous interest in the intricacies of relationships between members of the British royal family and their European cousins.

'That was nice of you,' said Daisy to Justin after Rose had left them.

'Not in the least,' he said indifferently. 'At least I'll

have fun while dancing with her; most of the girls here are such affected bores.'

And once again his eyes went to Violet, who was laughing at one of David's jokes.

'Dinner is served, Your Grace,' announced the butler.

'I know what you should do for an ending to your film,' said Justin when they reached the fish course. He took a sip of his wine and then turned to the Duchess. 'You must know, Your Grace, that Daisy has made a movie and it is about to be snapped up by a leading film producer.' Justin's voice was trained to reach to the back of a law court and everyone stopped talking and looked at him and then at Daisy.

'Well, we must drink to the success of that,' said the Duchess graciously. 'Robert, champagne for everyone and then we'll drink a toast! What a shame that the Duke is not here. He would be so interested. He is forecasting that if the present trend goes on everyone will eventually have a private cinema in their house.'

To Daisy's embarrassment, once everyone, even Rose, had a glass of champagne, Justin himself called for the toast. Violet's eyes narrowed slightly as she looked across the table at them but Justin ignored her and proceeded to give a quick and dramatic summary of the film.

'The only thing is that Daisy has to find a new ending. It ended rather sadly with this noble and self-sacrificing chauffeur being dragged off to prison, but Hollywood would like a happier ending. And I've just thought of one.' Justin smiled wickedly across at Violet, though he pretended to address Daisy, and said, 'What if the hero is now released from custody – he comes back, meets the heroine, she falls into his arms, they exchange a passionate kiss and then they ride into the sunset, leaving the tragic figure of the chauffeur gazing after them. What do you think, everyone?'

'Lovely,' said the Duchess, applauding delicately with her bejewelled hands. 'How clever you are, dear Justin.'

'If ever I need a lawyer, old boy, I shall come to find you,' said an elderly cousin of the Duchess, eyeing Justin with approval. 'Clever young fella – gave me some great advice about that troublesome affair of . . .' His voice sank to a whisper into the Duchess's ear and she nodded vigorous approval.

'Cross your fingers for me, Daisy.' Justin kept his voice to a low mutter. 'That fellow has big interests in the city. I put him wise to a few things last night. If he said the word he could get me a job. Must see if I can have another chat with him.'

Won't be good enough for Violet, thought Daisy as she nodded and wished him luck. She wants a brilliant marriage, not just enough to live on. Her thoughts turned to the letter, and the mysterious baby that had been born to its writer. 'Justin,' she said, 'tell me about the law regarding birth certificates. Does everyone have to have one? And does it always have to have a date of birth on it? And are they all kept at Somerset House?'

'Every birth in Britain,' said Justin with his mouth full

of lobster. He chewed, swallowed and continued. 'It's the law that every birth must be registered with the date of birth given on it. Time is important, you know. Friends of mine at Harrow, twins, were the eldest sons of their father, an earl. Mark was born at six thirty in the morning and Adam at eight o'clock. So Mark was the heir – and Adam, poor devil, like myself, was just a younger son. They were identical twins too. Used have a lot of fun at school with that! But to go back to the heir business, apparently as soon as Mark was born, a silver bracelet was locked on to his wrist and never taken off until he was about three years old just in case some nursemaid swapped the babies.'

'How horrible,' said Daisy. 'Poor little baby – bet he tried to bite it off as soon as he got teeth.'

'Not so poor,' said Justin. 'He's got everything now. Just has to sit there. Adam, only an hour and a half younger, has come down from Oxford and now he has to find something to do – get a job, or else marry a rich heiress, like me,' he finished rather bitterly, looking across at Violet who was giving David a taste of her choice of dessert from her own fork.

'What about people like me and my sisters who were born in India? Do they have birth certificates?' asked Daisy hurriedly.

That interested Justin and he turned the thought over in his mind.

'I'm not sure about ordinary people,' he said eventually, but I would say that because your father was in the army it would go by British law – yes, I remember now. All the Indian Army records are kept at Somerset House. Why do you want to know? I suppose you're wondering who was born first, you or Poppy.'

'That's right,' said Daisy.

'Do you no good, old girl,' said Justin affably. 'No money at all for girls, you know.'

Chapter Eighteen

The ballroom at the Mayfair house was magnificent, thought Daisy when they went through after dinner. It was the first time that she had been in there. It was very different from the long, bare room on the top storey of Beech Grove Manor. This was a splendid and lofty apartment built on to the back of the house. It had glass walls and a glass roof and there were several small rooms leading off the central hall, including a suite of ladies' cloakrooms, a men's cloakroom and a caterers' kitchen. A forest of potted palms stood around the walls interspersed with the elegant gilt chairs, carefully arranged in friendly groups of varying sizes. These would be for the chaperones and for those young ladies who were unfortunate enough not to have a partner for a dance. High above the hall was the musicians' gallery and the sound of instruments being tuned floated down as the dinner party guests walked in through the side door that led from the dining room. Each girl, even the younger ones, linked arms with a partner and made a stately procession from the dining room until they reached the ballroom and melded into one large chattering group.

Catherine and the Duchess took their places in front of a row of potted palms and waited for the guests to arrive. Most of them would have been entertained to dinner by other hostesses, friends of the Duchess. She, in her turn, would do the same thing for their daughters' balls. The house party chattered eagerly while waiting, each girl keen to tell what had been planned for her season. To Daisy's appalled ears it sounded as though six months of non-stop parties, balls and other events were already arranged. It would take a fortune to do all this. Unless the Duchess sponsored Violet and allowed her a share in Catherine's season, it would be impossible for Violet to have the same as these other girls.

Catherine was very flushed and for the first time Daisy thought that she looked pretty. I suppose she has been looking forward to this for months, if not years, she thought and was half sorry that she had not made a point of admiring the girl's splendid dress earlier in the evening. The rich magnolia with pale pink rosebuds suited Catherine's fair colouring and her hair was expertly dressed, though the style was a little old-fashioned.

'Catherine looks lovely, doesn't she?' Daisy turned towards Paula, hoping that Catherine's sister would pass on the compliment, but she was wasting her time, she thought, as Paula's only response was to turn to Violet and demand loudly, 'What are you doing for your season, Violet? You're being very quiet.'

Every head turned at that and all eyes were fixed on Violet, who coloured up and was suddenly at a loss for words.

'What date is your ball planned for?' asked a girl called Sybil, while Paula whispered in the ear of another girl.

'You are going to have a ball, aren't you?'

'Have you sent out the invitations?'

'Have you had an invitation, David?'

'No, we haven't been asked – none of us.' Paula's voice was so loud that the Duchess looked across at the little group.

'I say, everyone,' interrupted Justin, 'why doesn't Daisy take a photograph of us all before the rest arrive? Come on, girls, let me get you all lined up, beauty in the front and the rest at the back. All the fellows stand in a straight line and I'll arrange the girls at the front. If I don't get a job in the law, then I'll turn to flower arrangement. Stand here, Marjorie – you will be a lily, and Esmé – you'll be a rose.'

Justin chattered on while Daisy darted across to the shelf where she had put her camera. Violet's cheeks were flushed, she noticed when she came back, but she had been placed at the end of the line beside a quiet, shy girl who was unlikely to cross-question her. In any case, as soon as the photograph was taken, Violet took David by the arm and strolled over with him to examine one of the portraits that lined the walls.

The new arrivals swarmed in and after removing their coats in the suite of cloakrooms they came up to greet the Duchess and Catherine one by one. After this they moved to the centre of the floor and stood around chattering. Most seemed to know each other and greetings were called out and hands waved. As the line of newcomers started to grow thin and peter out, Catherine began to look uneasy. Nothing could start until Prince George arrived and there was no sign of him yet.

'I think I'll take some film now before they start dancing,' Daisy said to Justin, and taking her camera from her bag she positioned herself unobtrusively by the door and began filming. After a while everyone would forget about her, but in the beginning, she had learned from the film she had taken yesterday, it was best to be at a distance.

Oh bother, she thought. I suppose that if the Prince has the first dance with Catherine I will definitely have to film that and I'll miss my dance with Justin.

'No sign of His Royal Highness yet, Robert,' she murmured to the footman as he obligingly shifted a small table out of her way.

'No, my lady,' he whispered back. 'Mr Curtis is walking up and down the hall, peeping out every minute.' But as he spoke the butler came through the door, went up to the Duchess, gave a stately bow and said something.

The Duchess had stood in the one position for almost an hour without slouching or showing any signs of fatigue but at the butler's words she stretched up to her full height, her elaborately dressed hair seeming to grow an inch nearer to the ceiling and her tiara sparkling in the light from the chandelier overhead. Catherine straightened up too.

Another footman came in at that moment and said something to Robert about it just being the photographer and journalist from *Tatler* who had arrived.

'Trust them,' muttered Robert. 'They'll be out there

waiting until he gets out of the car. We'll see His Royal Highness in a minute now,' he said, nodding his head wisely and speaking to Daisy out of the corner of his mouth. 'Those photographers are always just ahead of the game. They track the four young princes all around London trying to take photographs of them. You keep your camera ready, my lady. I'll block the magazine reporters and you can get a good scoop of the Prince greeting Her Grace. Trust me.' He slipped through the door after Mr Curtis.

And then there was a strong draught. Not just the door to the hall, but the door to the outside world was opened wide and held open. Daisy shivered with excitement. London was out there. London – full of street lights that made starlight look dim, London – full of radiance and energy, of young talent, of people who were breaking the patterns of stuffy behaviour and old-fashioned rules of conduct. She wanted to be part of it and she had only courage, a good eye, a feeling for a picture and a Kodak camera with which to achieve her dreams.

From a distance, she thought, lifting her camera to her eye.

Yes, from a distance would be good – symbolic, really. The long empty path between the Duchess and the door ... The young royal would tread it lightly, airily, like a prince in a fairy tale. And the Duchess would greet him, introduce him to her daughter. The archetypal story of romances – the fair young girl and the handsome young prince.

And Daisy lifted her camera, ignited her flash, and as Prince George came in swiftly and charmingly, two hands outstretched, she filmed the greeting between him and the Duchess, filmed the bow to the charming daughter and the perfect curtsy that returned it, filmed the signal to the orchestra from Mr Curtis, the butler, filmed the slow start to the stately waltz, filmed the handsome perfection of a young prince who held the world in his hands, filmed him and Catherine waltzing, the expression of ecstasy on Catherine's face. Daisy hoped that it might stand for every girl's young dream come true. Some day, she thought, she would make another film – a prize-winning film that would demonstrate what Sir Guy called 'a universal theme'.

And then the first dance was over.

Daisy went up to the Duchess. The look of excitement on the woman's face touched her. 'I think that the film will be marvellous,' she said with sincerity. 'I got everything. I'll get it developed tomorrow but I'll have to work on it at home. Don't worry – I'll make it good. Catherine looked lovely.'

And then she left her and went over to Justin.

'You stood me up,' he grumbled, but there was a smile on his face.

'You'd do the same thing to me if it was a question of a job with a top London law firm,' she retorted, and he laughed. She didn't feel guilty. He had quickly got himself another partner, she had noticed. Justin with his charm, his decided profile, his handsome face, would never lack partners. Quickly she struck out the first dance and inserted his name into the second. He had booked Violet for her third dance – she remembered that.

'All right for the second?' she queried, showing it to him, and noticed that a photographer, accompanied by a smartly dressed young woman, was at the door, blocked by the faithful Robert while the butler went to check matters with his mistress.

In a moment the Duchess had arranged a posed photograph of Catherine and Prince George and, when that was taken, Mr Curtis and Robert, aided by the second footman, tried to remove the two from *Tatler*, who had got their photograph and a few lines for a headline. They were having problems, though, as the journalist and photographer smoothly eluded them and darted in and out of the crowd, taking photographs and noting names.

'*Prince Dances with Young Debutante. Will the Beautiful Eighteen-Year-Old Daughter of the Duchess of Denton Be the Debutante of the Year?*' said Rose in Daisy's ear.

'Hold my camera,' Daisy started to say, and then she stiffened.

Violet was laughing with David. She was parodying children at a dancing class, dropping stiff little curtsies and looking apprehensively over their shoulders in case their teacher scolded them. It was a clever piece of acting and Daisy felt that she had underestimated her sister. Perhaps Violet could become an actress after all.

But she was not the only one watching Violet.

Prince George politely disengaged himself from the Duchess. He walked across the ballroom floor and bowed before Violet, She gave a parody of the curtsy offered by the Duchess and her daughter and he laughed. Laughed! The Prince of royal blood, fourth in line to the throne of England, threw back his head and laughed with Violet Derrington, who was wearing a second-hand dress cut down from a seventeen-year-old-gown found in an old trunk in the attic of a semi-derelict house.

And then they began to dance.

The music played a slow waltz.

Violet and Prince George danced it as if they had been dancing together for years. Cheek to cheek they drifted around the ballroom floor, moving perfectly in step with each other. Daisy looked at her camera, started to lift it, and then saw the Duchess's face and lowered it. But the photographer from *Tatler* could not be so easily restrained. His camera clicked and clicked again as he dodged around the room, taking photographs of the Prince dancing with this unknown girl. The reporter was already eagerly cross-questioning Marjorie and scribbling frantically in a notebook. Daisy did not need Rose at her elbow to imagine the headlines in *Tatler*.

Prince Dances with Earl's Daughter. Will Lady Violet Derrington Be the Debutante of the Year?

Daisy hardly dared to look at the Duchess's face. How could Violet be so silly as to infuriate the woman at this stage?

'Let's dance,' she said to Justin. Poppy, she noticed, was dancing with the elderly cousin – the big business-man who had said he would come to find Justin if ever he needed a lawyer. Poppy was looking bored but extremely beautiful as he exerted himself to charm her. 'Now's your chance,' said Daisy as they took to the floor and she saw Justin's eyes leave Violet for a moment. She had to distract him. 'Now's your chance,' she repeated. 'Look who Poppy's dancing with. When this dance finishes, what could be more natural than for me to join my sister? And then you can chat up the big noise in the City while Poppy and I have a girlish gossip.'

'About your sister and her prince,' said Justin, but there was a gleam of interest in his eye.

'You don't need to make conversation with me; you can just run over points of company law in your head,' said Daisy obligingly.

'Stop ordering me around, young woman,' Justin said loftily, looking down at Daisy. 'I know you manage everyone in your family but you're not going to manage me. I have everything to do with company law on my fingertips. When I waltz with a girl, I chat. I don't study.'

'Have it your own way,' said Daisy with a shrug. She looked around the ballroom and then laughed. 'Look at Rose,' she said with a chuckle.

Rose had just refused, with a polite smile and a shake of the head, an invitation from one of the boy cousins. She had opened her bag and was using the tiny pencil from her dance programme to make notes on the back of a paper dance list. From time to time she looked up, glanced at her sister in the arms of the young Prince and made another note.

'It's for the grand novel,' said Daisy, but Justin was not as amused as he usually was by Rose's ambitions. He frowned and began stiffly to discuss the orchestra. He was purposely engineering their steps so that they came nearer to the Prince and Violet, but Daisy didn't mind. She, too, was curious to know what Violet was talking about that kept the twenty-one-year-old Prince in gales of laughter.

'Of course, she is a bit pathetic, really. These Victorians find everything so unmentionable, don't they?' And Violet embarked on a cruel imitation of Great-Aunt Lizzie's horror at overhearing Rose giving a funny version of the 'facts of life' to one of the farm children.

'I say, we mustn't lose touch with each other, Violet,' said Prince George. 'Are you going to Millington next weekend? You know Lady Diana Cooper, don't you? I'll get her to send you an invite. Do say that you'll come.' The Prince was obviously enamoured; Daisy was glad that her father wasn't present. He would not have been happy at the way the two of them were dancing. 'Dance with Justin,' she whispered to Poppy just before the next dance. This time Prince George had come to a sense of his social obligations and had gone up to Catherine with a smile on his face and his hand outstretched. She curtsied and he grinned, no doubt remembering Violet's ridiculous mimicry.

Daisy filmed this dance from the first to the last minute, making sure that she crossed in front of the Duchess several times so that their hostess noted what

215

she was doing. But she had a sinking feeling that it was all too late. There was no mistaking the fact that Prince George's eyes continually wandered in the direction of Violet. When the dance with Catherine finished, he left her after a bow and crossed the room towards the spot where Violet was chatting to David.

'Don't you go filming them.' Justin's voice was savage in Daisy's ear. This was Violet's fifth dance with Prince George.

'I don't want to,' she said sadly. And she didn't.

She remembered something said by Fred, the boy with malaria, when she was at Sir Guy's studios. It now struck her as profound.

'One should never get the impression that the author of the film knows the end of the story all the time.'

She did not want to film Violet in the arms of Prince George. She did not want to film the lovely face of her sister – not in love, no, it wasn't that. Violet's expression was more that of a once-starving cat who had a saucer of cream set before her.

Violet was lapping up the experience of being the focus of all eyes.

And she was spoiling Catherine's coming-out ball, not just for Catherine herself, but for the Duchess of Denton, who had dreamed of this moment for years.

And Daisy knew quite well what the ending of this particular story would be.

Chapter Nineteen

The farewells the following morning were brisk and efficient – and inevitable. Violet had ruined Catherine's coming-out ball; it would be too much to expect the Duchess to sponsor her through a presentation to their majesties.

'Goodbye, Daisy dear; we're so looking forward to the film. The bits you have shown me look wonderful. How clever you are, my dear. Here's a little something for you in the meantime.' Some coins chinked in the Duchess's hand and were transferred to Daisy's.

'Goodbye, Rose, my dear, I've so enjoyed our chats, and Poppy – goodness, you are so like your dear, dear mother! It was lovely to see you. Goodbye, Violet. Do remember me to your father and to your dear great-aunt. Have a lovely journey, my dears.'

And then they were out through the front door and into the big, old-fashioned car and they were driving through the streets of London.

'You're all very quiet,' commented Morgan as he pulled smoothly out into the morning traffic. He glanced over his shoulder and said sympathetically, 'Didn't things go well?'

'Very enjoyable, thank you,' said Violet stiffly.

'You sound like Great-Aunt Lizzie,' remarked Poppy.

'Blood will tell,' said Rose wisely. 'Though there is still quite a distance between Violet's nose and her chin.'

'Shut up,' said Violet viciously.

'What about us all having an ice cream at Gatti's?' asked Morgan. 'I made a bit of money on selling a drums recording that I made. There's a market for that sort of thing now with all the new films that are coming out. It was only a few minutes long but I got a guinea for it. Here's the Strand now.' He slid the car neatly into a parking space and escorted them across the busy street.

It was so early in the morning that there was no one else in Gatti's ice-cream parlour and Morgan found them a nice table beside the window where they could sit and watch the crowds walking down the Strand. A smart girl in a frilly apron and cap brought them a colourful menu and they settled down to choose, Rose decreeing that everyone should have something different so that they would get to sample five out of the ten varieties.

'And the next time you come to London you can choose the other five,' said Morgan.

'I'll never come to London again,' said Violet mournfully.

'The Duchess hasn't made any offer to present Violet at court,' Poppy explained to Morgan with her usual frankness.

Morgan shrugged. 'Present yourself,' he said. 'I'm all in favour of people doing things for themselves. This is 1923, you know. Walk up to Buckingham Palace and shake the man by the hand.'

This made them all giggle – Daisy even felt slightly hysterical – halfway between tears and laughter. She hoped that Violet wouldn't soon dissolve into tears again. However, her younger sister came to the rescue.

'Oh, Morgan, my dear man,' said Rose with a clever imitation of Great-Aunt Lizzie's condescending manner, 'you really don't understand these matters. A girl can only be presented to the King by a lady who has been presented herself – even in the dim and distant past, like the Duchess,' she added.

Morgan grinned. 'Well, I'm only a poor boy from an orphanage, my lady,' he said with mock humility, 'but what about asking your great-aunt to do it, then? I bet she was hobnobbing with kings and queens when she was growing up.'

Violet shook her head tragically. 'She'd never do that. She hasn't a penny herself, you know. Remember her clothes. Everything has been darned so much that there are more darns than cloth in them.'

'What about another relation?' persisted Morgan. 'What about any aunts or cousins or anything like that?'

Suddenly Daisy had an idea. She swallowed the last spoonful of the delicious ice and then asked: 'Morgan, where is the Savoy Hotel? It's on the Strand, isn't it? I'm sure that I heard the Duchess talk about it.'

'That's right – just down there.' Morgan pointed.

Daisy made up her mind quickly. It was worth a try. She took from her handbag the guineas that the Duchess had given her. 'Let's buy some clothes with these,' she said impulsively. 'Violet, you take Rose into that shop over there. Poppy and I will join you in a minute. Morgan, will you be all right here for half an hour or so?'

'I expect so,' said Morgan affably. 'I'll buy a paper and have a cup of coffee. Enjoy yourselves.'

'Where are you and Poppy going?' asked Violet as they reached the door of the shop.

'Something to show Poppy,' said Daisy rapidly as she pulled her twin sister away and began to run down the broad pavement of the Strand. In a few minutes they had reached the stately entrance to the Savoy. Daisy slowed down and put her hat straight.

'Enlighten me,' said Poppy as they walked down the hill towards the front door of the hotel. 'What actually are we going here for?'

'Elaine,' said Daisy. 'The boy at Sir Guy's studios who told me that he met her on the boat coming back from India said that she mentioned she was coming here to the Savoy Hotel.'

'And you suddenly thought that she might present Violet,' finished Poppy. 'Unlikely, I'd say. There must have been some big row or there would have been letters, Christmas cards – that sort of thing.'

'Worth a try,' said Daisy. She didn't care for the look of the starchy individual in the Reception Office, or of the way in which he glanced disdainfully at their shabby coats, but she marched bravely in.

'I'm looking for a Mrs Elaine Coxhead; I understand that she is staying here,' she said, trying to sound a little like Great-Aunt Lizzie, but not succeeding.

'Nobody of that name, here, miss,' he said after scanning a few pages.

'She came back from India a month or so ago and drove straight here,' said Daisy firmly. 'Her name must be somewhere.'

He turned over a few more leaves, and then stopped, a stubby finger pointing at an entry.

'Left here two weeks ago,' he said triumphantly.

'Have you an address for her?' persisted Daisy, but he shook his head.

'No, miss,' he said. 'Will that be all?'

Daisy didn't bother answering but stalked out, followed by Poppy, who touched a note on the piano in the foyer and said in clear, carrying tones. 'Out of tune. Oh dear, what a shame! I couldn't bear to take afternoon tea here and listen to an out-of-tune piano, could you?'

Daisy giggled and felt better. 'I'm glad that I didn't say anything to Violet,' she said as they walked back up the short road to the Strand. She looked around at the crowds. How on earth could they find Elaine in a city the size of London?

Morgan was with Violet and Rose outside the ice-cream cafe.

'Did you buy anything?' called out Poppy when they had reached the pavement in safety.

Violet shook her head. 'No,' she said. 'The clothes are terribly expensive, but I've got lots of good ideas from looking at them. I can alter some more of the dresses in the trunk to look like the latest fashion from London.' She seemed much happier, though she did add, 'Not that I'll have any occasion to wear them.'

'I've an idea,' said Poppy. 'I was thinking of what Bob here said about Great-Aunt Lizzie. Couldn't we use one of the guineas to buy her something to wear? Or all of them? You can have mine if you like.'

'Yes, but I need to have a season in London – and I need to have a ball, and things like that. Father would never agree to spending money on that, and Great-Aunt Lizzie won't do anything without his agreement,' objected Violet, but her colour had deepened and there was a calculating look in her eyes. 'But one of Catherine's friends has asked me to a house party in Berkshire,' she added. 'And . . .' She hesitated and blushed, the colour in her eyes intensifying.

'Save your guinea for new riding breeches,' interrupted Daisy quickly. She had overheard Prince George's casual invitation to Violet and knew that there was no possibility of Great-Aunt Lizzie or her father agreeing to her visiting a house where the hostess was unknown to the family. 'Riding is something you do so well, Violet, and Berkshire is great horse countryside,' she ended hurriedly.

'Let's all have another ice cream before we go back,' said Morgan.

'Gorgeous,' said Poppy. 'What are you having, Rose?'

Rose was taking a long time to decide so Daisy walked back to the table and set down her ice cream. Morgan's newspaper had been left on the chair – the London *Times*. She began to scan through the personal column on the first page, hoping to find something funny to show to Rose – she was a little worried that Rose might have been more upset than was apparent at Sir Guy's decision to get Fred to redo the design of the title cards.

'*Could DM urgently get in touch with RW of Chelmsford. Address and phone number lost.*' That was the first advertisement that she read.

And suddenly she had an idea. Surreptitiously she extracted the middle page from Rose's splendid new notebook, took from her handbag the tiny pencil still attached to her dance programme, and wrote:

COULD ELAINE COXHEAD PLEASE CONTACT DAISY.

And then she looked at the address at the top of the newspaper – Fleet Street.

'Morgan,' she said when they all had finished their ice creams, 'is it possible to stop off at Fleet Street on our way home?'

'Only down the road from here,' he replied, looking at her closely.

'The dear Duchess getting her to do her errands – you were quite a favourite with her, Daisy,' said Violet acidly, and Morgan nodded understandingly and turned to scan through the pages of the discarded copy of *The Times*.

'I have an idea,' said Daisy. 'While we are here in London, why don't we spend the money on a new pair of riding breeches from Aquascutum for the four of us?

That's one thing that Vi can't make and they would be essential for any country house parties. What do you say? I really don't see Great-Aunt Lizzie agreeing to take those guineas.'

'You're the one that earns the money; you make the decisions,' said Poppy with a grin. 'But wait until Baz and I set up our jazz club – I'll be the rich twin then!' She gave Daisy's hand a quick squeeze.

Chapter Twenty

The house seemed dark, gloomy and very, very cold when they returned from London. Michael Derrington was prostrated by one of his frequent sick headaches which left him lying on his bed in a darkened room for a few days and sipping from a glass of milk from time to time. Any sympathy, any enquiries about his health and any attempts to make him more comfortable drove him into fits of rage and the girls learned to keep well away from him.

'It's just the war, that terrible war,' Mrs Beaton used to say to the children. 'He was the nicest, kindest, most cheerful man before the war. It was a terrible thing that war – left nobody in the country untouched. All those young men shell-shocked, maimed and even slaughtered. The only consolation is that they say it was a war to end all wars. Britain will never go to war again.'

And that left Great-Aunt Lizzie.

Tense, tired and disappointed, suffering from a heavy cold and sore throat, she was, decided the girls, in no mood to consider a trip to Buckingham Palace to present her great-niece to King George and his wife.

However, Violet was in good spirits. From the day after their arrival, she sewed like one inspired. Ball gowns, cocktail dresses, lunch outfits, walking costumes – the picture rail in the schoolroom was hung with so many clothes that Justin took to calling it the milliner's shop. He was back in Kent with his tolerant uncle and aunt whose heir lived in another part of the country and who were glad to have a lively young man around the place.

'You're getting better and better at this, Vi,' said Daisy one day, examining how cleverly Elaine's blouses were altered and how expertly her tweed jackets were taken in at the waist. 'Perhaps you could set up a dressmaking firm in the west end of London and make pots of money.' She smiled nervously but it was obvious that Violet was not listening to her. She was completely obsessed with the idea of being a debutante and having a season. Will I feel like that in a year or two years' time? wondered Daisy, trying to take her mind away from her fears and uncertainties. Her godfather, Sir Guy, was keen for her to have a season; he had told her that, pretending it was for the sake of all the wonderful film she might be able to shoot of her fellow debutantes. She turned her attention back to Violet, who had taken down a long dress made from white satin with elaborate white lace trimmings.

'The great thing is that Elaine's presentation dress looks just the same as Catherine's,' said Violet exultantly. 'The style hasn't altered at all. They still wear those long flowing dresses, nipped in at the waist and with a train. I've shortened the train a little. Catherine said that the palace has issued instructions that it need not be more than eighteen inches long now. And the three ostrich feathers that you have to have are there in a box. Look at them.'

Daisy gazed dubiously at three fluffy white feathers, each about a foot long. 'They're a bit yellow,' she observed.

'Oh, that doesn't matter,' said Violet impatiently. 'Marjorie told me that she will be wearing her grandmother's ostrich feathers. She said that she was going to be the tenth girl in the family to wear them.' Violet giggled at the thought of the lovely gossipy conversations with the other girls at the Duchess's house party and then her face darkened as she thought of the abrupt end to her stay.

'I don't know why you are criticizing and moaning, Daisy,' she said in an irritated way. 'You're very sour these days. What's the matter with you? Don't walk off; I was going to show you—'

The matter with me, thought Daisy as she closed the door on Violet's angry voice, is that nothing is happening. And I'm sick of lying in wait for the postman and finding that nothing but bills are arriving at the house. She had spent her last few pennies on sending the completed film of the ball to the Duchess and the revised version of *Murder in the Dark* to Sir Guy and on buying *The Times*. Her advertisement had appeared ten days ago but there had been no repsonse. She had clipped it out, shown it to Poppy and then hidden it in her underclothes drawer. From time to time she took it out and looked at it.

'Everyone who is anyone reads the Court Circular,' Great-Aunt Lizzie had said one day, laying down the law as usual.

'You mean everyone reads the personal column.' Michael Derrington, now in a good mood, had chuckled at this and had forced his aunt-in-law to admit that she did usually glance through it to see whether any old friend was trying to get in touch.

But perhaps Elaine did not take *The Times*. Perhaps she had no friends who would have spotted the advertisement and called it to her attention. Or perhaps she had returned to India?

Daisy didn't know and the uncertainty was terribly hard to bear. She tried to throw herself into the plans for Violet's presentation and had even read up on the requirements for court presentations in an ancient book of etiquette that Rose had unearthed from the library, but she found it very hard to keep her mind on it. It had suddenly occurred to her today that Elaine might have replied with another advertisement in *The Times*, giving a box number and telling 'Daisy' to contact her through this. And if Daisy had not replied then she might have been secretly relieved. Daisy felt that her head was splitting with all the thoughts that were rushing through it.

She would try to distract herself, she decided, and grabbed a basket, going out through the back door to collect the eggs from the hen house. There was something soothing about this occupation and by the time she came out with a basketful she felt better. She waved cheerily at Justin who was just dismounting from his horse.

'I've got the list of costs from my aunt for my cousin's coming-out dinner and dance,' he said. 'Should have been an accountant, that woman! She's got it all written down. Writes down everything, apparently.'

Daisy took the notebook from him. There they were, all the prices. 'Lend it to me, Justin, just for the moment. I want to copy them out. I won't take long.'

'No hurry,' said Justin carelessly. 'Is Violet in the schoolroom?' He didn't wait for an answer but went towards the back door, patting the pocket of his Norfolk tweed jacket and saying, 'I've followed your advice and bought *The Times* at the village shop. Hilarious some of the advertisements in "Situations Vacant"! I thought I would read them out to Violet to help pass the time while she's sewing.'

'Let me have a look,' said Daisy. She almost snatched it from him and felt her hands tremble as she searched for the personal ads. She read through them twice, but there was nothing there so she handed the paper back to Justin.

'Anybody advertising for a brilliant young lawyer and offering a princely salary?' She put her question quickly before he could ask her what she was looking for.

'I fear that the secret of my brilliance is remaining somewhat too hush-hush for my liking,' he retorted with a grin. 'However, I live in hope.'

He should go up to London rather than hang around kicking his heels and dangling after Violet, who has no intention of marrying him, thought Daisy as she went into the drawing room. Great-Aunt Lizzie, still rather shaken after her illness, had retired for her afternoon rest so she would have the place to herself. She opened up Lady Pennington's Household Accounts Book at the page that was marked by a helpful slip of paper and gazed at the page headed in neat capital letters: PAMELA'S COMING-OUT PARTY.

The prices were all there arranged in neat rows of pounds, shillings and pence:

	£	s	d
BAND:	18	18	0
FOOD:	14	1	10
DRINK:	17	17	0
HIRE:	4	0	0
EXTRA HELP:	15	15	6
EXTRAS	1	10	0
TOTAL:	72	2	4

And underneath that was:

DINNER FOR EIGHTEEN PEOPLE

	£	s	d
FOOD:	4	0	0
CHAMPAGNE:	3	0	0
HELPERS:	2	0	0
	9	0	0

Well, thought Daisy, at least we could cut out that eighteen guineas for the band; the jazz boys and Morgan would do it for the fun and for their supper. *Hire* was probably for those chairs for the chaperones – that would be unavoidable. Perhaps, she thought optimistically, the whole thing could be done for about forty pounds. And Sir Guy was talking about paying her forty pounds for her second film. He had been delighted with the new ending – particularly the shot of Violet and Justin riding off past the lake, and Morgan standing there looking after them.

'Yes,' she murmured aloud, feeling a rush of excitement at the thought of her earning power. 'I think I might be able to do it if only Violet would be happy to have it here. After all, she keeps getting letters from men and girls that she met at the Duchess's place so she will have enough people to invite. She could have a small dance.'

The food and drink were expensive, but perhaps the champagne could be skipped. There were still lots of bottles of wine down in the cellar and the price of the food could be cut down if they used plenty of eggs and potatoes. She giggled a little as she thought about the giant Spanish omelette and reached into her great-aunt's desk for a piece of scrap paper on which she could write down the prices.

The drawers were full of thick, expensive writing paper and gilt-edged visiting cards and invitation cards, but Daisy did not like to use any of these without permission. The little centre door only had pens and ink bottles behind it. Impatiently she got to her feet. She would have to go up to the schoolroom to get some paper.

As she rose her foot caught in a hole in the carpet and caused her to stumble, pressing against the ornately carved ridge below the pull-out, baize-covered writing surface. Suddenly a drawer shot out, almost causing her to lose her balance. So Great-Aunt Lizzie's desk had a secret drawer! There must be a spring under one of those carvings, but Daisy did not waste time investigating this. Her whole attention was on the contents of the drawer. It was stuffed with old photographs and she picked some out and started to leaf through them.

A very much younger Great-Aunt Lizzie, with a small blonde child in her arms and a tall girl standing beside her, stared out of the old brown photograph at her – Mary and Elaine with their aunt, guessed Daisy.

And then she came across something that made her catch her breath in astonishment. First of all she thought it was a photograph of herself. The blonde-haired girl in the picture looked to be about fifteen or sixteen. But that was not the surprising thing. Beside her was a boy of about the same age and this boy was the image of Justin – a square, determined chin, dark eyes, crisply curling black hair and a well-shaped mouth curving into a broad smile. If it were not for the old-fashioned clothes, then it could be a picture of Daisy herself with Justin by her side.

'Rose,' called Great-Aunt Lizzie from the stairs, her voice still rather hoarse and followed by a fit of coughing.

Hastily Daisy stuffed the photographs back and managed to click the drawer closed. Then she picked up Lady Pennington's book and went out. 'Were you looking for Rose, Great-Aunt?' she asked. 'I'll fetch her for you. I think that she has taken her dogs for a walk.'

'Never mind, I suppose the fresh air will do her good; I'm worried about her education though. She'll slip behind if I don't keep pressing her to work.' The old lady's voice sounded fretful, but it was also feeble and Daisy felt sorry for her.

'Shall I ask Maud to light the fire in the drawing room?' she asked, but her great-aunt shook her head. 'No, thank you, dear. It's not worth it. I just have a few letters to write and then I think I'll go back to my bedroom,' she said. 'I'm not feeling quite the thing today.' She tried to smile and then added, 'I'll be better when the weather improves.'

This is the best spring we've had that I can remember, thought Daisy, watching with concern as the old lady dragged herself down the remaining stairs, leaning heavily on the banisters. 'I'll find Rose and see if I can set her some work to do,' she promised as her great-aunt went into the drawing room. There was no doubt that Rose's education was being neglected.

If I had forty pounds, should I spend it on Violet's coming-out or send Rose to school for a few years? she wondered. There was a girls' grammar school in the large town of Maidstone, but Great-Aunt Lizzie might disdain that – and Daisy had no idea of the fees. Thinking hard, she went through the hall and out of the front door.

And then she stopped, her eyes widening. There was a car coming towards the house. Not the ancient battered old black Humber driven by Morgan, but something quite, quite different.

The red Rolls-Royce moved in a stately way up the avenue, passing under the overhanging branches of beech trees, skirting the untidy bushes of rhododendron and dodging the odd pothole. It looked like a very expensive car. Daisy's eyes widened at the sight. Who did they know who owned a car like that? For a moment she wondered whether it could be the Duchess's car, but then remembered that had been blue.

But who was this sitting in the back of the sumptuous, brand-new Rolls-Royce? It was a woman. Through the back window Daisy could just make out an elegant close-fitting hat. She took two steps backwards. Her father was in a bad mood – hands shaking, nerves in pieces – and Great-Aunt Lizzie was tired and ill. It was up to her to deal with this stranger.

The car had stopped now in front of the door. The chauffeur had got out and had opened the door. A small figure climbed out. A small, slim figure dressed in the latest fashion with a short dustcoat over an even shorter dress. Daisy quickened her step and the woman turned to face her.

And it was like staring into a looking glass. This woman had blonde curly hair, creamy skin, cornflower-blue eyes, a curvaceous figure, and she was no taller than Daisy herself.

'Good morning,' said Daisy politely, well trained in good manners by Great-Aunt Lizzie. 'Have you had a good trip?'

'I've come from London.' The woman's voice was

husky and to Daisy's alarm she saw tears well up in the blue eyes that had moved from looking up at the ivy-encrusted house to studying her intently. Daisy waited, feeling uneasy. The woman had a maid sitting in the front of the car, but the girl had obviously been given instructions not to move so she sat there, looking straight ahead.

'Are you . . . ? Are you . . . ? Which of the girls are you?' There was no doubt – Daisy had not imagined those tears; the woman's voice was choked.

'I'm Daisy.' The words were no sooner out of her mouth than she saw, with relief, that Bateman, alerted by one of the maids, had appeared on the steps leading up to the hall door. He hesitated for a moment and then came down the steps more quickly than Daisy had ever seen him move.

'My lady,' he said, and his voice was full of emotion.

'Dear Bateman.' To Daisy's astonishment, the visitor flung her arms around the butler and hugged him. And what was even more astonishing, Bateman forgot all his manners and put his arms around the shoulders of the woman and hugged her back. A tremor seemed to move the two figures as if a sob had passed between them and then Bateman stood back, fighting to return his old face into its usual lofty expression.

'My lady, it's wonderful to see you again,' he said in a low voice. 'Lady Elizabeth and his lordship will have a marvellous surprise.'

'Didn't you get my wire then?' The woman was half laughing and half crying. 'The same old post office!' she said. 'Always late with everything! I suppose that's the telegraph boy coming up the avenue now. I just arrived back in England a couple of weeks ago. Popped over to Paris to buy a few clothes from Chanel and then back to dear old London again.' She turned and saw Daisy's worried expression and smiled reassuringly at her.

'This is Lady Daisy; your aunt, Lady Elaine, my lady,' said Bateman. He nodded to the lady's maid who now got out of the car, carrying an elaborate dressing case. The chauffeur went around to the back of the car and took out a large stylish leather suitcase.

'Take my purse, Bateman dear, and pay off the chauffeur. I just hired this car in London.'

While Bateman was doing this, Elaine smiled again at Daisy. 'You look like me, don't you think? Much prettier, of course. Who does Poppy look like?'

'She looks like my mother,' said Daisy promptly. She hardly remembered her mother's appearance now, but the house was full of photographs of her and there was a magnificent oil painting on the stairs which showed the full glory of her flame-coloured hair.

At that moment Morgan came driving up the avenue from the village. Lady Elaine laughed with a slightly hysterical note in her voice. 'That can't be the same old Humber still here!'

'Yes, my lady. That's the same car. Not many things have changed since you were here last. The chauffeur is new, of course,' he added loftily and Daisy suppressed a giggle. Morgan had been chauffeur at Beech Grove Manor for the last four years, but to Bateman and Mrs Pearson he was still 'the new chauffeur'.

Daisy gazed at the bobbed hair. That was just the way that her hair should be! Bobbed in a pageboy cut, with the ends turned under so that it swung when its owner moved her head from side to side as she looked at the house, the stables, the beech woods and the old Humber car with the air of one who could hardly drink in the familiar sights quickly enough.

Daisy waited at the bottom of the steps as they went through the porch door. She would allow Bateman to show Elaine into the drawing room. She hoped that Great-Aunt Lizzie was alone and that her father had not joined her. Aunt and niece should have a little time together in private. They had not met for about seventeen years, she thought; let the first five minutes be for them alone before the rest of the family arrived on the scene.

Then when all was going well – when Elaine had been introduced to the family, had been amazed by Violet's beauty, was rested, fed and in a receptive mood – then possibly Daisy could broach the subject of a possible sponsorship of her eldest niece through a Court Presentation and hopefully a London Season.

There was one relief, anyway. One glance at Elaine's clothes, at the handsome luggage, at the stylish lady's maid, at the hired Rolls-Royce had been enough. There was no doubt in Daisy's mind that Elaine was wealthy enough to make Violet's dream come true.

Chapter Twenty-One

Justin was having fun with the 'Positions Vacant' section of *The Times* as Daisy reached the door of the school-room.

'*Young person wanted to do general work around the house and to dress the young ladies' hair,*' he was saying. 'What do you think, Violet? Could I hold down a position like that? Would you let me practise on you?'

'I wish you'd stop talking nonsense. Look what you made me do. Now I'll have to take out those stitches. Great-Aunt Lizzie would have rapped me over the knuckles for sewing like that when I was ten years old.' Violet was surprisingly happy these days, despite her chances of a debut looking bleak. Daisy had come to suspect that Justin's constant presence in the house was the reason for this. Ever since the night of Violet's birthday party, when Justin had chopped wood, peeled potatoes and shifted furniture, he had behaved not like a visitor but like a member of the family, strolling in through the back door unceremoniously, swinging an axe in the wood yard, inspecting the home farm with her father, contentedly swallowing bread and cheese for his lunch and staying until darkness fell. Daisy found it difficult to know whether Violet was in love with him though, or whether she was just treating him as an older brother. She and Poppy confided in each other, but Violet kept her own counsel.

'Guess who's arrived,' said Daisy dramatically as she came into the schoolroom. 'In a Rolls-Royce,' she added, feeling surprised at her ability to sound casual when her heart was thumping irregularly within her chest.

Violet's face went completely white and her eyes were enormous as she stared at her sister. 'The Du—' she began, but Daisy shook her head quickly.

'No, not the Duchess,' she said. 'She watched with sympathy the light die out of her sister's face. She hadn't realized that Violet still hoped that the events of that fatal evening of the Duchess's ball could be undone. 'More exciting than that!' she said quickly. 'It's Elaine back from India. You know, Vi! Elaine of the Dresses!' She decided to say no more until she had a chance to talk to Elaine. It would be too cruel to raise Violet's hopes only to have them thwarted once more.

However, the look of disappointment was quickly replaced by one of horror as Violet turned to look at all the short, jaunty dresses that had been ruthlessly cut from Elaine's flowing gowns.

'What's she going to say?' she breathed.

'She'll probably sue; I wonder whether she would like me to act for her,' said Justin with relish. 'Now let me see,' he said a crisp, authoritative tone. '*M'lud, we ask for exemplary damages of one hundred guineas per gown to cover material damage to property and injury to the very natural feelings of sentimental attachment on the part of my client.*' He counted the line of dresses and said: '*My client is willing to settle out of court, m'lud, for the sum of twelve hundred guineas – and costs, of course,*' he added hastily.

Daisy couldn't help giggling and even Violet started to laugh.

'What does she look like?' she asked.

'Like me,' said Daisy. 'But she's very well dressed and her hair is bobbed.'

'Well then, she won't want her dowdy old clothes back,' said Violet decisively, 'and don't you say a word about suing, Justin,' she warned, 'or I won't mend that tear in your jacket for you. Now you can help to carry all of these down to my bedroom. I'll hide them in my dressing room. She probably won't stay more than a night or so. This place will seem freezing to her after London – never mind India.'

'I'll just pop down the back stairs and fetch Poppy,' said Daisy. She had heard the sounds of jazz from Morgan's cottage earlier in the morning and she guessed that was where Poppy and Rose had hidden themselves.

By the time she had turned the handle of the door, however, it was too late. There was a click of heels coming quickly up the stairs.

'Ah, there you are, Daisy,' said Elaine nervously. 'Aunt Lizzie thought you must be in the schoolroom.'

She entered the room, her face full of curiosity, her gaze already going to the faded, much-mended curtains, when Justin, putting back the dress that he had unhooked from the picture rail, turned towards her.

Elaine stopped suddenly. Her face, thought Daisy, wore the expression of someone who had seen a ghost. Her lips parted and she stared at him in horror.

'Who are you?' she breathed.

'Just a young person who helps around the house and dresses the young ladies' hair,' said Justin amiably, and then looked bewildered as Elaine continued to stare at him. Daisy and Violet exchanged puzzled looks.

'This is Justin Pennington, a nephew of a neighbour of ours.' Violet gave Justin an annoyed look and made the introduction with a little of the Duchess's quelling manner about her. 'Justin, this is our Aunt Elaine.' She came forward with her hand outstretched. 'How do you do? I'm Violet, the eldest of the family.'

'I'll go and fetch Poppy and Rose,' said Daisy. Before anyone could say anything she turned and went rapidly down the back stairs. By the time she had reached the gallery Justin had caught up with her.

'Coward,' he remarked.

'What about you?' retorted Daisy.

'I made a considered judgement that it would be against the interests of my client, or perhaps I should say my potential client, to be present at any preliminary and informal conversation,' he said haughtily. 'In any case,' he added in his normal voice, 'I think that Violet will do better with a girlie chat and laying the secret of the family poverty before her aunt. She does that sort of thing well.'

'Race you to Morgan's cottage,' replied Daisy,

shooting out through the back door and starting to run. He caught up with her easily though and they jogged companionably through the trees.

'You get them; I'm out of breath.'

Daisy waited until her sisters came out with Justin before saying, 'Come on, Poppy. Show some interest in a long-lost relative, especially one that provided your party dresses.'

'Oh, I can't wait to see her; what a romantic moment in the middle of my dreary life,' intoned Rose. She began to run back towards the house and Justin followed her. Poppy and Daisy, left alone, stared into each other's eyes.

'Has she said anything yet?' asked Poppy, and Daisy shook her head and explained about Bateman, Great-Aunt Lizzie and then Violet.

Dinner was a strange meal – completely dominated by talk of India. One by one, Michael Derrington and his aunt enumerated acquaintances and places and cross-questioned Elaine for up-to-date news. It was as if they feared to leave a silence at the table. Rose made a little game of slipping in wise remarks like, 'Ah, the Rana, not the Maharana, I see,' but the other three girls ate in silence. Coffee was served in the drawing room – an unusual piece of grandeur these days, and when that was over, Great-Aunt Lizzie said decisively, 'Well, dear, what brings you back to England after all this time?'

'Nigel Coxhead died and I had to come over to sort out some of his affairs,' said Elaine quietly. 'That was my husband,' she continued, turning to the four girls sitting primly on the sofa. 'He was quite elderly,' she explained as Violet opened her mouth to say something. Violet shut it again and gave an uneasy glance at the other two.

'You were left well provided for, I trust?' Great-Aunt Lizzie raised a delicate eyebrow, her back as straight as a ramrod, her old eyes hooded.

'Very well,' said Elaine quietly.

There was an uncomfortable silence. The Earl looked at Lady Elizabeth but she said nothing.

And then Elaine broke the awkward silence by turning to Violet with a warm smile. 'We must have a long talk in the morning about your clothes – for your coming-out,' she said, and Violet's face lit up.

'Next year, perhaps,' said the Earl firmly and Violet's face fell again. She stared fixedly at the fire, her eyes bright with tears. Elaine looked at her and hesitated and then she took a deep breath, almost as though she were summoning up courage, and turned to face her brother-in-law.

'No reason why it shouldn't be this year,' she said courageously. 'There's time enough to arrange everything. I can present Violet and look after her season. This is something that I would enjoy, Michael. I've decided to hire a house in London for the next couple of months. There's no reason why I should not present Violet, is there, Aunt Lizzie? As you will remember –' now she looked across at her aunt, and her soft-featured face grew a little hard – 'as you will remember,' she repeated,

'I was presented myself when I was only seventeen years old. It was King Edward then,' she said with a smile at Rose, who nodded wisely, but refrained from slipping in a short biography.

Rose, like all of us, thought Daisy, was breathless at the sudden drama that had erupted. All through dinner when the servants had been in and out of the room, Elaine had appeared sweet, shy and docile, following her aunt's choice of conversational topics, but now, with the family gathered around an unusually hot fire, she seemed suddenly to have seized the initiative and to have become brave.

'No, no,' Elaine repeated the word firmly. 'I remember my season very well and I am sure that I can steer Violet through all its problems and be a support and comfort to her at this very important time of a young girl's life.'

And once again her eyes met Great-Aunt Lizzie's, and the two women stared at each other for a long minute, both faces slightly flushed in the firelight.

And the older woman was the first to drop her eyes.

'You know, Michael, that might be a very good idea,' said Great-Aunt Lizzie, and the girls held their breath.

But the Earl was in a good mood. He had enjoyed reliving his life in India, and though a little sadness had come into his face at the memories of his dead wife, he had laughed at some of Elaine's stories and had chortled with glee at the report that one of the most dashing young officers of his day was now bald, overweight and suffering from gout.

He smiled at his sister-in-law. 'Well, it's very generous of you, Elaine, and we would appreciate it. Are you sure?'

'Mary would have wanted it,' said Elaine gently, and Daisy held her breath. They all avoided mentioning the name of Mary Derrington, but now the only reaction was a look of gentle melancholy and a slow nod of the head. He put his arm around Poppy, who sat beside him on the sofa and hugged her, but looked across at his eldest daughter.

'Well, Violet . . .' he started to say, but Violet had jumped up and thrown herself on Elaine.

'Oh Elaine, no one has ever done such a lovely thing for me in my whole life.' Daisy saw her father wince and was pleased when Rose said, 'You should promise to be her slave for the rest of your natural life.'

Even Great-Aunt Lizzie, who tried to discourage Rose's odd remarks, laughed with relief at this.

'And the other girls will be company for her and we'll all have such fun shopping,' said Elaine. 'And don't worry, Aunt Lizzie, I'll make sure that they have lots of educational visits to the British Museum and . . . and . . . places like that,' she added. 'I'm staying at The Ritz for the moment. I'll have to see about hiring a house, but I suppose the lawyer might help.'

'I know what,' said the Earl, suddenly inspired. 'You take Bateman with you; he'll do everything for you. Find a house in a suitable place and hire staff. You can leave everything to him. He's used to doing that sort of thing. He did it for Mary and myself when we were young. He'll have you sorted in a couple of days. We'll send him up by train so that he has everything ready by the time you arrive. And take Morgan too. The man has nothing to do here but go on errands to the village. In London he will be wonderful. He's a very reliable chauffeur. You can get him to drive Violet around to all those little lunches that girls have and take the other girls to museums and everything like that; and the girl Maud – she can trail around with them so that you don't have the bother of chaperoning, Elaine. Lizzie, you can manage without Morgan, can you? No visits planned for the next few weeks, and anyway,' he went on without waiting for an answer, 'he can always come back if you need him – you'll have a telephone, won't you, Elaine? Well, there you are, Violet, your old father has had a few good ideas on the trot.'

'You're a genius,' said Violet, bestowing a warm smile on him but then turning back to Elaine with a pleading look on her face. 'Do you think that we could have a coming-out ball for me – just a small one?'

'Most of those town houses have folding doors between the drawing room and the dining room, dear,' said Great-Aunt Lizzie knowledgeably. 'You'd have enough room for twenty or more couples to stand up in the ones that I remember.'

'And Bateman will organize everything for you,' said the Earl.

'It will be wonderful to have dear Bateman, and a chauffeur and a car.' Elaine sounded as if great wealth had descended on her and her brother-in-law smiled benevolently on her as she got to her feet.

'You'll have to excuse me,' she said. 'I think I will retire early – after the journey . . .'

'Into darkest Kent,' put in Rose helpfully.

'I'll go up with you and see that you have everything you need,' said Violet. Her face was aglow with pleasure and her eyes shining with excitement.

Chapter Twenty-Two

❀

Money simplifies everything, thought Daisy. They had left Beech Grove Manor four days before. Daisy, accompanied by Elaine's maid and Maud, travelled by train and the others came up in the car, driven by Morgan. Bateman had found a lovely mews house in Mayfair and there was even a garage for the Humber with a bedroom over it where Morgan could sleep.

'All the other chauffeurs in Mayfair will laugh at your ancient car,' teased Daisy when he met them at the station.

'Then they'll show their ignorance,' said Morgan with a shrug. 'This is a good car – very comfortable.'

'That's true.' Daisy nodded. She had enjoyed the journey in the steam-puffing monster and felt that it was like the first step towards being an independent young lady, but there was no doubt that the Humber was a very comfortable car. It was nice sitting in the front seat with Morgan, who had fetched her from the station; Great-Aunt Lizzie would never allow them to do that, no matter how squashed they were in the back seat.

Poppy had claimed a bedroom at the side of the house, overlooking the busy main road, and had hung a sign on the door, much to Violet's disdain, saying: TWINS. KEEP OUT. Rose had a tiny room which she christened

THE BOUDOIR. Violet and Elaine had the only rooms with dressing rooms attached so it was settled that the two lady's maids should sleep there.

And the following morning the shopping began.

'Harrods, Morgan,' murmured Elaine as they trooped into the big car. Violet had decreed that the shabby tweed coats should be left in their bedrooms so they were cold until they stepped inside the hothouse atmosphere of the shop.

'It's like fairyland,' said Violet in a whisper, and Daisy suddenly felt very fond of her. The yearning, ecstatic look on Violet's face showed how deeply she had suffered when it had looked as though all of her dreams were doomed to die.

'Let's go to the children's department first. A nice soft wool coat with a velvet collar for you, Rose, I would think,' said Elaine decisively.

'I don't think I can carry all of these clothes,' said Rose after an hour had passed. She stared in a bewildered way. 'I feel like Sara Crewe at the beginning of *A Little Princess*, or else her doll,' she added.

'Wear the coat and that dress and the rest can be parcelled up and put in the car,' said Elaine. 'Now, Daisy, I think it's your turn. Violet, dear, we'll leave your things until after lunch. Morgan can take the other three girls home and you and I can have a wonderful afternoon.'

Sometimes in the course of the next few days, Daisy was reminded of the doll called Daisy and all her outfits. Elaine got such huge pleasure out of selecting clothes for the four girls and was tireless in pursuit of perfection. On one occasion, in Harrods, the saleswoman stared fixedly at Daisy for almost a minute before rushing off and returning with a single dress on a hanger.

'This is *parfait*,' she declared.

'Bet she's just pretending to be French,' muttered Rose, but Daisy only had eyes for the dress.

'Black!' exclaimed Elaine, looking doubtful. 'But she's only sixteen.'

'*Oh, mais Madame, mais Madame.*' The woman became even more French in her agitation. '*Le bon dieu* created *Mademoiselle* to wear black. Look at that hair, that skin!'

'I thought perhaps pink; I don't know what her father will say,' Elaine murmured weakly, but she smiled then, her blue eyes lighting up with admiration. 'It is gorgeous on you, Daisy. If you like it you may have it.'

Daisy looked at herself. The black brought out the blonde of her hair, made her skin look very white, her cheeks the palest pink, slimmed her slightly plump figure and made her cornflower blue eyes glow.

And it made her look incredibly poised and sophisticated.

'And this little cropped white linen jacket from Chanel,' murmured the saleswoman, slipping it over Daisy's shoulders and standing back to gauge the effect.

'She'll need a hat,' said Rose, looking with interest at her sister.

'Something girlish,' said Elaine nervously, but it was

she who, after scanning the shelves, came back with the perfect hat – more of a headband really, but with a beautiful coiled feather which would curl itself around Daisy's head and show up the blonde of her hair.

'*Parfait*,' said the sales assistant. 'Madame has such taste. *D'accord*, your daughter resembles you so much. You know what will suit her.'

'She's not her daughter,' said Rose.

'I should have said "sister",' said the woman rapidly.

'Wrong again,' said Rose cheerfully. 'She's her niece.'

'Rose!' said Elaine, looking most embarrassed, but Daisy was too occupied with looking at herself in the looking glass to scold Rose. I look perfect, she thought, and then she looked at the price on the hat and got a shock.

When the saleswoman went off to put away the discarded hats, Daisy tackled Elaine.

'I say, Elaine, that's an awful lot of money you are spending on me – and you've given us so much already. And then there are all Violet's clothes for her presentation and everything.'

Elaine looked surprised. 'I never think about the price of things when I am buying clothes.' Her voice was sincere and Daisy thought she would say no more. It must be nice to have always had money, she thought. And then she wondered whether money had made Elaine happy.

Next day, Elaine and Violet settled down with a pack of invitation cards and a list of caterers and the arrangements for the ball began. They were blind and deaf to anything else and only too happy for the other girls to amuse themselves. Poppy and Daisy came quickly to an agreement that Rose would accompany one or other of them on alternate days. So she went either to the music shops of Denmark Street – where Baz was liable to appear – or to the film studios of West London. Morgan was quite happy to trust to Daisy's godfather to look after the two girls, but informed her privately that he stuck like a limpet to Poppy and Baz.

'Some funny folk in the music scene,' he said with a grin. 'Not sure your father would think much of them, but I'll make sure they are safe.'

Eventually the great day of Violet's coming-out ball arrived. Daisy was the first to be ready and when she came downstairs she found Bateman reassuring Elaine.

'I wouldn't worry, my lady – everything will be fine. The hired staff are all very adequate – need telling, of course, but so far they've carried out their duties in a most satisfactory manner.' It had been a wonderful inspiration on the part of her father to have sent Bateman with them to London. Elaine was shy, diffident and wary of trusting her own judgement about anything other than clothes. Now, with Bateman in charge, she could concentrate on getting new outfits for the three girls and making sure that she and Violet would be splendidly dressed for the presentation to the King and Queen.

Daisy looked around the house with approval. It was such a change to live in a place where the curtains and carpets were new, the paintwork was shining, the pictures were light, fresh landscapes, not gloomy, smoke-smeared oil paintings, and the furniture shone with a high polish.

There were mirrors everywhere – every wall opposite a window was lined with them and they filled the house with light. Daisy looked at herself in one of them with satisfaction. She herself was as smart as the paintwork, she thought. Her hair was bobbed in the latest fashion and it swung around her neck, giving her head a lovely light feel. Her dress was incredible: closely fitting around the shoulders and then falling straight down to just above the knee in cascades of pale pink frills, set on a rich, deep pink background. Over it she wore the long rope of pearls given to her by her godfather and they added the perfect touch.

Daisy took a few experimental dance steps and watched how the dress shimmered and the colours blended as she moved. The dress was so short that for the first time in her life her legs, encased in white silk stockings, looked quite long. She pointed a toe and pirouetted and then came face to face with Justin, who had wandered out of the dining room and into the back hallway. He had been on business in London and was as much of a fixture in the house here as he had been at Beech Grove.

'You look like one of the flower fairies in my little niece's book,' he said with a grin.

'Your favourite reading material, of course.' Daisy wasn't going to admit to being embarrassed.

'That's right,' he said. 'I'm a great fan of the flower

fairies. I love the way that you can see them at the bottom of your garden when twilight comes, don't you?' His voice changed as he looked around. 'Where's Violet?' he asked.

'She'll be down in a moment.' Daisy studied him. He looked pale and his eyes were heavy as though he had a headache or something.

'Have you had a bad day looking for a job?' she asked. She herself had had a wonderful day with Sir Guy at his West London film studios. She had worn her latest outfit, a little close-fitting pink velvet hat and an elegantly cut, tan-coloured coat made from wool so fine that it clung to her figure like a silk dress. The young men in his studio had all been watching a film and shouting praise and criticism when they arrived, but they had fallen silent as she had stood in the light of the opened door.

However, what came next was even more satisfying as all these young men viewed her revised film, exclaiming, voicing comments and suggestions, and showing how they appreciated the artistic decisions involved in making cuts and re-jigging scenes from the original film. And eventually, prompted by Sir Guy, they had estimated its commercial worth as forty pounds – something that made Sir Guy exclaim that he would soon be bankrupt if this sort of extravagance went on.

Remembering the fun, she smiled involuntarily, but then frowned as she thought of how she had begged Elaine to ask the boys from the film studio to Violet's coming-out ball, but Elaine, usually so pliable, had refused.

'These are not the sort of young men that you ask to a dance, Daisy,' she had said, commenting, 'They are not our sort, dear,' and explaining that it might spoil Violet's chances if riff-raff were allowed to attend her coming-out ball.

However, she had acquiesced happily to Poppy's request to issue an invitation to Baz and his friends, who were all in London for the season. None of them were rich – all were younger sons – but all came from aristocratic families. Daisy eyed Poppy enviously as she came down the stairs and Justin gave a whistle of admiration, saying, 'I say, what a dress!'

'Pretty good, isn't it?' Poppy glanced over her shoulder at the tall looking glass. Her dress was of wine-coloured silk and Justin was right: it certainly looked spectacular with her mane of dark red hair.

'You must never cut your hair.' He seemed anxious to talk to Poppy now and not to resume his conversation with Daisy about getting a job.

'I certainly will!' declared Poppy. 'But we thought it might be best to do it one at a time in case Father dies of apoplexy. Daisy and I drew lots to see who would be first.'

'Hope you two silly girls don't try to persuade Violet to cut her beautiful hair. I don't know why women are bobbing their hair all over the place. Not a man that I know likes it.'

'Perhaps the girls do it to please themselves,' said Poppy coolly. 'Perhaps that is more important than trying to please men.'

'I'll go and fetch Violet,' said Daisy. A peep into the front hallway showed that the first guests had already arrived. Bateman was welcoming them and would take them into the long drawing room and introduce them to Elaine. Violet should be there – it was supposed to be her coming-out ball after all. Elaine had told Daisy and Poppy that they were to stay in the background and let Violet shine.

These first guests were a family party – a woman who had known Elaine in the days when Elaine and her younger sister had been debutantes together. She was accompanied by her son and her striking-looking daughter, who was sporting a haircut as short as any boy's. This must be the Eton crop, thought Daisy as she sped upstairs to fetch Violet, who was in her room, looking through copies of *The London Illustrated News* showing last week's debutantes arriving at the palace. Next week would be Violet's turn. Elaine had insisted on buying a new dress for the occasion. Full-skirted and slightly old-fashioned so as not alarm their majesties, the dress was hanging in the wardrobe, the regulation ostrich feathers placed on the top shelf, carefully wrapped in tissue paper.

'Are you ready, Vi? The guests are starting to arrive.'

Violet looked up at her and Daisy saw such a storm of emotion in her eyes that she sat down beside her and put an arm around her.

'I can't believe it's actually happening, Daisy – I never really believed it could. This is it – I have to be perfect or it will all be for nothing.'

Daisy squeezed her sister's shoulder. 'Well, you look perfect, so that's a jolly good start. Come on, let's go downstairs and you can see your dreams come true.'

Violet's dress for the ball was quite spectacular. It was made from emerald green silk, but the silk was barely visible because thousands of tiny blue feathers – just fluffy pieces of down – were sewn on to the fabric. The rich green-blue colour enhanced the intense blue of Violet's eyes. Daisy escorted her sister downstairs and enjoyed the effect that she made.

'Look at Justin. His eyes are standing out on stalks.' Daisy whispered the remark into Violet's ear when they reached the door of the long drawing room. Justin was standing in the background, but his eyes had widened at the sight of Violet.

And then everyone turned and saw Violet and gasped. Lord Elbury, heir to a dukedom, sprang forward and seized her by the hand, smiling down at her. Violet continued to hold his hand, but went from guest to guest welcoming them with smiles, and then went to stand beside her aunt who was dressed in pale yellow – Violet looking like a bird of paradise beside a pretty, though nervous, farmyard chicken.

And still Lord Elbury kept his place beside her, engaging her in conversation, laughing from time to time. Daisy stole a glance at Justin and saw that his eyes were full of sadness. When he saw her looking, he rapidly readjusted his features and turned away with an air of indifference and began to flirt with Violet's friend Marjorie.

How many people are really enjoying themselves? Daisy wondered as she looked around the room. The orchestra had struck up the first few notes – Poppy and Basil, now joined by George and Edwin, were openly laughing at the prim genteel sound they were making as they played an old-fashioned waltz, but the rest of the faces were serious. Violet floated in the arms of David the Heir. There was exactly the same smile on her beautiful face as when she danced with Lord Elbury, but she didn't look as she had on the night she had tangoed in the arms of Justin. Some of the girls were dancing, but most were standing by the side of the room, looking glumly certain that no one was going to ask them to dance. Young men were in short supply – even numbers of male and female had been asked, but the young men were obviously going to arrive late. Daisy looked at Elaine's worried face and felt sorry for her. She certainly didn't look as though she was enjoying herself. Many of the older women there had been older sisters or cousins of people she had known during her debut year, but they seemed to have little to say to her.

She moved a little nearer. Elaine was hesitantly smiling at the father of a girl of Violet's age, who was looking down at her with his eyeglass.

'We've never met,' he was saying, 'but I've heard of you, of course.'

And Elaine winced, then caught Daisy's eye and tried

to smile. There was some sort of mystery about Elaine; there was no doubt about that. This man seemed to be implying something as he peered at her through his eyeglass before letting it fall and shaking her hand with that look of curiosity still on his vacant-looking face.

Men! thought Daisy, feeling suddenly irritated. She marched down to the jazz band boys and Poppy. Simon was lost in an unhappy dream, staring moodily at Violet, his passion for her unabated, but the others were amusing themselves. Edwin was pretending to play a violin, Basil was at an imaginary piano, and George tapped daintily at an invisible tambourine.

'You're supposed to be dancing,' said Daisy crossly. 'Go on, Poppy, you can have one of them. The rest of you must go off and select some girl without a partner and ask her, very politely, to dance. If you don't do that, I shall personally see that you have a very poor supper and won't get asked again.'

'What's got into you?' Poppy raised her eyebrows in amazement, but grabbed Basil by the arm and steered him on to the floor. The other three boys gave Daisy an astonished look, but obediently crossed the dance floor, huddled together for reassurance, and appeared to be asking the nearest girls to dance.

Daisy looked over at Justin, who was still staring at Violet in the arms of David. She couldn't quite treat him the way she had treated the jazz band, and tell him to dance. But then she tilted her chin and thought, why not? This is the 1920s, not the Victorian era. Women have rights as well as men.

'Dance with me, Justin,' she said casually and took his hand.

He moved obediently after her and even smiled at her once they reached the dance floor. He opened his mouth – probably to talk about Violet, but Daisy was too quick for him.

'I'm a woman of means now, Justin,' she said as he swung her around.

That got his interest, she thought, but then he laughed.

'Got a rise in your pocket money?' he said teasingly.

'No,' she said smugly. 'I got paid for a job well done – just like you would get paid for defending a client in court.'

He was still smiling but he looked puzzled.

'Done a few successful burglaries, have you? Got yourself hired as an organizer of Debs' Events by Buckingham Palace?'

'No,' she said proudly. 'It's to do with my chosen profession: I sold a film that I made.'

He nodded infuriatingly. 'Sir Guy, I suppose,' he said. 'Wish I had a rich godfather.'

'It wasn't a present,' said Daisy. 'He showed the altered film to his team and asked them how much he should pay for it. He told them to forget that I had made it. Some of them said thirty-five pounds and some forty-five, but most said forty so he gave me forty pounds. What do you think of that?'

It had been a wonderful moment. She had still been

hesitant about taking it, but Sir Guy told her that he could get double that by the time he sold it to some cinemas.

'It's just the sort of thing that they are looking for in a "short",' he said. 'I'll sell that to perhaps five hundred cinemas – remember there are more than twenty million people visiting cinemas these days, so you can see why there's money in producing films.'

Daisy looked at Justin to see the effect on him of her words.

'Justin, did you hear me?' she asked impatiently.

He didn't answer. His eyes had gone to Violet again. The music was slowing and then stopped. Everyone clapped politely, Basil with exaggerated gentility, bringing his hands gently and slowly towards each other, but not allowing them to touch. He and Poppy went towards the champagne and the other three members of the jazz band joined them with evident relief. Most girls returned to their mothers or chaperones, who were sitting on small gilt chairs – perhaps the same chairs that had been hired for the ball at the Duchess's party – but Violet still kept a white-gloved hand tucked into David's arm.

Daisy glanced at Justin and saw the look of gloom intensified on his strong-featured face. He jutted out his chin and looked as if he were about to accost the two of them. It's not fair, thought Daisy. He can't ask her to marry him as he is a younger son with neither money nor a job, so he should really just leave her alone. If it had been up to her, she would have chosen Justin in preference to that slack-jawed David with his weak chin and his blonde hair slicked back from his narrow forehead, but she wasn't Violet. Violet was a romantic – she wanted to be a princess, not the wife of a younger son, or even of a busy barrister.

Annoyed with herself for mentioning her film, Daisy went across to the table, picked up two glasses of champagne and walked up to a fair-haired young man standing with what looked like his mother and sister. She gave him a bright smile and said with a fashionable drawl as she handed over the glass, 'Fizz! Don't you just love it!'

And then she smiled flirtatiously at him.

She was just about to ask him to dance – why not? she asked herself – when there was sharp ring at the hall door and one of the footmen beckoned to the butler. A moment later Bateman opened the door with a flourish.

And he was followed by one of the most devastatingly handsome men that Daisy had ever seen. He was dark-haired and dark-eyed, immensely tall with very broad shoulders – he had the build of an athlete and he was dressed in a splendid uniform of red and gold. Bateman marched straight up to Elaine and the crowd parted to allow the newcomer to follow him.

'His Excellency, Mr John Nelborough,' announced the butler, and Elaine, to Daisy's amazement, blushed like a sixteen-year-old, and came forward with both hands stretched out.

'Jack,' Elaine said. 'How on earth did you manage to get here on time?'

'Ship docked half an hour ago, got togged up on

board, sent my man with the luggage to The Ritz and came straight on here.' The mysterious stranger lifted both of Elaine's hands to his lips in a manner which Daisy thought to be rather dashing.

'Let's dance,' he said, and whispered in her ear. And Elaine, still blushing, went across to the orchestra and said something. The conductor lifted his baton and began to play 'Danube Waves' and the newcomer lifted his voice and began to sing almost as though he and Elaine were the only ones in the room:

'Let this be the anthem of our future years,

A few little smiles and a few little tears.'

And Elaine gazed up at him as if he were the answer to all her dreams.

'Excuse me,' said Daisy to the blond boy and made her way around the edge of the dancers until she reached the butler, who was watching Elaine and the mysterious stranger with an indulgent look in his eyes.

'Who's he, Bateman?' asked Daisy, noting with interest how Elaine almost lay back in the muscular arms of the new arrival.

'High Commissioner of the Indian Police, my lady,' said Bateman. He had a look of satisfaction on his elderly face and nodded gravely when Daisy said, 'He looks rather dashing.'

'Good voice, nice bass-baritone.' Poppy had appeared at her elbow with the jazz band boys in tow. They stared critically across at His Excellency, who was laughing as he sang: *'Tell me this is true romance.'*

'From India,' said Daisy with emphasis, but Poppy wasn't interested in that.

'Wonder how he would sound with a good jazz-band backing,' said Edwin.

'Like to hear him sing "Everybody Loves My Baby" with a voice like that,' said Baz. He hummed a few lines of the jazz tune in his half-broken adolescent voice.

'Any possibility of getting some decent music, Daise?' asked Simon.

'Wait until it's Poppy's coming-out dance,' said Daisy with a grin. 'Tonight is Violet's special night.' And Elaine's, she added silently to herself as she watched her aunt, looking as young as Violet, whirling around the room in the arms of her dashing suitor. 'Why are you standing around here? Ask Rose to dance,' she ordered Simon, and he saluted and went off.

No one asked Daisy for that dance, but she sipped her champagne and felt quite happy. She was interested in what was going on. Violet had at last given Justin a dance and he was holding her very close and murmuring in her ear. Daisy suddenly felt rather sorry for her. She thought of Poppy's revelation that Baz's grandfather had died and he had been left a London mews house. Did Justin have any wealthy relatives who would leave him a legacy – not just a house, but an income? Of course, sooner or later he would get a job as a lawyer, but she guessed that his family would put pressure on him to marry money. There were supposed to be lots of rich American girls in London whose wealthy fathers were on the lookout for

Englishmen of good family to marry their daughters.

And then the waltz finished. Elaine's eyes had gone to Daisy. She said something to her escort, standing prettily on tiptoe to whisper in his ear. He nodded and he too looked across at Daisy. He tucked Elaine's arm under his and strolled across the floor, smiling at her. He would be in his mid-thirties, she thought. He had an air of assurance and of authority that made him very attractive.

'Jack, may I introduce Daisy, my niece. Daisy, this is a friend from India, Mr Nelborough.'

'So you're one of the twins,' said Mr Nelborough casually as he moved Daisy around the dance floor in an expert manner. 'And that's the other twin, the girl with the magnificent hair, is that right? You're quite unalike, aren't you?'

'Yes, we are,' said Daisy. 'But after all, we are not identical twins so there's no reason why we should be any more alike than sisters: Elaine and my mother Mary were completely unalike – Mother was very like Poppy.' She eyed him sharply, wondering why Elaine, who had been so well schooled in etiquette by her Aunt Lizzie, had asked him to dance with Daisy rather than with the eldest of the family, Violet.

'Why did you come over to England?' she asked casually. He was a wonderful dancer, she thought. It was quite an exciting experience to be whirled around by him.

'Well, I had a bit of leave coming and a friend of mine – an equerry at Buckingham Palace – got me a pair of tickets for the royal wedding so I thought of Elaine.'

He spoke her name lovingly and tenderly and his eyes wandered in her direction before they looked back again at Daisy. 'What was I saying?' he enquired.

'The royal wedding,' prompted Daisy. Everyone in London was agog at the prospect of the ceremony at Westminster Abbey between Prince Albert and Elizabeth Bowes-Lyon. Rose was already an authority on anything to do with it.

'Oh yes, of course. Well, I thought Elaine would love it – she's very romantic. So I hopped on a ship and came over to have a little holiday. I thought she might like an escort around London, that sort of thing, you know.'

'I'm sure she'd love that,' Daisy said sincerely.

'It's a lovely surprise to see her four nieces – like sisters to her. I never expected to meet you all.' He smiled down at her. He really was incredibly handsome and charming, she thought.

Chapter Twenty-Three

❀

'You can't believe what a crush there was. We were all queuing up in this long corridor, about a hundred debutantes and their presenters with them – and it was just so hot and I kept thinking that I could smell these ostrich feathers that we were all wearing and I thought that I would faint. And then the girl ahead of me made a mess of her curtsy. She wobbled terribly when she tried to stand up and she almost over-balanced. And I was shaking with nerves when my turn came.'

'But you didn't overbalance – I bet you were the best of them all,' said Daisy. Violet would have risen to the occasion, she knew – even this morning she was still floating on a wave of joy and excitement.

'Was Prince George there?' asked Rose.

'No, just ladies-in-waiting – that sort of thing.' Judging by Rose's annoyed face, Violet was not making a good story out of it – not enough to satisfy her anyway. Rose was already well into a novel called *The Girl Who Married the Future King*.

'What were you all saying to each other?' she urged, pencil at the ready.

'Nothing really,' said Violet vaguely. 'We were too nervous. It was just so exciting.'

'Start from the beginning and tell it properly,' said Rose firmly.

Violet sighed. 'Well, we went in that hired Daimler. Wish we had gone with Morgan – he probably would have found a short cut. It took us about an hour to go down The Mall, everything was queuing from start to finish – we even queued at the railings outside Buckingham Palace. At last we were inside, and there we were in a brightly lit crowded corridor, everyone had bare shoulders because we had to leave our wraps behind, and there was a funny smell from all these ancient ostrich feathers, and we all went up the grand staircase, and past those Carrara marble statues.

'Was the balustrade made from gold?' asked Rose, scribbling frantically.

'No, bronze, I think,' said Violet vaguely. And then she took pity on her youngest sister and told her all about the red carpet and the soldiers, members of His Majesty's Body Guard of the Honourable Corps of Gentlemen at Arms with their plumed helmets and heavy gold epaulettes. 'And they had these pointy things in their hands,' she finished.

'Medieval halberds, held ready to root out the traitors in the crowd,' put in Rose, turning to a new page.

'I had to pinch myself when we got to the antechamber, the ball supper room,' admitted Violet. 'I kept saying to myself, "In another minute I will be presented." But of course we sat there for hours, or it seemed like it.'

'What were you sitting on?' asked Rose eagerly.

'These gilt chairs – like the ones that are hired for dances,' said Violet. 'We sat in rows on stiff gilt chairs for what seemed hours.'

'And then?'

'And then Marjorie and I were discussing her house party and she was telling me all about who was going to be invited and how *Tatler* were sending down a reporter as well as a photographer . . .'

'I wish you'd tell me more about the palace,' complained Rose. 'You and Marjorie are always chatting about parties. What happened next?'

'And then it was my turn. Well, I've told you all about that – you have enough to make up a story. I must go and get ready. I'm having lunch with Marjorie and some of the other girls so I must fly.'

'Don't worry, Rose, you'll make a much better story out of it – Violet has no imagination,' said Daisy.

Chapter Twenty-Four

'Doorbell – someone for me!' called Violet, running down the stairs. She was revelling in her status of being, according to *The London Illustrated News*, one of the most popular debutantes of the year. She was already dressed in a stylish purple overcoat, knee-length with four prominent buttons and a velvet-lined stand-up collar. The style suited her slim figure and brought out the intense colour of her eyes.

The housemaid was already on her way to the door and Violet waited on the last step, smiling broadly at the sight of a chauffeur on the doorstep. He touched his cap deferentially.

'Lady Giselle is waiting in the car for her ladyship,' he said politely.

'I'm off, girls – be good,' said Violet gaily. 'Where's Elaine? Oh, of course, she has taken Rose to see *Peter Pan*, hasn't she?'

And then she was off, high heels tapping down the steps, and the parlour maid closed the door behind her.

'Well, I'm off to see—' began Poppy, but Daisy interrupted her.

'Poppy, will you come somewhere with me?' she asked. 'I'd really like you to come,' she added.

'Sure. Where do you want to go?'

'Just down the Strand,' said Daisy. 'Let's get our coats.' But then she hesitated. This concerned Poppy as well as herself. She had to talk to her first. 'Come into the morning room for a moment,' she said. 'I want to tell you something.'

The morning room was a cheerful place, facing south so that the spring sunshine poured through the windows, and with a bright coal fire burning in the well-swept grate. Daisy sat down on the easy chair beside it and held her hands out to the flames. Her thoughts were so complicated that she found it hard to disentangle them. She looked across at Poppy, that face so familiar. It was so unlike her own and yet the bond was so strong that it almost seemed as though the girl opposite her was part of her own body.

'Poppy,' she said. 'I don't think I am your twin after all.'

'What!' Poppy stared at her. She began to laugh. 'You're thinking of that old nurse, aren't you? The one that kept going on about how small you were. Well, it's not possible, you know. You'll have to get Rose to tell you the facts of life. You're either my twin or you would have to be about a year younger.'

'Not . . .' said Daisy, hearing her own voice as if it were the voice of a stranger, '. . . not if we had different mothers.'

There was a long silence then. Poppy's face had gone white. She stared across at Daisy. 'What do you mean?' she asked eventually.

'It's like a jigsaw,' said Daisy dully. 'You know the way you get all sorts of pieces that are obvious-looking and yet they don't make sense until eventually one tiny, little, almost meaningless piece suddenly makes everything else fit together? Well, it's been like that with me.'

'What little piece?' Poppy tried to smile, but her mouth trembled. Daisy felt tears blur the face opposite her. She pulled the backs of her hands across her eyes, blinked twice, bit her lip and began to speak as resolutely and calmly as she could.

'I suppose the letter was the first clue,' she said bravely. 'We got distracted by Maud and her tragic story, but of course that letter could be nothing to do with her. She was born in 1909. The child of the woman who wrote that letter was born in the last months of 1906 – the year when we were born. So who wrote it? And then came the mystery of Elaine. Why did she suddenly disappear – in the middle of her season – aged only seventeen? Why did she suddenly go out to India? And then there was the finding of the photograph, you in the arms of Mo – I mean of Mary Derrington, but not me. And then the other photograph – one bouncing, well-grown baby and one tiny one – and then there was the nanny at the Duchess's place.' Daisy began to laugh, gulped a few times, took a deep breath and quoted: 'Very backward – a three-month-old baby, looking like a six-week-old one.'

'There could be a perfectly simple explanation . . .' began Poppy, but Daisy interrupted her.

'Don't think that I haven't said all this to myself,'

she went on, half laughing, half crying. 'But there's the way that Elaine looks at me, especially when she thinks nobody is looking – the way that doll was called Daisy and then, the other night, when she brought His Excellency from India over, I could see her watching me the whole time. She didn't bring him to Violet, or to you; she wanted him to dance with me, she wanted to see how we got on – funnily enough, that seemed to make everything real to me.'

'What are you going to do? Can't you just forget about it?'

'I think I have to know so I am going to go down to Somerset House. Maud found her birth certificate there and if I am your twin, mine will be there too. Justin told me that twins have separate birth certificates. It proves which is the elder twin in the case of inheritance. Will you come with me, Pops?'

'Of course I will,' said Poppy. She held out her hand, hooked Daisy's little finger with her own and said, 'Twin power.' Then she went to the door: 'I'll get Morgan to drive us,' she said. 'You look very white. I might be the bigger twin, but I don't fancy carrying you down the Strand. We'll get him to wait by the Embankment and then we can just walk up to Somerset House. I'll make up an excuse – I'll say that Sir Guy asked you to plan something that could be filmed on the Embankment and by the river. He'll be quite happy sitting in the car and reading one of his magazines.'

*

Once inside the cool, dim depths of Somerset House, Daisy felt better. As she and Poppy walked up from the Embankment she had planned what she was going to say.

'My sister and I are twins,' she said, smiling at the clerk behind the counter. 'Our father, Michael, Earl of Derrington, has forgotten which of us was born first. To settle an argument, could we have a look at our birth certificates?' She gave both names, the place of birth, the names and titles of Michael and his wife, and then waited calmly. The clerk looked puzzled, but he was quite a young man and she could see him deciding that he didn't want to cross-question the daughter of an earl. After a minute he disappeared.

It seemed to Daisy he was away a long time. Poppy was looking worried. A few times she opened her mouth to say something and then shut it. Daisy was grateful to her. She knew that she was past speaking. In another moment, either she would be completely reassured, or else her life would have been turned upside down.

And then the clerk was back. And in his hand was just one piece of paper.

'I'm sorry that I have been so long,' he said, looking rather bewildered. 'There's some sort of mix-up, I'm afraid. I can only find one birth on that date and in that place. I've looked at the days before and the days after and there is nothing else. Here it is. Father: Major Lord Derrington; Mother: Lady Mary Derrington née Carruthers.' He held out the certificate.

The name of the only baby born to the couple on 11 October 1906 was Poppy Mary Derrington.

Daisy felt strangely calm as she walked down towards the car. She would get in the car, she planned, allow Poppy to cross-question Morgan about his music magazine, sit quietly there, and when they arrived home she would go up to the bedroom, lie on the bed and have a sleep.

And after dinner she would talk to Elaine.

And then something occurred to her. She stopped suddenly. 'Poppy,' she said in an undertone, 'I've thought of something else. I know who my father was.' She felt a cold, shivering feeling come over her, and then Poppy linked arms and dragged her across the wet grass. There was a seat there with a large plane tree behind it and in front of it a straggling bush. Daisy sat down and felt Poppy's arm across her shoulders. She took a deep breath and was glad to hear that her voice sounded fairly normal.

'Poppy, do you remember when we were having the drag hunt and Violet was teasing Justin about being afraid to jump the hedge?'

Poppy shook her head. She wore a look of concern that touched Daisy. It was not often that Poppy worried about anything other than her music.

'You were with Baz, I think. But anyway, Justin shouted at Violet. He said something about his Uncle Clifford being killed jumping a hedge and that he was about five years old at the time – on his first pony. But this is the important thing. Clifford Pennington was seventeen and the year was 1906.'

Poppy stared at Daisy. 'The letter,' she breathed.

Daisy nodded. 'That's what I was thinking. It was dated in the spring of 1906. And you remember what it said: *They can't say we're too young now.*'

Tears flooded her eyes and she put her head in her hands.

'Oh, Poppy,' she sobbed. 'They were my parents. And they were not much older than I am now. What must she have felt like when she heard of his death?'

'Don't cry, don't cry,' said Poppy. She had her arm around Daisy and with her other hand pressed her sister's head against her shoulder. 'Don't cry,' she begged and her voice broke.

'I have to,' sobbed Daisy, and Poppy said no more, just sat on the bench beside her and kept her arms tightly around her until the sobs began to slow. Then she hooked her little finger inside Daisy's and said: 'We'll get through this together. And don't start going on about not being my twin; I've thought about it in Somerset House and decided that we'll always be twins.'

Somehow that made Daisy feel worse. She broke into a loud wail that surprised even herself. Poppy held her tightly and said nothing this time, just allowed the wail to continue. And then footsteps sounded on the nearby path and before they could escape a man's voice was saying in alarmed tones, 'Is someone hurt?' and Morgan appeared in front of them.

'Oh, Bob. She's so upset,' said Poppy.

Morgan was much more than a chauffeur – he was a friend. By now he was kneeling on the ground in front of them. He took Daisy's hand and said in a comforting voice, 'Now, what's the trouble?'

Daisy shook her head. It was impossible for her to stop crying. She didn't want him to go away though. Somehow it was very comforting to have her hand held in that large, firm grip.

'It's a secret, but—' began Poppy and he interrupted her. 'Then don't tell me it,' he said firmly. 'Old buried secrets should be kept buried. Sometimes it does no good to dig them up.' He gave Daisy's hand a comforting little squeeze. 'You're a brave girl,' he said unexpectedly. 'You take the world on your shoulders too much though. Now dry your eyes and come down to the car. We'll go for a drive along the river and I'll show you all the sights – Tower of London and everything.'

For the whole of the drive down by the river he chatted like a tour guide, pointing out sights on river and land that neither girl looked at, but gradually Daisy began to feel better. I've known for a long time, she thought. I think I guessed when I saw the doll. I was just keeping it buried inside me. Perhaps Morgan is right. Perhaps it should have stayed buried. But then I don't think that I could be like that. I'll talk to Elaine tonight – she still could not really think of her as her mother – I'll talk to her and then I'll just leave it. Father – at least Michael Derrington, she amended – he knows the truth and of course so does Great-Aunt Lizzie, and I wouldn't be surprised if Bateman and Mrs Pearson and Mrs Beaton all know it too.

Everything worked out well for the conversation that evening. It was one of the few nights when Violet was not going to a ball so she took herself off to bed early with a copy of every magazine in the house tucked under her arm. Rose was in the throes of writing a play so she disappeared with a large notebook and Poppy gave a few exaggerated yawns and then she went off too. Only Daisy and Elaine were left beside the fire.

Now that the moment had come, Daisy did not quite know how to start. It was all so difficult, she thought, and then she wondered how she would film the scene. In the end she said simply and quietly, 'I went to Somerset House today and I tried to get my birth certificate. They didn't have one for me – just one for Poppy. I'm your daughter, am I not?'

'Who told you?' Elaine's face flushed up angrily. And then she added defensively, 'I was going to tell you as soon as I found the right moment.'

'Yes,' said Daisy. 'I suppose you were.' But it was easier to go on buying clothes and chattering about dances, she thought silently. 'Nobody told me,' she added. 'I just guessed. I found a letter that you wrote – I found it in the stables.' She stopped and then said, 'Tell me about my father.'

Deliberately she did not look at Elaine, though she

was sure that she heard a sharp intake of breath or even a stifled sob. Resolutely she suppressed the pity, resolutely she stopped herself saying *Never mind, let's talk about Violet's season.* I have a right to know, she said silently.

After a moment's silence Elaine said in a wavering tone, 'Michael—' There was a question in her voice.

Daisy interrupted her impatiently. 'Was it Clifford Pennington?' She took from the pocket of her skirt the weather-stained envelope with its sheet of paper inside.

From the corner of her eye, she saw Elaine take it out and read it through, and then – before Daisy could stop her – she threw it on the fire. For a moment they both watched it ignite, blacken, curl and fall away in tiny specks of grey ash.

'He was killed the day I wrote that.' Elaine's voice was bleak and hard.

'What did you do?'

'Waited, hoped, feared, despaired . . . and then one day I saw Mrs Beaton look at me oddly and I realized that I had begun to show. I could wait no longer then, so I confessed it all to Aunt Lizzie. It was either that or drown myself in the lake. I suppose I lacked courage for that.'

Daisy thought about it. Elaine had not been much older than herself. If that happened to me, would I have considered suicide? she wondered, and knew that she would not. I would have gone to London, she thought but did not say.

'You were an heiress though, weren't you? You would have had plenty to live on.'

'Not until I was twenty-one. Aunt Lizzie was my guardian – Aunt Lizzie and some law firm in the city – but they did everything that she told them to do.' Elaine paused for a moment as if expecting Daisy to say something, then continued, 'She made all the arrangements. Mary was expecting a baby. It was Aunt Lizzie's idea to tell everyone that Mary was expecting twins. She took me out to India – supposedly on a holiday as I was tired after all the balls I had been going to. She took a house up in the hills – there was plenty of money – engaged a midwife and a wet nurse, and a few weeks after you were born, you were taken down to Mary and Michael and I was married within three months. Aunt Lizzie thought an older man would be good for me and would steady me.'

'But you named me first before you handed me over.' Daisy turned to look into her mother's face.

'How did you know that?' For the first time Elaine smiled slightly.

'Your doll was called Daisy. I found it under the floorboards. I've got it safe for you.'

Daisy got to her feet. She should kiss Elaine; she knew that. But somehow she could not. 'I'd better go,' she said lightly. 'Poppy will moan if I wake her up and she did look very sleepy, didn't she?'

Poppy was in her nightdress with her hair braided in one long plait, but she was not in bed when Daisy opened the door. She had a bottle in her hand and was pouring some sherry into two small glasses.

'I brought up the biscuit barrel too,' she said. 'It's nice to be living in the land of plenty. Now drink down that sherry. There's plenty more in the bottle and I'll replace it before anyone sees it.'

Daisy tilted the glass and felt the warmth run down her throat and into her stomach. She took a bite of a chocolate biscuit and then had another swallow. She smiled at Poppy. 'You're a genius,' she said.

'Tell me all about it,' said Poppy, tossing back the contents of her glass.

Daisy shrugged. 'Not much to tell, really,' she said. She was determined not to cry. 'It was a Romeo and Juliet story, except that this Juliet gave in to her family. She did what Great-Aunt Lizzie told her – gave up her baby and never bothered to try to see her again. And married a rich Anglo-Indian Great-Aunt Lizzie picked out for her, of course, just to give herself the final touch of respectability. I don't think she cared too much about me. Anyway, let's not think about the past. Let's make the most of our visit to London. What does Baz think about the chances of a jazz club doing well?'

Chapter Twenty-Five

The weeks are just flying by, thought Daisy as she and Poppy relaxed by the cosy fire in the morning room. Violet was back from her weekend at the house party, but had given them very little detail about it. Poppy and Rose were due to go back to Beech Grove Manor the following day, but Elaine had begged for Daisy to stay until the end of the month when the house lease would be finished, saying that she would be company for her as Violet was out for most of the day and almost every evening. Daisy was pleased to stay on – she had fallen into the pleasant habit of spending a few hours every day at Sir Guy's studios and knew that she was learning a huge amount about how to make films. She was thinking now about what Sir Guy had said to her yesterday, when there was a sound of running footsteps on the stairs outside and Rose came in clutching her large notebook.

'Want to read something?' Rose's voice was casual, but it did not deceive her sisters. Daisy buried her head in a book that Sir Guy had given her and Poppy hurriedly picked up *Tatler* magazine.

'I say, Rose,' she said, holding it out. 'Do you want to read this? Violet's in this one three times! "*The lovely Lady Violet Derrington looked exquisite in a robe of shimmering satin.*" And there's more. Loads of pictures of the house party at Marjorie's place – most of them of Prince George, of course. Vi only gets a look-in because she was dancing a lot with him, and she had supper with him.'

'I've seen it,' said Rose. 'But do you want to read my story?'

'How long?' asked Poppy with a yawn.

'Forty pages,' said Rose proudly.

'Forty pages!' Poppy was horrified. 'I'm a slow reader – give it to Daisy. Anyway,' she continued, glancing up at the pretty clock on the mantelpiece, 'I must go – meeting Baz. It's his last day of freedom too.'

'Don't *you* want to read my story, Daisy?' pleaded Rose. Daisy stretched out a reluctant hand but then said, 'On second thoughts, why don't you read it to me?' The fire was warm, the room was cosy and she could sit looking into the glowing coals, thinking her thoughts, while Rose read her latest story to her – inspired by Violet, guessed Daisy, as she listened to the sentimental love scenes. It had what Rose said triumphantly was a lovely romantic ending where the poor girl gave up the heir to the throne, telling him that he had to marry a princess.

Violet herself came into the room just as Rose said dramatically, '*and the waves breaking on the shore seemed to her to be the very sound of her breaking heart.*'

'Oh, Rose,' shouted Poppy from the hallway, 'Morgan says that it would be nice if you came too, and Maud, and if you do, he's going to take us to a lunchtime jazz club. Do come. Morgan says that I can't be the only girl, but it would be all right if I have a maid and my sister to chaperone me. He's so old-fashioned,' she added with a giggle.

Rose was out of her chair in a flash, dropping the notebook on the rug as she went flying upstairs, shouting for Maud at the top of her voice. Daisy listened until the slam of the front door and the clatter of footsteps on the steps outside had died away. Then she leaned forward, picked up the notebook and put it on the small low table by the chair, arranging it tidily with its edges square to the outside rim of the table. Only then did she say, with a half-smile, 'So you've turned down a prince.'

'He just wanted to have fun,' said Violet indifferently. 'It was a lovely house party though.'

Daisy said nothing. Violet was temperamental these days, one minute snubbing her younger sisters and telling them that they were just children, and the next minute reacting bad-temperedly to any joke. She seemed to want to talk now, though, and Daisy prepared to listen.

Slowly and dreamily Violet went through her weekend: the arrival at Marjorie's place, the names on the bedrooms, everyone's titles carefully written up, the elaborate dinner on the first night and the moonlit walk afterwards.

'They have an old abbey attached to the house,' she said. 'It's just a ruin. But Prince George said that he could not wait until daylight to explore it. And of course everyone was keen. We all had plenty of champagne – and you know how you feel after that.' Daisy said nothing but continued looking into the fire.

'I'm having such fun with my season,' went on Violet. 'Oh, I hope and hope that Elaine doesn't go back to India. I want you and Poppy to have the same fun that I'm having – you could come out next year. People whose birthdays are in the autumn usually come out when they are seventeen.'

'Tell me about the moonlit walk,' said Daisy, and Violet laughed softly.

'You can imagine what it was like. We were all rushing upstairs to put on something warm and Marjorie's mother was fussing a little but no one took any notice. And, of course, it was Prince George who wanted to do it, so she didn't dare say no. I was so thankful that Elaine bought me that fur wrap – so much more romantic than that awful tweed coat.'

Violet stopped and shuddered slightly as if at the thought of their past poverty-stricken wardrobes.

'It's beautiful, the abbey,' she went on dreamily. 'You just can't imagine what it's like. There was a big window – the eastern window – over the place where the altar used to be. No glass in it, of course, but those soaring pointed arches, and the moonlight making the stone seem so dazzlingly white, and the dark trees on the hill beyond showing through it – just as if the window framed the picture.'

It *was* romantic, thought Daisy, feeling a little envious of her sister. She had something that she had to tell Violet, but she would wait for a while, for the right moment.

'Any ghosts?' she asked lightly.

Violet didn't answer that for a while.

'It must be a strange thing to grow up being a prince,' she said after a moment. 'Everyone is so deferential to you – even Marjorie's people, who are very grand. Her mother looks as though she would happily throw herself on the ground and be trampled by Prince George – and he's only twenty-one years old.

'So when the Prince and I wandered out of the church and into the cloisters, no one followed us, no one shouted out teasing remarks the way that they were doing with Marjorie and Brian when they slipped upstairs to the old ruined dormitories. There were about thirty of us there that night, you know, and yet nobody came too near us, nobody joked with us, the way that they were joking with each other, laughing and calling out when someone put an arm around a girl.'

'So you wandered in the moonlit cloisters with Prince George,' commented Daisy. 'I'm not surprised that Rose found that romantic.'

Violet smiled a little. 'I made up a nice ending for her. You know – about honour and duty and all that sort of thing.'

'What did happen?' asked Daisy, looking closely at her sister.

'Nothing really,' said Violet with indifference. 'We were pacing the cloisters all by ourselves. He had his arm around me. I didn't mind that – I was a bit flattered, to be honest. And then all of a sudden he gave this stupid artificial jump and said in a sort of idiotic squeal, 'A ghost!'

and then he grabbed me in his arms, really crushing my dress, and tried to kiss me, and . . . well, you can guess . . . And I didn't particularly like him doing that so I just pulled away and said, "No, Your Highness; that was just a rat."' Violet giggled. 'You should have seen the jump he gave that time! It was a real genuine jump. He let go of me and started to look all around and I just slipped back into the abbey church again.'

'And that was the end of that,' said Daisy regretfully. 'I wonder if Prince Albert did that sort of thing to win Lady Elizabeth.'

'Well, she turned him down three times before she accepted him,' said Violet with a nervous laugh. 'And that's not all. I kept away from Prince George the next day, but then David started haunting me. Even at breakfast time he was pestering me for loads of dances. I gave them to him, because I was pretty sure that Prince George wouldn't ask me but the others might think that I was booked by him. I didn't want to be a wallflower.'

'So you danced with David. Don't tell me that he tried something on – you didn't go out into the cloisters with him, did you?'

'No, it was raining,' said Violet with another giggle. 'But we found a little nook among the potted palms and –' she faced her sister – 'he asked me to marry him.'

'Goodness,' said Daisy. 'You have had a busy weekend! What romance!' She felt rather envious. Prince George paying marked attentions and then a proposal from David the Heir.

'The proposal wasn't actually that romantic,' said Violet after a minute. 'He was so keen to tell me about what his father "would do for him", as he put it – all about him having the Barrington estate, and what the house there was like, and the revenues, and that when the first child was born some other estate would be added. You won't believe this, but he actually asked his father if he could marry me before he even proposed.'

'And what did his father say?' Daisy bit back a smile. It was a pity that David had not kept his mouth shut about asking permission of his father but had to blurt it out to a romantic girl like Violet.

'Apparently he said, "*Gel's got good blood, good family; the Derringtons have a good name; no money of course, but that's not a problem with us, my boy.*"' Violet spoke in an exaggerated imitation of an upper-crust accent.

'What did you say? Did you say "yes" straight off or . . . ?'

'I said I would have to think about it,' said Violet eventually.

'And now you've thought about it, you don't really want to do it,' said Daisy with a sigh. So much for all the planning, she thought. So much for the dreams of ending their poverty. Elaine, she guessed, would go back to India at the end of the month – once Jack went she would have no particular friends to keep her in London – and Beech Grove Manor would return to normal.

'Well, he's nice, but he's – well, he's not very entertaining, is he?' said Violet in a complaining tone of voice. 'It's a funny thing, but even as he was proposing I suddenly thought of the night when we made that Spanish omelette and ate it on the kitchen table, and I was thinking that I might never have that sort of fun again if I married David. He's a bit strait-laced, a bit old-fashioned, and his mother . . .' Violet shuddered.

And then when Daisy said nothing, she said crossly, 'Well, all right, I'll marry him if you want me to.'

'No,' said Daisy, and she was pleased to hear how strong and positive her voice sounded. 'No, don't do that. Marriage is for life and you're only eighteen. I don't think you should marry anyone you can't visualize liking when you're about sixty.'

'Sixty might be all right,' said Violet with a slight giggle. 'It's just the years between then and now that are the problem. But if I don't marry him, who shall I marry? He's the only offer I've had so far.'

'There's another possibility,' said Daisy hesitantly. 'I wasn't going to tell you for a while – Sir Guy thought that I should wait until it was more certain – but a man from Hollywood has bought that film *Murder in the Dark* and he would like to meet you, would like you to do some tests . . .'

'Me!' Violet went white.

'It's not definite yet,' warned Daisy. 'But . . .'

'Mr Justin Pennington,' said Bateman, opening the door with a flourish and ushering Justin in as if he were one of the royal princes.

'I say, girls, you'll never guess! I've got a job!'

Justin was blazing with excitement.

'Oh, Justin, how wonderful!' Daisy came forward and gave him her hand, but he grabbed her and hugged her exuberantly and then before she could object he hugged Violet too.

'Five hundred pounds a year,' he said. 'That's what they are paying me. What do you think of that? Five hundred! It was that fellow who was at the Duchess's house party – you remember him – he was there – one of the directors – well, that's one in the eye for my father. He kept scolding me about wasting my time socializing when I should be looking for work. This fellow remembered me as soon as I came into the room and he told the others that I was a smart young fellow and then they all had to smile and make polite remarks. I knew things were going well once the interview started. They were all leaning forward and nodding their heads. I even made a few witty remarks, and as soon as I heard the first laugh, I knew it was in the bag.'

'Oh, Justin! A job! Real money!' said Violet with rapture.

'You'll be able to get yourself lodgings now.' Daisy could hear the envy in her voice.

'I'm thinking of getting myself a house,' said Justin with his haughty air. 'Fellow I know swears that it's better in the end than going into digs and having landladies cheating you. Just one servant to start with – fellow I know says that you can always hire extra servants when you're throwing parties and that sort of thing.'

'Parties!' said Violet ecstatically. 'Oh, Justin, will you invite me?'

'You'll be the hostess,' said Justin. His tone was light-hearted but there was a gleam in his dark eyes and Violet looked at the carpet. After a slightly awkward pause, Justin produced a newspaper from his pocket. 'I say, you wouldn't come with me to have a look at a few houses, would you?' he asked, aiming his question at a midpoint between the two girls. 'My father promised me a couple of hundred pounds to set myself up "like a gentleman" – those were his very words – as soon as I got a job in a law firm. Even he is going to be impressed by five hundred pounds a year. Wait ... till ... he ... hears!' Justin spaced his words emphatically and gave a whistle.

'I'm sorry, Justin, I have some letters to write,' said Daisy.

'Violet, will you come and help me in my quest?' Justin was saying. 'Oh, dear, dear Violet, take pity on a poor fellow. How can I inspect kitchens and ... what is it that this advertisement says?' He inspected the newspaper. 'Oh yes, "the usual offices". How can I inspect "the usual offices" without a knowledgeable person by my side?'

Daisy heaved a sigh when they had gone out. Somehow she felt rather lonely. Poppy and Rose would be having a wonderful time at the jazz-club lunch – she could just imagine the fun and the jokes. Violet and Justin – well, that would be fun too. She wondered whether to go to the studios, but she had told Sir Guy that she would not come today as it was going to be Poppy's last day in

London. She would miss Poppy and Rose, she thought, and Violet had so many friends in London. The phone rang continually and the mantelpiece was covered with invitation cards.

In any case, the atmosphere at the studio had changed. She was now extremely sorry that she had mentioned to Sir Guy that Harry had asked her out to lunch. Her godfather had been quite shocked, in his old-fashioned way, and told her that her father would be most upset if she were allowed to go out with the young men who worked at the studio. 'Nice lads,' he had said dismissively, 'but not what your father would want for you.' And he had added that when she had her season the following year she would have plenty of young men running after her. 'I'm responsible to your father for you, you know.'

Daisy suspected that he had spoken to his workers because they had all been rather stiff with her the next day. Fred, in particular, had hardly looked at her since, though he had been very friendly and helpful to Rose, teaching her how to letter title cards when Daisy had brought her there for a morning.

And then she heard the front door open. For a moment she thought that Justin and Violet had returned, but there was no sound of voices, just a few light footsteps in the hallway, and then the door to the morning room opened and Elaine came in. Her face lit up when she saw Daisy and she immediately shed her coat on to a chair and came over and sat on the armchair opposite. She said nothing, but looked affectionately at her.

'That was a short lunch,' said Daisy after a minute.

'Was it?' Elaine had a bewildered, slightly delirious air about her. 'Well, I rushed back. I hoped you would be here. I need to talk to you. I hoped I would find you by yourself. I must talk to you.' The short sentences poured out from her almost in a series of gasps. Daisy smiled invitingly. She had begun to guess what had happened.

'Jack has asked me to marry him,' said Elaine in almost a whisper.

Daisy got up and kissed her, giving a warm hug before she returned to her own chair. 'Now that's a surprise,' she teased. 'What kept him so long?'

Elaine smiled a little. 'He has been mentioning it,' she admitted, 'but I've always put him off. You see, I couldn't – I couldn't agree to marry him without telling him the truth.'

Daisy's smile died away. She sat up very straight. She was not sure that she wanted Jack to know the truth about her parentage.

'And then today, after lunch, I finally got up courage. We went for a walk in Green Park. It was cold, but very nice.' She smiled to herself. 'We were walking along, arm in arm, and he just said, "I don't know what I'll do unless you promise to marry me!" and then I told him the truth about myself and about you. And do you know what he said?'

Daisy shook her head. No words were needed.

'He said that he wanted you to come back to India with us. You'll be a bridesmaid at our wedding and you will live with us until you get married yourself. Oh darling, you would have the most wonderful time. India is the most beautiful place and you'll find it's full of handsome young men. You will have a wonderful, wonderful, wonderful time. It will be so lovely for me to have you with me at last. And Jack is so fond of you too. He says that you are the most sensible of all the girls. Oh, and darling, you will have everything that you want. Between Jack's salary and my money and the money that my husband left me – well, this sounds a little vulgar, but we will be extremely rich. You can have everything that your heart desires – your own little car, clothes, furs, whatever you want. There's just one thing though. Jack wants me, and you, to go back with him next week instead of waiting until the end of the month. But don't worry, he's promised to escort us to Paris for a few days' shopping before we go.'

Chapter Twenty-Six

Daisy was already coming down the stairs for dinner by the time that Justin, Violet, Poppy and Rose all came through the hall door in an exuberant cluster. She was glad to see them. She had asked for a little time to think matters over and the thought of Elaine waiting in the morning room made her thankful to see the noisy crowd.

'We've had the most wonderful day,' shouted Poppy when she saw Daisy. 'We heard King Oliver and his Creole Band. They were playing a tune called "London Café Blues". It was sen-sa-tion-al!' Poppy looked as if she would fly with excitement. She grabbed Rose's hands and danced around the hall.

'Sensational! You don't know the meaning of the word, young Poppy!' Justin tried to make his voice sound superior and elder-brotherly, but his eyes were blazing with triumph.

'Shh,' said Violet, but she too couldn't suppress her excitement. She dragged him into the morning room, putting her hand over his mouth to stop him speaking. Poppy and Daisy exchanged knowing smiles and followed them, Rose sliding in behind.

Elaine looked up from her happy dream when they came in. 'Has Daisy told you my news?' she asked with a smile. 'I'm getting married to Jack when we return to India.'

'Oh, Elaine, that's wonderful!' Violet went across and kissed her. Poppy glanced enquiringly at Daisy, but said nothing.

'India!' shrieked Rose. 'Oh, Elaine, I do feel that I would make the most wonderful bridesmaid. I would strew roses before your feet, like they did at the wedding of Lady Diana Cooper. Oh, do, pray consider my application for the post. I know all about India. I must have read Mr Kipling's novel *Kim* about forty times at least. I know pages of it off by heart.'

'We'd have to think about that, see what your father says.' Elaine was taken aback. Her eyes went to Daisy.

'That means no, of course,' said Rose sadly. 'Oh well, I shall wend my weary way to my bedroom, shed a tear, wash my hands and come down to dinner my usual composed and radiant self. But I do hope you will be very happy, Elaine, and that my misery will never cast a blight over your marriage.'

'Wait a minute.' Justin put an arm around Rose's thin shoulders. 'We all wish you well, Elaine,' he said formally. 'Jack is a lucky fellow. Is he coming here tonight? We want to congratulate him.'

Elaine dimpled and smiled radiantly. 'He did say that he would come for dinner. And bring some champagne. I'm expecting him any minute now.'

'Champagne,' said Rose thoughtfully. 'Well, that might "*minister to a mind diseased and pluck from the memory a rooted sorrow*". Shakespeare,' she added, looking a little more cheerful.

'We've got some news too,' broke in Justin. 'Wait till you hear this, Rose. You might be a bridesmaid after all – without stirring out of Beech Grove Manor.' He put his other arm around Violet, drawing her close to him, and looked around triumphantly. 'Violet and I are getting married,' he said.

'Oh, my dears!' Elaine was startled out of her preoccupation, but she was drowned out by the joyful exclamations of Violet's sisters.

'Oh, Justin, pray, pray tell me all about it,' begged Rose. 'This is what I lack as a novelist – real life experience, and Violet is no good at telling these things. Tell me how you proposed.'

'Well,' said Justin, facing her solemnly, 'the important thing with these affairs is to get the right setting, don't you think, Rose?'

'*A jug of wine and thou beside me singing in the wilderness*,' said Rose dreamily.

'Actually, it was in the pantry,' said Justin apologetically. 'Or was it the scullery? Well, we were looking over this house for me to live in when I get my huge salary of five hundred pounds, and I thought that Violet looked so beautiful in every one of the rooms that I didn't care what the furniture looked like or anything, I was just determined to take it. And then we got to the pantry and she looked like an angel in that terrible little dark room so I just couldn't help myself – I told that awful woman who kept dogging our footsteps that I would rent the house and I sent her off for some papers. And there we were in that awful pantry, and I suddenly knew that I could not bear that dreadful little house without Violet in it, so I proposed. What do you think of that, Rose?'

'Well,' said Rose, 'it may not be terribly romantic, but I do appreciate your honesty in telling me all this, Justin. If you had consulted me beforehand I would have given you a few tips. *A violet by a mossy stone . . .*'

'Not too many mossy stones in London,' said Poppy, entering into the fun.

'Let's all go down to Beech Grove Manor tomorrow,' said Justin with the air of one struck by a good idea. 'I shall approach your father and humbly ask permission to pay addresses to his eldest daughter – after I have impressed him with my new-found wealth, of course; and then Violet and I will wander out into the beech woods, find a mossy stone, and . . .' Justin interrupted his speech as a sharp ring came from the front door. 'Ah, the man with the champagne,' he said as Poppy ran to open the door and Jack came in, followed by the cab driver carrying a box.

'Come in, sir, come in,' said Justin to Jack, with the air of the man of the house, at the same time relieving the cab driver of his load. 'Come into the morning room; we're all a bit delayed tonight. Exciting events, pressure of business. First of all, may I offer you, on behalf of the family, our sincerest congratulations and best wishes to you both for your happiness, and secondly, perhaps you might like me to give this box to Bateman. I'm sure that he can handle it.'

Jack smiled and shook hands with the four girls, his eyes lingering longest on Daisy. She returned his smile warmly. He was very nice, she thought. He and Elaine would, she was certain, be very happy together.

'Let's all put on the dresses that we wore for your birthday party,' she said to Violet with a sudden inspiration. After all, she thought, the discovery of the dresses was the start to everything. 'You're happy, Vi?' she asked when they got into the hall.

'Deliriously,' said Violet. 'I feel as though I've had the champagne already. I have that floating and fizzy feeling.'

'Will you be able to live on five hundred a year?' asked Poppy.

'I think so,' said Violet dreamily. 'Anyway, I have expectations. Tell her, Daisy.'

So Daisy went through the story of the man from Hollywood who had liked her profile and would visit London next autumn and wanted to meet her. Violet smiled and looked like an angel and surreptitiously admired her profile in a looking glass on the landing.

'You'll be like Lady Diana Cooper in *The Miracle*, won't she, Daisy?' asked Poppy generously. 'All London will flock to see you.'

Violet smiled and, rather unusually for her, kissed them both. 'We'll plan the bridesmaids' dresses tomorrow,' she said, 'but now I must get ready. I'm exhausted. What a day!'

'You seem a bit quiet, Daise,' said Poppy when they

reached their bedroom. 'Oh, isn't it so lovely to have someone light a fire and bring up hot water every day at just the right time! Is something the matter?' she asked, looking closely at her sister when she didn't answer.

Just then there was a knock at the door and Maud came in to do Poppy's hair. Daisy managed her own these days – that bob was just so easy to comb.

'I'll tell you later on,' she said to Poppy and waited until her sister was ready before going down. She felt shy about confronting Jack and Elaine on her own. Did he really want her to make a home with them? What would Poppy think when she heard about the small car for Daisy's use?

The dinner was probably the most relaxed and the most enjoyable that they had ever had in the pretty house. Elaine was dreamily peaceful, like someone who had reached a safe harbour, thought Daisy; Violet was radiant with happiness, Justin outrageously witty, Rose matching him quote for quote, and Poppy less in the clouds than Daisy had ever seen her. She and Baz had made out a two-year plan, she informed Daisy in a whisper; they were full of ideas for setting up this jazz club. Morgan had driven them to see the house that his grandfather had bequeathed to Baz and by a piece of luck the caretaker was there and had shown them all over it.

'It even has a cellar – we thought that would be good for the club,' she told Daisy. 'Morgan agreed with us about getting rid of the kitchen and all those pantries and things – just turn it into one big room and then the morning room on the ground floor can be a cloakroom. We'll get Vi to help with the decorating – she has a good eye for colours. We thought we might buy some cheap materials in Petticoat Lane or places like that and—'

'Now how about a toast to true love,' suggested Jack, rising to his feet. Already he had assumed the air of the master of the house, giving a whispered command to Bateman to substitute lemonade for champagne in Rose's glass after she had downed the champagne in three large gulps. He would suit Elaine very well, thought Daisy. She was someone who found it hard to make up her mind about anything and Jack would be the perfect husband – affectionate, loving, but decisive and organized.

'I can't wait to introduce my wife at those formal dinners out in India,' he said when the toast had been drunk, looking proudly at Elaine. 'These Maharajahs have a wonderful sense of style and of occasion. You eat off gold plates—'

'Gold!' exclaimed Rose. 'Oh, Elaine, how lucky you are to marry a man who is invited to eat from gold plates!'

'You could always take a large handbag and slip one in,' suggested Justin, but he didn't look envious. He and Violet were having fun talking about their house and planning to put swathes of cheap, artificial silk over the gloomy pictures that lined the walls. It was the jolliest dinner they had had since they came to London. There was no strain and everyone seemed very happy.

'Now what's on your mind?' asked Poppy as soon as they reached their bedroom. Jack and Justin had gone off together, Violet was talking to Elaine downstairs in the drawing room, and Rose was so sleepy after the champagne that she could hardly keep her eyes open.

'Elaine has told Jack all about me,' said Daisy. She tried to say it lightly, but she still felt a sense of betrayal. It had been her secret as well as Elaine's. She met Poppy's eyes and saw that she understood, so gave a little shrug. It wasn't that important, she supposed. However, an answer had to be given to Elaine by the following morning. It should have been given that evening really.

'Poppy,' she said. 'Elaine and Jack want me to come to India with them – to live with them. She says that they will have pots of money – she didn't quite put it like that – but she promised me anything that I wanted: clothes, everything – even a small car.'

Poppy was very still, very silent, her amber-coloured eyes very wide.

'But it will be your decision,' she said eventually.

'That's right,' said Daisy. 'It will be my decision.'

And, she thought, it should be an easy decision. On the one hand was life in a freezing cold, poverty-stricken house where money seemed to be limited to penny stamps, grudgingly dealt out one by one; where food was monotonous; where she was, she admitted to herself, the least appreciated of four neglected girls.

On the other hand was India: warm and welcoming, a land of sun and luxury where the mangos grew ripe, soft and ready to be picked, and people dined off gold plates; a place where she would have every luxury that she could imagine, even a little car – she pictured it red – which she would use to dash from party to party at high speed. India, where uniformed young gentlemen would fight over her favours, ready to escort her to balls and dances. India, where she would watch polo matches and saunter in lush green enclosures with the winners – a luxurious home where the bath water was always hot and a servant always available to give her whatever she wanted at that moment; a home, moreover, where she would be the most beloved child, instead of knowing, deep down, that she was the least loved. And now she knew why.

The contrast with the life that she had led for most of her childhood was stark. A cold, damp house. No money, no clothes, no prospects. Her needs, her desires, her interests of no importance to any adult in the house. A life led in close proximity to three other girls, her nature always urging her to consider her sisters, to worry about them, to try to do something for them. How could she go back there, knowing she didn't really belong? Poppy was the only one who knew the truth, but things would never be the same. She felt like an intruder.

The decision, she thought, certainly should be an easy one.

She looked across at Poppy and then hesitated.

'I'm not sure,' she said eventually.

Chapter Twenty-Seven

The next few days seemed dreary after all the excitement. Poppy was caught up in the world of jazz and as Morgan was insistent that she should not go to lunchtime concerts without another girl with her, Rose went out with her each morning. Violet and Justin were also out every day, shopping for Justin's little house and planning their future. Sir Guy and his workers were absent from their London studios, shooting some sea scenes in Dover, so Daisy was very much alone.

Her mind was busy, though. She had her decision to make. Elaine kept looking hopefully, waiting for a word from her, and on that morning Daisy had decided that by dinner time her decision would have to be made. As soon as the others had left the house she took a piece of paper, ruled it down the middle and put INDIA at the top of one column and ENGLAND at the top of the other. By the time she had finished writing, the first column was full of exciting prospects and the second was sadly bare.

There was no doubt about it, she told herself. It made such good sense to go to India and to make her home with Elaine and Jack.

At that moment the doorbell rang. Someone for Violet, or for Elaine, thought Daisy, throwing the list into the fire and dreamily watching the burned embers go sailing up the chimney. And then she stiffened. That was her father's voice in the hallway – Michael Derrington's voice, she amended. She listened to his heavy footsteps and then the door opened.

'I'm afraid that Elaine has gone out, and so have the others,' she said. He did not look well, she thought as she looked up at him, and she wondered whether he had one of those devastating headaches that had afflicted him since his return from the war.

'It was you that I came to see,' he said, closing the door behind him. He walked across the room and leaned over the fire, picking up the poker and rattling the coals vigorously.

'How are you?' he asked. His eyes did not meet hers.

'I'm fine,' she said, feeling rather puzzled. 'We're all fine,' she went on when he did not respond. 'Rose is having a wonderful time. She does enjoy her visits to the British Museum and Elaine has taken her to lots of plays. London has been very good for her. And Poppy—'

'But what about you?' he interrupted and she looked at him with astonishment.

He put down the poker, straightened himself, took a deep breath and then looked away again.

'Elaine told me that you . . . that she . . .' he muttered.

'Told you . . .'Daisy began, but before she could finish he pulled her into an awkward, one-armed hug. Then he pulled a crumpled and much-read letter from his pocket, thrust it at her and walked away, standing by the window with his back turned to her.

'I should have told you myself,' he mumbled. 'I shouldn't have allowed you to find out like that. I'm selfish. Mary and I had planned that we would tell you when you were about fifteen or sixteen – old enough to understand. She would have done it so much better than I could, but that's no excuse.'

Daisy smoothed out the letter and began to read.

'*Dear Michael,*' it began and beside the words was a half-scratched-out blot as though the writer, looking for the right words, had held the pen poised over the paper long enough for the ink to drip from the nib.

'*I'm afraid that Daisy knows the truth about her birth,*' the letter went on.

It's not my fault, Michael. I didn't say a word. Somehow or other, she guessed. She went to Somerset House and couldn't find her birth certificate with Poppy's.

Don't tell Aunt Lizzie, will you, Michael? She's bound to blame me for it. But I thought you'd better know and I wanted to tell you that it wasn't my fault.

I have invited Daisy to make her home with me in India. I will enjoy having her; it will be a great opportunity to throw some lovely parties. Nothing need be said to anyone else – she will come as my niece.

Your affectionate sister-in-law,
Elaine.

Daisy put the letter down. Not really about me, she thought. Elaine is more worried about being blamed for the news getting out than she is about how I feel. She walked across the floor and touched his arm.

'Father,' she began, but suddenly he turned around and enveloped her in his arms.

'I'm going to miss you terribly when you are in India,' he said, his face turned from her. 'You must know that I've always thought of you as a daughter, since the first moment I held you in my arms. We loved you like you were our own – I often forgot that you weren't. Mary always said how well you were named – little Daisy, *Day's Eye* – a little ray of sunshine in the house, that's what she used to say. I don't know what we will all do without you.'

Daisy said nothing. She moved a little closer and nestled into him and he put his arm around her shoulders and held her tightly.

'Still, we mustn't be selfish. It will be a wonderful thing for you,' he said and she could hear the amount of effort that he put into making his voice sound cheerful. 'The others will envy you. Elaine will be rich enough to buy you anything that you want. You'll have a fantastic time out in India.' He released her and said rapidly, 'I must go, darling; I'm due at the lawyers; that wretched Denis is making trouble for me. You stay here in the warmth. Tell Elaine that I'll be back at dinner time.'

And then he was gone.

Stay here in the warmth, repeated Daisy to herself. And, indeed, she did feel warm all over. She had never known how much he had cared for her; she had forgotten about being called a 'ray of sunshine' by her mother, but now it came back to her. They had taken her in and cared for her, Michael and Mary. She and Poppy had been twins for more than sixteen years and nothing could change that now. And then there was Rose, and Violet. And even Great-Aunt Lizzie. They were her family and she had her place there.

Daisy was sitting dreamily by the fire when Elaine came in.

'Jack has taken Rose to see the Tower of London, but I thought that I couldn't stand it so I came back home,' she said. There was a slight effort in her voice and she looked enquiringly at Daisy. Indeed, thought Daisy, it was time that an answer was given to her invitation of a few days ago.

'Elaine,' she said. 'I've decided that I will stay in England. It's very nice of you and Jack to invite me to India, and perhaps I could come out for a holiday some time, but for the moment, I think I should stay here.'

She expected questions, lamentations, but Elaine, after a moment's reflection, seemed almost pleased at her decision. After all, thought Daisy, Jack and she would be a newly married couple – an almost-grown-up daughter might be a problem. Elaine, like herself, had probably been thinking over the situation during the past few days and had, perhaps, begun to regret her hasty invitation. She beamed at Daisy.

'It's whatever will make you happy, darling,' she said

tenderly. And then a cheerful thought seemed to strike her and she said, 'But, of course, I will come over in the spring and present you and Poppy at court. I'll hire a house and we'll give some balls. You will make a lovely pair of debutantes.'

'I've made up my mind.' Daisy had waited until she and Poppy were alone in their bedroom getting ready for dinner. She was still determined to keep the secret from Violet and Rose. Let it be forgotten, she thought.

Poppy's eyes widened at her words, but she said nothing; just waited, a half-smile on her lips.

'Of course, it was an easy decision,' said Daisy mischievously.

Poppy's smile broadened. 'You're staying!' she shrieked.

'What? Staying in London? You lucky thing!' Rose had come into their room and had overheard the last words.

'No,' said Daisy hastily. 'I'm coming back to Beech Grove Manor with you all. I can work on my films there, but Elaine is coming over next spring and she will present Poppy and me at court. You will probably also be allowed to come up for the season, Rose.'

'I shall try to get myself accepted as a roving reporter on *The Evening Post* before then,' said Rose seriously. 'In the meantime I shall practise writing some wonderful headlines about you two.' She thought for a moment and then said triumphantly:

'How about this?'

She seized a pen from the writing table by the window and printed in huge letters:

Derrington Debutantes Are the Season's Sensation! Dynamic Duo Takes London by Storm

Daisy linked her little finger in Poppy's and grinned.

'We might,' she whispered. 'We just might . . .'

Acknowledgements

First and foremost must come a huge vote of thanks to Rachel Petty at Macmillan Children's Books – one of those wonderful editors who combine enormous enthusiasm with an unhesitating eye for material that needs to be firmly chopped out. She, like me, loves this period in history, and it was great to have a fellow enthusiast by my side during the writing process.

Thanks also to my agent, Peter Buckman of Ampersand Agency, who is so knowledgeable about the film world; and to my family and friends, who still encourage and admire.